A husband, trying to rekindle his marriage in a lonely seaside village, meets a strange young woman from his forgotten past; a man taking a garden gnome to a museum gets an unwelcome surprise; a lonely widow encounters an enigmatic character from an embryonic pop group; a group of scientists make an horrific discovery at a big cat conservation centre; and a baby hare comes of age with a momentous idea.

Continuing in the spirit of *To Cut a Short Story Short,* [volume one], these and 83 other stories, varying from 100 to 5000 words, are found in this eclectic and scintillating collection of 'flash fiction' by Simon J. Wood.

To Cut a Short Story Short, vol. II

By Simon J. Wood:

To Cut a Short Story Short

A young magician in a pub opens his hands to release a cloud of tropical butterflies; a female bookseller is forced to attend a dance in drag to atone for a misdemeanor; a lonely man searches for a mysterious woman on a cruise; four school friends experience terror on a caravan holiday, and a macabre stranger wanders the streets at midnight, stealing dreams.

Ranging from just 100 up to 4000 words, these and 106 other memorable little stories are found in this eclectic and tantalizing collection by Simon J. Wood, an exciting new voice in the Flash Fiction genre.

256 pp.

ISBN-10: 152134311X, ISBN-13: 978-1521343111

eBook: ASIN: B071ZQGBR4

Bound in Morocco

A short story of intrigue and subterfuge set in Morocco.

Marcus Slater decides to forgo the cold, wet, wintry weather of England to join a walking party in the sunny climes of Morocco. There, against a backdrop of the curious, ancient towns of southern Morocco he meets the enigmatic Sylvia and finds himself embroiled in a game he cannot possibly afford to lose.

42 pp.

ISBN-10: 978-1521324660, ISBN-13: 978-1521324660

eBook: ASIN: B071ZBK245

N.B. Both books are also available as audiobooks, narrated by Angus Freathy. Obtainable from Amazon, Audible, and iTunes.

To Cut a Short Story Short, vol. II

88 Little Stories

Simon J. Wood

Dedicated to the memory of my father, John Wood.

Preface

Following on from *To Cut a Short Story Short,* I am pleased to present another volume of 'more of the same.' In this instance, however, the stories are generally considerably longer, but still under 1200 words for the most part.

I have reproduced *Clarissa's Missives,* parts one and two, from *To Cut a Short Story Short* [vol. I], as it was extended to a trilogy through requests on my blog of the same name, and is now published as one complete story.

I also make no apologies for including *The Optimist Creed* by Christian D. Larson with the hope that readers will find it as inspiring as I have.

The stories are in *approximate* alphabetical order but adjusted to give the minimum page turns per story, for a better reading experience.

For the curious – and/or flash fiction *aficionado* – the word count for each story is given in the appendices.

I would like to express my appreciation to Angus Freathy for his wonderful narration on the audiobooks of my first two titles – *Bound in Morocco* and *To Cut a Short Story Short.*

For their help in the choosing the final selection of stories for *this* title, I would like to thank Mary Mahan-Deatherage, Nancy Richy, and Peter Runfola. I would also like to thank them for their helpful suggestions.

Finally, it remains for me to say a sincere 'thank you' to Shirley Hargrave for permission to use her experience as the inspiration for the story *In Dulce Jubilo*. I am extremely grateful to her.

Thought reaches its loftiest activity when plunged into its own mysterious depth; when it breaks through the narrow compass of self and passes from truth to truth to the region of eternal light, where all which is, was, or ever will be, melts into one grand harmony – CHARLES F. HAANEL

Contents

A Flying Visit

My story starts one sunny day in August. I'd spent the morning setting up bookcases, then bringing in box after heavy box of old books from an outbuilding, with the intention of getting them into some kind of order. They belonged to my uncle Josiah who had died at an unexpectedly early age after being pushed onto the live rail of a tube train at Holland Park station by a 'random madman,' described as a 'fakir lookalike,' yet to be apprehended.

The books had been left to me, Ruben Winterfield is my name, in uncle Josiah's will, possibly as I'd worked in the antiquarian book trade for a number of years, although I'd only met him on occasion. Well, the ones I'd looked at so far were fairly weird. There were books on various forms of astrology, tarot, angels, demons, witchcraft, clairvoyance and the like. There was also a collection of old hardbacks by William Walker Atkinson, the famous occultist, also known as Yogi Ramacharaka or Theron Q. Dumont, which I suspected to be very valuable in the first and early editions, which these were.

Needing a break, I decided to take a stroll and get some fresh air. I walked along a footpath outside my house, to a track along the edge of a field, where a stream bubbled in a gully which ran alongside. I reached a huge, gnarled oak tree, where there was a short path to a small waterfall. On impulse I took it and was amazed to find that, for the first time ever, I was not alone there.

A lady in a purple cloak was situated on the far side of the stream, bending over with her hands in the water, presumably searching for something. On my side of the stream stood a young girl, perhaps six years old, holding the lead of a beautiful honey-coloured rough collie. The girl had a pretty face, bright blue eyes and mid-length blonde hair, held back in a pony tail with a blue band.

The lady seemed startled by my appearance and stood up, looking flustered. The little girl simply turned to me and smiled. "Hello, I'm Esmerelda, this is Solomon, and that's my mummy."

Well, it seemed that the mother, Tameka, had been performing some kind of ritual, to Neda, a goddess of waters, when in her excitement of shouting an invocation, a talisman she'd been holding went flying into the waterfall. It was eventually found, a leather pouch, stamped with strange symbols, and containing now-sodden herbs.

Esmerelda rolled her eyes at me. Apparently, this wasn't the first time her mother's 'occult activities' had gone awry.

I'd invited them back for a cup of tea, a glass of orange squash, and a bowl of water respectively, and had taken a shine to them. Tameka had wavy blonde hair and was not unattractive, but somewhat odd, rambling on about archangels and goddesses, as if they were personal friends.

Esmerelda, on the other hand, seemed bright as a button, and, mentally well in advance of her six years. Solomon seemed a gentle soul, content to sit in the corner, close his eyes and meditate on whatever dogs meditate on.

"Mummy's got a magic carpet," Esmeralda said.

I laughed. "Well, I'd like to fly to Iceland, they've got some pretty big waterfalls there!"

Tameka perked up. "Actually, I do have one. It was left to me by my great-uncle, Henri Baq. He wrote a history of the flying carpet."

"I thought it was just fairy tale nonsense," I said.

Tameka's face became serious. "Fairy tales are usually based on fact."

So, to my astonishment, I'd wound up at their place one afternoon, an old castle-like mansion, only part of which appeared to be habitable. Tameka led us into a large book-lined study and went over to an old cupboard. She extracted a rolled-up piece of fabric, approached the centre of the room and unfurled it.

I gasped in astonishment. It appeared to be woven from green silk with a gold weft, perhaps eight feet by five. We all clambered on board, Solomon too, who barked several times, whether in assurance or alarm, I couldn't be sure. We humans sat cross-legged in time-honoured fashion for riding carpets.

2

Tameka took a piece of parchment from a shoulder bag. "This carpet was made under the supervision of Ben Sherira, from the Kingdom of Ghor," she translated. "Is everybody ready?"

"Yes, mother," sighed Esmerelda, whilst Solomon opened his eyes and gave a soft bark.

"What about you, Ruben?"

For the first time, I realised this might not be a piece of total insanity. "Well, er, if you're sure it's safe ...."

Tameka didn't reply. She read some incomprehensible words from the papyrus, clapped her hands and, *Wham*! I found myself looking down on an amazing sunlit cloud-scape through a translucent bubble, surrounding our carpet.

We whizzed over deep blue oceans, mountains, glaciers and forests, until Esmerelda exclaimed, "Oh, look, mummy, there's *Akureyri*!" whilst Solomon whined, presumably wishing to be on *terra firma*.

I gazed down on the picturesque fishing town, situated in the north west corner of Iceland, as we headed over the brilliantly coloured flowers and shrubs of the botanic gardens, allegedly the world's most northernmost, and then shortly we were hovering over *Godafoss*, the 'Waterfall of the Gods.'

Curtains of thundering water pounded down from multiple falls, deafening, even within our supernaturally-protected environment. Suddenly our 'bubble' disappeared and we were exposed, enveloped in the mist of rebounding water, our ears reverberating to the clamour of its unimaginable crashing weight, our noses assailed with the odour of liquid energy. Solomon was barking furiously.

After a few minutes our sphere of protection reappeared and our now somewhat soggy carpet soared upwards once more.

The sun dried the carpet, even through our protective bubble and I also found it was safe to move about, a welcome relief after squatting for so long. "I'd like to see the Niagara Falls," I ventured. "I've never been there."

Esmerelda pulled a face, and Tameka took the hint. "Sorry Ruben, Esme's going to a party. It's her friend, Rosalina's birthday and they're having a magician."

3

I laughed at the irony. Then I noticed that the sky had turned dark and our carpet was being buffeted by high winds. It turned cold, then after a while it began to snow.

"I don't like this, mummy," said Esmerelda, looking tearful. Solomon rubbed his face against her cheek, as if to reassure her.

"Don't worry, we're safe in our bubble," said Tameka. "Hey, d'you remember those glass globes that you shook and then they were filled with falling snow?"

"Yes, of course," I said. "There'd be a little Christmas scene inside."

She laughed. "Well, we're like that, but the other way around!"

Later that day I stood on a terrace outside the Brampton Hotel's *Riverside Room,* where the party was being held. From inside came the excited squeals of young children enjoying the fun. I stood with a glass of wine, gazing down on a small waterfall which cascaded alongside a glass wall of the hotel. Had I dreamt the Iceland adventure? it seemed too incredible to be true. Suddenly I felt a warm, soft hand in mine and a kiss on my cheek.

"Thank you for coming today." It was Tameka. With a flowing red dress and wearing makeup, she was barely recognizable as the soggy female above *Godafoss* earlier.

"Oh, you're welcome, it was … something different, I suppose," I said, rather lamely.

She smiled. "I hope you'll come with us again."

I noticed she was still holding my hand. My heart beat a little faster. "Yes, I'd like that." I guessed I could use her magic in my life.

A Girl Like Alice

With any luck it would blow over. I wouldn't miss her, though. In fact, now I thought about it, I could quite happily live without Alice wandering around the empty, echoing corridors of Thurkett Grange, dressed in nothing more than a long-sleeved shirt – pale green stripes on white – with her small, hard breasts showing through the material like two cherry tarts. As often as not she'd be humming tunelessly, frowning, pacing up and down, sometimes muttering to herself. And as for 'Steve'!

I couldn't even be sure how we came to be together. I'd met her somewhere, a restaurant, a party, my mind's hazy on that point. She had a lean, smooth face, with mediumly-full lips, neat white teeth and large grey eyes, all framed by an inverted 'v' of tight curls in straw coloured hair, cascading down to her shoulders.

She wasn't especially pretty, but attractive, if you know what I mean.

"Hello, I'm Alice, who are you?"

"Stephen, … well, people call me Steve."

She'd seated herself opposite me, plonking a large glass of lemon-coloured wine down on a table between us, so that some splashed onto the tablecloth. She giggled. "Whoops! … That's a coincidence, my cat's called Steve!"

"Why did you call him Steve?"

"I didn't. He told me that was his name."

I laughed. "Sounds like an unusual cat!"

"Someone said you live in the old manor house. On your own. Do you get lonely?"

I'd blushed. Truth was I did sometimes. Since Lorraine had left a year ago. "Not really."

"Can I come and see the place?" She smiled a quizzical, endearing smile, smoothing her short black skirt down over long slim legs with orange-painted fingernails.

So, as a patron of the county art society I'd shown her round my gallery, which housed a number of the society's finer works.

5

She'd traced her fingernails over a moody seascape, executed in oils.

"Careful! That's a valuable painting!"

"This was painted by my uncle Maurice. He lived out by the coast – in Mablethorpe."

"Really?" Maurice Sotherton had indeed lived in Mablethorpe and the painting was signed just 'M.S.' "That's a coincidence."

Then the library. Thousands of volumes rubbing shoulders from floor to a high ceiling, where light entered through small leaded windows in the sides of a white-painted cupola.

"I wrote a book once," she said.

"Really? What was it about?"

"It was called *The Seven Spiritual Laws of Excess* ... it was supposed to be funny."

"Did you sell many copies?"

"One. To my husband."

"Oh ...."

"Actually, you know him."

"I do?"

"Tom Prince. You play pool together at the Blacksmith's Arms. Or did."

Well, that was strange. I did know Tom, a friendly guy, aged about thirty, but we'd mainly played for different teams. Then one day he'd vanished. No one knew where he'd gone and his house was looking rather dilapidated. I'd never heard him refer to a wife.

But all that was in the past. Alice had left as suddenly as she'd moved in, taking her vociferous Siamese cat, Steve, with her. I could honestly say I missed him like a hole in the head. But Alice? Well, she wasn't all bad. We'd had good times together, not just in bed. She was a font of bizarre and irrelevant knowledge and a frequenter of odd galleries and museums. The type that lay hidden down ancient cobbled alleyways and which hardly ever seemed to open.

My finger hovered over her number on my speed dial. I reckoned it wouldn't do any harm to give her a call. Just to see how she was doing, nothing more, you understand. *Here goes!* I pressed the number just as the doorbell rang. I thought I heard the yowl of a cat. Another damned coincidence! My heart beat a little faster and I found myself smiling. 'Better the Devil you know' came to mind.

A Tall Story

Feeling the plank bending slightly under my weight, I crawled to the end, trying to avoid looking at the impossible drop beneath me. Although I had a good head for heights, I still felt queasy. My fingertips felt the surface, roughly planed and unfinished, whilst I smelt the scent of freshly worked wood. A mild, warm breeze blew on my face, and above, the yellow disk of the sun burned down on me.

Reaching the end, I closed my eyes and turned around on the plank by feel. Then I opened them again and looked back at Jessie, silhouetted against the top of the tall spire. I couldn't see her face, just blonde hair blowing in the breeze, against the slate-grey tiles.

She was stood on a platform close to the top of the steeple of St. Stephen's church, Budhaven, one of the tallest in Britain. Above, on the very tip of the spire, a small but ornate metal cross surmounted a thick strip of copper lightning conductor which ran down the side of the steeple and ultimately into the earth.

"You OK, Ben?" she called.

I gave a thumbs up sign. The plan was to photograph me for Facebook, standing at the end of a narrow plank with a four-hundred-foot drop below! Now, out here, the reality was a bit different. It was really quite breezy, it might be dangerous. I decided it would be safer just to dangle my legs over the sides. It would still look impressive.

Suddenly, a workman with a yellow hard-hat appeared behind her. Her father owned the firm undertaking reparations, that's how we'd got access to the spire, although he would never have given us permission to do what we were doing, had he known.

The man walked quickly towards Jessie, his yellow hat pulled down at the front and his face in shadow. She heard his steps and began to turn around, though not in time to prevent him from shoving her hard in the back, sending her crashing onto a low barrier surrounding the platform. I heard her cry out in surprise. Before she'd had time to regain her balance, he bent down, took her by the legs, and hurled her out and over the edge.

8

She didn't make a sound and in total disbelief I watched her spiralling downwards, making an odd bounce before crashing onto a corner of the church roof with a distant, sickening, thud. I looked up and the man had gone.

Just then, I felt a sharp pain in my right hand. *Ow!* I looked to find a half-crushed wasp. I could see a dark mark at the base of my thumb where its sting had gone in. In a state of panic, I scraped it off and crawled back along the wooden plank to the platform, pulling myself over the barrier, oblivious to the pain. I needed to get down and get help. Jessie might still be alive.

The platform had been constructed using a huge crane and access to it was now via internal steps in the spire, then out through a door and up a specially erected ladder to a trapdoor in the platform. But, to my horror, the trapdoor wouldn't lift. It appeared to be bolted shut from underneath!

With my hand throbbing from the sting, I looked around, nothing but a big wooden chest. Inside were a number of coveralls and hard-hats, a large number of poles – about two feet in length – connected together with a type of elasticated rope, a roll of some kind of wire mesh, about the same width as the poles were long, about twenty pairs of thick socks and, of all things, a large flag of Bahrain. There was also a battered metal box that contained a few rudimentary tools. But even if I could somehow access the ladder beneath, I could imagine the spire door to be locked.

I looked over the edge and saw two tiny distant dots beneath me. "Help, I shouted, waving frantically. HELP!"

One of the dots turned pink, presumably someone looking up. Then I saw that they were waving back at me.

"No, you stupid idiots, get help!" I yelled at the top of my voice – but they got into a car and drove off.

There weren't many people about, there being no ecclesiastical service and the church tea room having shut some time ago. Those that were, either ignored me, assuming they could hear me from so far above, or else waved back, unsuspecting that I was in dire straits. In the meantime, Jessie's body lay, unmoving, far, far below.

I awoke to the deafening sound of rotors. I'd spent an uncomfortable and largely sleepless night on the cold, damp boards of the platform, trying to forget the fruitless hours of shouting and waving and the agony of my wasp-stung hand, the pain of which had now subsided, fortunately. Thank God I wasn't susceptible to anaphylactic shock, or I'd have been a goner! It had rained in the night too, so even having donned a coverall and hard-hat, I was wet and freezing. And, of course, there was poor Jessie. Tears of frustration filled my eyes. If only I could have got off this damned platform, I could have summoned help. Now she was doubtless beyond it.

But now I was astonished to see a rope swinging down from a helicopter and at the end of it was something, which as the chopper moved in and the rope swung closer, turned out to be a harness affair. I looked up but could see no one, just the orange underbelly of the helicopter and the whirring blades. I unclipped the harness and, seeing how it worked, quickly put it on. Looking up again, I now saw someone waving. I clipped the harness to the end of the rope and gave them a thumbs up sign, shortly feeling my feet lift off the platform. Thank God!

The chopper rose and the rope began to reel in. I was swinging around, looking down from maybe a thousand feet, but I felt so disoriented from an unprotected night on the platform that it all seemed surreal and I wasn't nervous. Soon two men were taking my arms and helping me aboard.

"Hello, Ben." It was Jessie's father, Maurice McIntyre, of the McIntyre Corporation.

I sat down and unclipped the rope. With tears in my eyes and a trembling lip, I said, "Maurice, I'm so sorry, I've got some terrible news. Some crazy workman pushed Jessie off that platform. I think she's dead."

"Oh dear." His face was sombre, then to my astonishment, it broke into a smile and then he began to chuckle. The chuckle turned into a laugh, and soon the other fellow joined in.

"What the …?"

Still laughing, he gestured to the front of the helicopter. The co-pilot removed a baseball cap and long blonde hair tumbled down. The airman turned and smiled. "Hello, darling!"

It was Jessie!

"Jessie! What the hell's going on? Is it really you?"

She came over and hugged and kissed me. Yes, it really was her.

So, it had turned out to be a bet, based on a stupid prank, organised by Jessie's brother, Fred, who had a YouTube channel for practical jokes. A drone had filmed me and someone on the ground had misled any would-be rescuers, telling them I was in on the 'joke.' Fred had bet his uncle Xavier a substantial sum that I wouldn't manage to escape, whereas Xavier, God bless him, although he was wrong, thought I had the initiative to somehow get down from the platform, unaided.

Seems they'd strung the church roof with a special kind of camouflage netting for Jessie to land on, complete with sound effect. She'd been a talented gymnast when younger. Then, when I'd been preoccupied with shouting and waving from the other side of the platform, she'd quickly climbed down and a dummy had been substituted. Thousands of YouTube viewers were no doubt chortling at my distress at this very moment!

I'd been fuming with anger but Jessie had been touched by how upset I was and mollified me by suggesting we get engaged, so now I'd be marrying into the McIntyre Corporation, no mean achievement! Fred, buoyed by the boost in viewings of his channel, and the subsequent potential increase in advertising revenue, had agreed, albeit reluctantly, to hand over half the wager, a not inconsiderable sum in my current circumstances. So, 'All's Well That Ends Well.' Though just *how* I was supposed to escape, I never *did* find out!

A Visit from Saint Nicholas – 2017 Version

'Twas the night before Christmas, all quiet in the house,
I sat at my laptop, with hand on my mouse.
I looked at the apps, so many to check!
E-mail, Facebook, WordPress and Tweetdeck.

I opened my mail and smiled with delight
at an e-card received, this cold Christmas night!
I clicked and watched Santa sail over roof top,
pulled by his reindeer, they ne'er seem to stop!

I clicked on 'reply' and sent thanks on its way
But Facebook was calling, no time to delay!
So on to my 'wall,' Christmas greetings to read
From friends near and far, and those I don't need!

Just then, from outside I heard such a clatter.
I opened the door, feeling mad as a hatter,
as in front of my startled eyes did appear
a sleigh pulled by eight, rather sweaty, reindeer.

They snorted and stamped their hooves in the snow.
Saint Nick in the sled called, "to the roof we must go!"
"Just a minute," I cried, a-pointing my phone,
"I must get a shot, for Facebook you know!"

"Quick friend," he said, "I've presents to deliver!"
He laughed and I noticed his belly aquiver.
"That was a good 'un," I said with some pride.
"But it's freezing out here, I'm off back inside!"

As I uploaded my photo, noises came from the roof.
'Twas the tapping and knocking of each little hoof.
Saint Nick down the chimney came, just like a ghost.
My hand o'er mouse button, about to click 'post.'

"Speed your hand, friend," laughed Santa Claus,
"I have presents for all, mamma, kiddies indoors."
So saying this, from his shoulder a sack,
he put down on the carpet, whilst rubbing his back.

He reached in and flung out packet after packet,
PlayStation, tablets, Xbox … what a racket!
He held up a game, shaking his head,
"In the old days, wooden toys, now Night of the Dead!"

"Times have changed Santa, it's electronic toys now.
Monopoly, Cluedo, all vanished, somehow."
Saint Nicolas sighed, his face it was long.
"Yes, son, I've had to get elves from Hong Kong."

"The old ones were sacked, they weren't internet savvy,
As you may guess, they weren't none too happy!
And Dasher, Dancer, Prancer and Vixen
They do their best, but Elon Musk's offered to fix 'em."

"He's made nuclear powered versions, don't you know?
It won't just be Rudolph who lights up the snow!
I'm undecided, though it'd save on the hay,
But the time it is passing, I must be away!"

So saying, back up the chimney he flew
"Come Comet, come Cupid, Donner and Blixen, yes, you!"
I looked back at Facebook, a comment from a mate,
"Nice pic of Santa and reindeer. Ain't Photoshop great?"

Then past the window they all came in flight,
Saint Nicolas, waving, puffed on his pipe.
And I heard him call as they vanished from view,
"Happy Christmas to All and a good night to you!"

An Eye for an Eye

I stared in total disbelief. I'd returned home from work to find my front door hanging from broken hinges and the whole house surrounded with yellow tape, stating POLICE LINE DO NOT CROSS. I looked around. There were no police vehicles, that I could see anyway, and nothing happening at any of our neighbours' houses. All seemed quiet and deserted.

I ducked under the tape and went in. A table in the hall lay on its side, but in the lounge, everything seemed normal. Then I looked in the kitchen. It looked as if a giant arm had swept everything onto the floor. There were broken cups and plates strewn around everywhere. I spied a mobile phone amongst them, my son Jack's, I thought. How odd. I picked it up and put it in a jacket pocket. As I did so, I noticed a dark stain on the brown kitchen carpet tiles, and what appeared to be speckles of blood all over the crockery. A saucepan on the stove, now cold, had a blackened base, as if it had boiled dry.

"You're not allowed in the house, sir!"

I turned around and jumped out of my skin. A man stood in a yellow suit with a huge clear visor. Through it, I could see he was breathing with a respirator. He wore black rubber gloves and shoes.

"What's going on. Where's my wife and son?"

"Your wife's in hospital and your son's … being looked after. Everything's being taken care of. Now, can you leave the house please, sir?"

"Why?"

"You need to go NOW, sir."

"No, not until I find out what's going on!" I felt an impact on the back of my head then … unconsciousness.

"Darling, come and look at this." I turned my lava rock paperweight around under the desk light. Yes, there it was again. In one of the mass of tiny holes, something moved.

Sandra came into the room. "What is it? I'm busy. And you need to get to work."

I laughed. "I thought it was my imagination, but I think there's something alive in this rock, in one of these little holes."

She showed surprise. "Where?"

I indicated the approximate hole.

Her interest perked up. "Let me see." She opened a desk draw and took out a magnifying glass. "Yes, I think I saw something move. Yes, I see it now, it's like a ... like a tiny red maggot." Ow! She dropped the paperweight and put a hand over her left eye.

"What's the matter?"

"Ow, if feels like there's something in my eye."

"Here, let me look." I couldn't see anything. I took the magnifying glass and looked again. Against the pale blue iris was a tiny red dot.

She must have noticed my concern. "What is it?"

"Oh, I think you've got a speck of ... er, dust or something in your eye. Here, let me look again. Hold your eye open." I peered into her eye once more. Suddenly, like magic, there were *two* tiny red dots.

So, I'd called for an ambulance and tried to stall a rising panic. When I'd next looked at Sandra's eye there'd been *four* red dots. I didn't dare look after that. She seemed agitated, pacing around with a hand over her eye.

"Just keep calm, darling, they'll know how to treat it." I became aware that I was crossing my fingers.

It didn't take long, although it seemed like an age. Two green-suited paramedics, a man and a woman, came in, carrying equipment. "Nothing to worry about, madam," the man said to Sandra after a quick examination. The paramedics exchanged concerned glances before the man came to me, speaking quietly and out of Sandra's earshot. "It looks like some kind of parasite. They can freeze the area and get it out with a laser. It's painless but her eye might be a bit sore for a few days. She'll be given some special eye drops. Just go to work normally, sir, we'll be in touch to let you know how she's doing."

And that was that. Once at work I was sucked into a department-wide panic at parts not being ready for a machine we were supposed to be marketing the following week. Heads were about to roll and I wasn't sure if mine wouldn't be one of them. At lunchtime there was a call for me from nearby St. Margaret's hospital.

"Mr. Jameson?"

"Yes, who's calling?"

"It's Doctor Menzies from Ophthalmology. Just to let you know your wife's fine and that she's been discharged. We're running her home in a hospital vehicle. She'll feel a little 'woozy' for an hour or two due to the anaesthetic, so she's been told to rest."

Now, I regained consciousness and the room blurred into focus. It seemed to be some type of hospital ward and I was lying on a bed. I got up and unsteadily made my way to a washbasin where I splashed my face with cold water. I looked at my watch. That was odd. It was two o'clock in the afternoon. I must have been given something to make me sleep, a whole day had gone by.

I felt in my jacket pockets and found my son's phone. I was surprised it hadn't been taken, but my wallet and other bits were there too. I took it out and looked at the messages. He hadn't set a password. They were the usual teenage nonsense, nothing untoward. But on the phone log, the last number dialled was 999. That was timed at 3.43 p.m. the previous day.

I clicked on Photos and, after pictures of Jack fooling around and pulling silly faces with equally silly friends, I noticed the last item was a video. I clicked it to play. It showed Sandra in the kitchen. Her left eye was covered with a gauze pad. "Jack, what are you doing?"

"Just filming the 'grand unveiling'!

"I'm only taking it off for a minute. I've got to put these eye drops in." She pulled on the tape holding the pad in place."

I could hear Jack gasp.

"Jack, what's the matter? Jack?"

I gazed in horror. Her eye was completely red and bulging outwards. As I watched, it pulsed three times, slowly, then suddenly exploded, covering the phone's lens with blood and tiny, wriggling red creatures. I recoiled at her shrill screams, feeling sick to my stomach. Through the blood spatters on the lens, I could see a gaping, empty eye socket. Oh ...my ... God.

"Yes, it was rather nasty wasn't it?"

I looked up in surprise. A man in a white coat had come into the room whilst I'd been absorbed with the horrific video.

"Unfortunately, the laser didn't do the trick. Those little buggers were more resilient than expected. Let me ask you, where did that rock come from, exactly?"

"I found it on a beach, Theddlethorpe St. Botolph's."

"Hmm. Well the boffins have had a good look at it. Seems it wasn't your ordinary volcanic lava rock after all. It's a meteorite."

"What? Then that ... thing that was in it was ... alien?"

"That's our presumption."

"What'll happen?"

"Don't worry, all those little critters were flushed out and your wife will be given an artificial eye. It'll be connected to her brain, so she'll be able to see, ... well, sort of. Jack's more problematic."

"How do you mean?"

"Well, this has got to be kept under wraps. A condition of us fitting the artificial eye is that you keep this ... ah, affair, to yourselves. We can't have the plebs, er, sorry, I mean the public, panicked by this. We're worried about Jack blabbing."

"Well, what'll happen to him then?"

"Oh, he's been packed off to a young offenders' institution for a year. We think the regime there should help him forget about it. No one there's going to believe him either, they've got ... other stuff on their minds."

"But, that ... that's horrible!"

"Look, you can say he's gone abroad for a year's study. We'll make it up to him when he comes out, OK?" He smiled. "Anyway, let's get you something to eat. You must be hungry?"

I was. I was starving. So hungry, in fact, I forgot to mention that when I'd picked up the rock, it had promptly broken in two. I'd donated the other half to a local charity shop.

Arse from His Elbow

"Promenaders, they get on my friggin' nerves! Pull over, Jacko."

The sleek black police car pulled up, just ahead of a man, tall, leaning forward as he walked, as if forward motion were the only thing preventing him from toppling over. He had a distinguished face, probably handsome when young, thinning grey hair, silver steel-rimmed glasses, and a long nose. He looked up with surprise.

Joshua got out of the police car. "Hi, Buddy, what are you doin'?"

"Who, me? Just walking."

"Why? Don't you know what's on tonight? The final of The World's Got Talent!"

The man's face looked blank. "I don't watch TV."

"Don't watch TV, you cannot be serious! Come on, man, *everyone's* glued to the screen right now!"

"Well, not me. I just wanted some … fresh air, exercise, you know."

"Actually, I *don't* know, buddy. Think about Little Thelma, right now probably singing her heart out with The Nation's Favourite Song. And you say you don't wanna watch her!"

"Who's Little Thelma?"

"*What*?" Joshua looked shell-shocked. "What? You don't know Little Thelma? You *must* do, buddy! C'mon, you're kiddin' me!"

The man remained silent.

"Hey, Jacko, c'mon out here. We've got us a live one!"

Jacko got out of the car and the two black-clothed cops stood up close, their sweaty bodies invading the man's space by design. Jacko took out a notebook and pen. "OK, buddy, name and address?"

"What, why, I mean, er …."

"Look, buddy, either you cooperate or you'll be spending the night in the cooler."

"It's Matthew. Er, Matthew Morris." Stammering, his thin lips revealed his street and house number.

"Why, that's over two miles away!" said Jacko.

"Yes, I've been walking for forty-five minutes."

"Forty-five minutes! Well, you'll have missed Suzy Chang and her dancing poodles, not to mention Jigsaw, the world's greatest contortionist! Come on man, tell me you're kiddin' us!"

Mathew Morris looked up and down the empty street, nervously. It was growing dark and he could see flickering coloured light coming from unlit houses along both sides of the road. Suddenly he felt emboldened. "Look, I'm simply going for a walk. When I get home, I'm going to work on an essay I'm writing – on Totalitarianism – and then I shall sit by the fire, drink a bottle of beer and read some poetry before supper!"

Jacko raised his eyebrows. "Meanwhile, everyone else in the world has a TV or can get near one and is cheering on their country's top star! But not Mr Mathew Morris, no, an essay is more important than Luther Steel's ventriloquism, Totalit … whassname, more important than Silvia de Fuego's amazing juggling, and goddamn poetry, if you *puhleeze*, more important than Fanny de la Mare, the world's greatest compère!"

"I've had enough of this joker." Joshua took out a radio and pressed a button. "Never heard of Little Thelma. Pah! Hello, Control, we need an ECT squad down here, *now*. Gotta guy who needs some serious rewiring!"

A raised voice came from the radio.

"Oh, my sweet Jesus!" Joshua turned, ashen-faced. "The show's been taken off air! Jigsaw got his elbow stuck up his arse, Little Thelma forgot her words and is having a nervous breakdown and Suzy Chang's going crazy with Silvia de Fuego for juggling her poodles!"

A Kind of Peace

"Hello, Darling, did you have a good morning?"

"It's half past twelve."

"Yes, I know it is. Is that a problem?"

"I'm due at the dentists at two and I asked you to be back by twelve. I wanted to pop round to my mother's first."

"For God's sake. It's only a twenty-minute drive to your mother's and twenty minutes to the dentist. You can still spend an hour gassing."

"No, I can't. She's got to go out at one. That's why I asked you to be back at twelve. Don't you ever listen?"

"Sorry, are you sure you told me?"

"Of course I'm sure! Now I'll have to go afterwards, so I'll be pushed to pick the kids up."

"I can pick the kids up."

"No, I want to make sure they get home in one piece."

"Don't be ridiculous. I drive up to the limit 'when it's safe to do so.' I don't dawdle along like you, holding up a bloody great queue of traffic!"

"Anyway, I need to speak to Miss Hughes, it's best I pick them up."

"What about?"

"What about!"

"Look, when we were kids, no one went running to a teacher to moan about being bullied. It was part of growing up."

"Yes, and look what happened. It turned us into a nation of neurotics."

"Better than a nation of kids without any discipline, or respect for their elders."

"Respect's something you earn, not something you deserve for … for just being alive."

"Don't be so bloody ridiculous!"

"Look, I just want to help him. Surely you can understand that. Even with your stupid, narrow-minded thinking!"

"What the hell's that supposed to mean?"

20

"Look, OK, I'm sorry. I've had a shit morning, since you asked."

"I thought you were going to your art class."

"I was. It was cancelled. I forgot to check Facebook. I only found out when I got there. Dawn had a left a note on the studio door."

"What happened?"

"Oh, her mum's in hospital again. She had to visit. So she says. A couple of hours wouldn't have made much difference I'd have thought."

"Perhaps she's worse than you think?"

"Hah! Are you kidding? She's made of cast iron, that one. Anyway, then I went to Tesco's and that stupid Mrs. Rheingold was there. You know, that ghastly Jehovah's Witness person. Keeps giving me their leaflets. Well, she was banging on and on about Jesus and the Bible. In the end I just told her to shut up."

"Oh dear."

"Yes, she didn't like that. Said she 'hadn't come to Tesco's to be insulted.' I admit I lost my rag. Told her to get lost and that I didn't want to hear another quote from the bible as long as I lived."

"Well, thanks for landing me in it. I'm playing golf with Frank tomorrow!"

"How was I to know. Anyway, you said you can't stand her either."

"Live and let live."

"Easier said than done when she's not in your face. Anyway, you can tell Frank I'm sorry. Tell him I had a bad toothache. That I didn't mean it."

"So I've got to lie on your behalf now?"

"Oh, come on, it's hardly against your nature!"

"What the hell's that supposed to mean?"

"You know what I mean. That … that floozy in your office. The one with the big nose and big tits, Natalie!"

"Look, that's over and done with, ancient history. I promised …."

"Look, Oliver, I'm totally stressed out – you shagging that bitch behind my back, Stephen being bullied, my friend's mum seriously ill, Mrs. Jehovah's Bloody Witness! I don't know how much more I can take!"

"Look darling, calm down. Just sit down, relax. Here drink this, it'll help …. Now, look, I'm not seeing Natalie, I promise, Stephen will be OK, he's strong and he's got lots of friends, Dawn's mother's got the best care she can get, she's every chance of pulling through and Mrs. Rheingold will have forgotten about it by tomorrow. Come on darling, don't cry …."

"OK … OK … Ollie, look, I'm going to go and lie down for an hour."

"Good idea, you have a nice little nap. You'll feel better."

"Can you come too?"

"What?"

"Keep me company … you know."

"What, you mean?"

"Well, I can't remember the last time, can you?"

"Come to think of it, no. Well, we are married after all … I suppose."

"For better or worse! Come on, Oliver darling, before I change my mind!"

Billy Bunter's Christmas Surprise

[A tribute to 'Frank Richards.']

Harry Wharton looked at the letter in disbelief. His hopes for Christmas had been shattered.

My dear Harry, we most deeply regret to inform you that we are currently undergoing extensive renovations at Wharton Lodge, and that they will not be completed in time for Christmas. So, your dear mother and I shall have to spend Christmas on a cruise to the tropics. Alas, funds do not allow for you to accompany us, dear boy, so, unfortunately you will have to spend Christmas at Greyfriars School.

Mr. Quelch has kindly agreed to stay on over the holidays to look after you and give you extra Latin tuition, very good of him, I'm sure you'll agree.

We realise this may be somewhat disappointing and have sent you a substantial postal order and a Fortnum and Mason's hamper, in the hope that some of your friends may be able to visit you over the Christmas hols.

A Very Merry Christmas from your loving pater and mater.

Harry felt his eyes wet with disappointment. Stuck here on his own with Quelch! And as for extra Latin drills, they were something he needed like a hole in the head!

Just then there was a knock at the door, and before he'd had time to answer, it crashed open, revealing the person who was presently least welcome – Bunter!

"I say old chap," Bunter blinked furiously, "I'm starving, you know. I was expecting a postal order from my pater but … but it must have been delayed. I haven't any food, old man. Could you … I mean, could you spare a bit of nosh, I mean, just a few, I mean quite a few, slices of ham perhaps, a loaf … or two, maybe a few cans of beans?"

Just then Hurree Jamset Ram Singh and Frank Nugent popped their heads in. "Hello Harry, is Bunter getting on your nerves?" Then, seeing the distress on Harry's face. "I say, old man, are you OK?"

Harry's face was red with rage. "Clear off, Bunter, I've got more important things to think about than feeding your fat face!"

"Oh, I say, Wharton, that's not very generous of you, old chap!"

"The generousfulness is *not* terrific!" laughed Hurree Jamset Ram Singh.

"I'll give you three seconds to get out, Bunter. One."

"I say, Wharton."

"Two."

"Just a pork pie … or two, perhaps?"

"Three!"

"I *could* manage them without mustard. *Yarooh!*"

A patent-leather shoe tip connected with Bunter's customary yellow pants, stretched to the limit by his fatness. "Ow, wow, I say, ow, Yarooh!"

"Kick Bunter!" encouraged Frank Nugent.

"The kickfulness is terrific," laughed the dusky-faced Nabob of Bhanipur, as Bunter was pursued down the corridor by the combined shoe tips of Harry Wharton, Frank Nugent and Hurree Jamset Ram Singh

"Hic, hec, hoc, hunc, hanc, hoc," intoned Mr. Quelch, whilst the other half of his mind was preoccupied with ecstatic thoughts of the marvellous works – as he thought – of Virgil, Horace and Ovid.

Harry Wharton stared through the window at the eddying snowflakes, trying to stay awake. What had he done to deserve this? He'd always been decent to the other fellows, perhaps not so much to Bunter, but then the Fat Owl had deserved it, but whilst the other fellows were at home with their loved ones, the Christmas crackers, roast turkey, gift-crammed stockings hung above roaring fires, and presents stacked high beneath sparkling Christmas trees, here *he* was, being drilled in Latin, in isolation, by probably the least popular master at Greyfriars; Mr. Horace Henry Samuel Quelch!

"Possim, possis, possit, possimus, possitis, possint …"

Harry felt his eyes begin to close. It seemed frightfully warm. His pen ground to a halt.

"Wharton!"

Harry jerked awake, "Oh, y-yes s-sir?"

Mr. Quelch's tone changed to a more sympathetic one. After all, he'd been young once. Or had he? He couldn't remember happy school days any more than he could remember not being a master at Greyfriars. "Look, Wharton, I know it's not your idea of fun being stuck on your own here at Greyfriars, but your father's a friend of mine. It's not so long ago he was where you are now, swotting up on his Latin conjugations and declensions, and bending over for 'six of the best' on more than one occasion too, I can tell you!"

"Sir?"

"And I've given my word to look after you and give you a boost in Latin. I daresay Matron will be doing something special for us on Christmas Day too!"

"Y-yes sir, th-thank you."

"Now, I want you to write out every tense of *habeo, video* and *venio* whilst I attend to matters in my study. All right, boy?"

"Yes, sir." Harry resolved to do his best.

When Mr. Quelch had gone, he put down his pen and went to the arched, leaded windows, looking out at the snowflakes swirling in the quad. There was an outside light and Harry was reminded of a snow globe he'd had when younger. He smiled at the thought of his former childish pleasure, shaking it and watching the snow falling onto a little Christmas scene – Santa and a reindeer standing outside a lighted cottage amongst pine trees.

Suddenly he gasped and rubbed his eyes. Outside, a procession of monks was heading across the quad! What the dickens were they doing in Greyfriars?

Although he didn't remember how he got there, Harry found himself outside. All was completely silent. It had stopped snowing and a heavy layer covered the ground. He realised he was wearing no shoes or socks, he could feel the soft, cold snow between his toes, hear it squeaking. In front of him, the line of monks proceeded, whilst his breath blew out like steam in the chilly night air.

Harry shivered and looked around. There were no lights on anywhere now, but a bright half-moon in the sky above, shining down on the crisp snow, gave an eerie light to the scene. He looked around at the dark, empty windows of the ancient school buildings. Nowhere was there any sign of life. Now he became aware of a soft chanting. He listened attentively, feeling a tear in his eye at the emotive words.

'Salve festa dies toto venerabilis aevo
Qua Deus infernum vicit et astra tenet ....'

The last monks were passing now and Harry felt emboldened. "Hey, excuse me." He approached the last monk. "Where are you from?"

But the monk ignored him, continuing to intone the chant until he disappeared from sight, seemingly headed for the ruined chapel beyond the cloisters. Harry stopped and stared in amazement. The snow ahead was pristine, no footprints anywhere!

"Harry, *Harry*?" It was the soft, friendly voice of matron. The room swam into view.

"H-hello matron, what ... what's going on?" It seemed an effort to speak.

"Mr. Quelch found you outside in the snow! You'd fainted. Thank goodness you hadn't been out there long, you could have frozen to death! You've been suffering from a fever. You've been in the infirmary for two days!"

Harry gazed down to see he was wearing pyjamas. "But ... but I don't remember. Just, just the ... monks."

"Monks?" Matron looked surprised, then looked up at Mr. Quelch who had entered the room with someone very familiar.

"Harry my boy! How are you?"

"Hello father, I'm OK, tired."

"Yes, you will be. You've been quite ill, my boy. Matron tells me that you must have been suffering from fever when you went

26

outside, to take your shoes and socks off like that! Thank Heavens Mr. Quelch here found you when he did!"

"Yes, you had a lucky escape, Wharton," said Mr. Quelch, "and I don't mean from conjugating those verbs I set you!" He smiled a rare smile.

Harry's father continued. "Anyway, I've got some good news, Harry. The reparations at Wharton Lodge were finished much sooner than expected, so your mother and I have cancelled our cruise and we've come to take you home!"

Harry smiled for the first time in a week and a weight lifted from his young shoulders.

The sound of laughter filled the drawing room at Wharton Lodge. A roaring fire blazed in the hearth and the mantlepiece was covered with Christmas cards. In a corner, a Christmas tree towered to the ceiling. It was covered in gold and silver baubles, tinsel, and twinkling lights. Underneath, lay an untidy pile of presents, wrapped in red, green, gold and silver, and with the names of the recipients inscribed on small gift tags.

"I say, Wharton, tell us that story about the monks again?" laughed Robert Cherry, his cheeks living up to his surname.

Harry's mother entered. "Come on, Robert, I think Harry's told all there is to tell already! And he's still not completely recovered from that fever, remember. Anyway, boys, the cook has just told me that dinner will be served in half an hour. There's a huge turkey, sausages, stuffing, roast potatoes, roast parsnips and … what else? Oh, yes, lots of vegetables!"

There was a groan from Frank Nugent.

"You need to eat your greens, you're growing lads!" laughed Mrs. Wharton.

Frank Nugent, Robert Cherry, and Hurree Jamset Ram Singh had been invited to join the Whartons for Christmas and now sat at a table playing cards, drinking lemonade and waiting for the much-anticipated call to dinner.

Outside a motorcar door slammed and the doorbell rang.

"That's odd, we're not expecting anyone else, are we mother?" said Harry.

"Not as far as I know."

"I'll go." He walked down the long hallway and past the grandfather clock, opening the door to a scene reminiscent of his snow globe, but the figure standing in the billowing snow wasn't Father Christmas but … Bunter!

"I, I say Wharton, old chap. I mean, can … can I come in?"

"What, which, why?" Harry laughed.

"Don't be a beast, Wharton! It's snowing for one thing. Look, Wharton, Bunter Court's flooded. Some pipes froze and burst. Mother and father have gone on a walking holiday in Africa and I'm stuck on my own!"

Fallen snow now covered Bunter's short wiry black hair, making him look like an albino.

"Well, thanks for calling and letting me know, Bunter, I'm sure you'll find something to eat in the pantry at Bunter Court. Merry Christmas!" He went to shut the door to find it wouldn't close. Bunter's fat foot was in the way!

"I say, H-Harry, old man, you … you wouldn't shove an old school chum out into the snow at Christmas?"

Harry thought of his own narrow escape. At this very moment he could be eating Christmas dinner with Quelch and Matron in Greyfriars refectory, listening to Quelch telling boring stories of ex pupils, and quoting Virgil!

"Oh, all right, come on in, Bunter, I daresay we can find you some Christmas grub!"

Bunter came in, wiping his wig of snow off onto the hall carpet. "Oh, I say, that … that's good of you, Wharton. I wouldn't want much, just a slice or two of turkey, well maybe three or five, and some roast spuds wouldn't go amiss, and …"

"Don't worry Bunter, I think cook's done enough to feed the five thousand!"

Just then a car hooted.

"Oh, sorry, Wharton, old chap, you couldn't lend me a few shillings for the taxi fare could you, old man, well perhaps a quid or two?"

"The cheekfulness is terrific," laughed The Nabob of Bhanipur, who had just appeared. He handed Bunter a five-pound note. "Give this to the taxi driver, *all* of it, mind! Wish him a Very Merry Christmas from us all!" He stood at the door watching to make sure Bunter did as instructed, as the Fat Owl trudged back to the cab in the whirling snow, whilst Harry joined the rest of his chums and family in the warmth and laughter of the drawing room. Even with the unanticipated presence of one William George Bunter, it looked like it was going to be a happy Christmas after all!

Blind Hope

Hard as winter ice, soft as summer grass. Her mind and fingers played with the forgotten contents of a bottom drawer. She fluttered her fingers over a mixture of bric-a-brac and clothing, plucking out something silky. She held it to her face and inhaled the faded scent of roses. A blouse! Yes, one she'd worn when she was young, twenty years earlier. She held it to her cheek, sensing the vibrations. Red or purple. Yes, of course, the blouse she'd worn to her grandmother's eightieth birthday party!

She pictured a photograph – herself, Flora, with a group of cousins, fifteen in number, all her grandmother's second-generation offspring. They all stood before a huge fireplace. The fire wasn't lit, it being summer, and the group had lined up in two smiling rows, symmetrically placed between two enormous bookcases that reached up to the high ceiling.

She'd stood at one end, her cousin Maurice, recently divorced, encroaching her space, touching her shoulders with his, showing an interest in a relationship with her perhaps? But she'd had her own *beau* then, Hector, Hector Simons. That was after the birth of Emma, but before her … accident.

She supposed she should feel sadness, loss, or something, but she felt nothing – empty, hollow, all longing and hope knocked out of her all those years ago. She wondered when she had last cried. At the death of her last guide dog, Billy, six years ago, she supposed. Six long years.

She wondered if the blouse would still fit. She took off a cardigan, then a T-shirt, feeling the air on her bare midriff and shoulders. Suddenly, for no reason, she unclipped her bra and threw it across the room. She sensed the weight of her small, hard, pointed breasts. She slipped the blouse on, feeling her nipples stiffen at the touch of the shiny, soft fabric. Yes, it fitted perfectly!

Then she remembered that the curtains were open over the window to the street. Oh, what the Hell! She didn't really care if any passersby saw her naked. She realised that was maybe the reason she didn't have net curtains.

The doorbell rang, and she heard Flossie stir in her basket. Normally she never answered the door, but she felt confident and curious. She felt the dog rubbing her leg, and reached down, holding its tail and letting the animal guide her through the door and down the corridor. There wasn't time to find and attach the harness. The bell rang again. "Just coming!"

She reached the door and undid the chain. Opening it, she felt a comforting blast of warm spring air in her face.

"Flora, it's me, Hector!"

She stepped forward and threw her arms around him, noticing the distinctive smell of coal tar soap that she remembered so well. She laughed. "You still use the same soap!"

"Emma told me where you lived," he said. "I've missed you."

Flora, hugging him tight, could say nothing more. Six long years were over.

Boxed into a Corner

The long white envelope had changed everything, but it had also changed the set of problems. Instead of, 'How can I afford to pay the mortgage this month and still have money for food?' it was, 'What part of the country should I move to and how many acres of gardens do I want?' Yes, those premium bonds sure came up trumps, even if they'd taken fifty years to do so!

So now one of my dreams was a possibility – a circular library! I'd envisioned burnished dark shelves, perhaps oak, stained a deep brown, areas of lighter brown and gold shining in the sun from a cupola high in the ceiling. Antique shelving would be nice, I thought, or I could get a skillful carpenter to make them. It'd take him some time, a lot of it *in situ* I guessed, but expense wasn't an issue, I could probably afford to have them made of silver, if not gold.

The problem was, how do you actually build a circular bookcase? Well, the most obvious thing was to have a circular room, but I'd found that houses with such rooms were in short supply in my locality. The other possibility was to have it constructed in a large *square* room. Now that was a much more realistic possibility. I even had one already, a kind of office cum junk room, high-ceilinged and barely used. But what about the corners? Surely, they'd be cut off, redundant, inaccessible, and gathering grounds for dust and cobwebs. Maybe even unwelcome rodents?

"What you need is EPS!" said my friend, Dave.

"What's EPS?" I said.

"Expanded polystyrene foam. Didn't you know that?"

"Well, why isn't it EPF then?" I retorted.

Anyways, it seemed if you got the right type, you could have it made into blocks that would round the corners of a room off, leaving a perfect circle for the shelves to be constructed around. Apparently, you could even have some cavities made in the foam for storage too, stuff that you would basically never need until you moved house, as it would to all intents and purposes be inaccessible. Anyway, that would get rid of some of the junk. Dave knew someone who could do the job.

We spent some time with graph paper and compasses working out the dimensions for the foam and in the meantime, I'd found a 'chippy' who would fabricate the shelving from antique mahogany in his workshop, then bring and install it in a couple of days or so. I'd seen examples of his furniture in a showroom and online, and I was very excited about his work. So much so that I'd also ordered a beautiful coffee table from him in an exotic solid wood – Amboyna Burl. A deep honey colour, with swirling, marbled grain. It was great when money was no object!

Life was looking good. There was just one fly in the ointment. Sandra. Thirty years of marriage had been twenty too many. Once an attractive young woman with flowing brunette locks, she'd now become 'dumpy,' to put it kindly, irritable and argumentative. Even my new-found wealth had barely cheered her.

Dave had a solution. "Look, I know a mate who makes these special, er, 'suitcases.' They're hermetically sealed. You can put, er, stuff in them, and there's no smell. Then when the heat's died down, you can dispose of the, um, 'contents' more normally like."

"What 'contents'?" I asked, already knowing the answer.

So, it was decided. I would take a fortnight's holiday on a cruise. The perfect alibi! Meanwhile Dave's 'mate,' the one who made the special 'suitcases,' would call round. Sandra would have an 'accident,' be popped into the case, placed in a cavity in the foam and sealed up. A car would be taken, so that it looked like she'd gone off somewhere and never arrived. Dave would then organize the carpenter.

The 'accident' wouldn't be cheap but Dave, a financial wizard, would take care of the 'laundry,' and my 'investment' would be untraceable.

OK, it'd be inconvenient to have to take all the books off the shelves and disassemble some of the shelving to extract the case at some distant future date, but it seemed like a foolproof plan.

Six weeks later I sat in my beautiful library with Dave. Everything had gone perfectly, police informed, all very sad.

Half the shelves were filled and there were boxes of books piled everywhere, waiting to be unpacked and assigned to their designated places. I estimated that there would still be perhaps twenty percent of shelf space available for further purchases, which could happily now be resumed, Sandra's resistance having been 'overcome.' Once the shelves were full maybe I could do it all over again with a smaller room? The house was certainly big enough, especially with only one occupant now.

Dave sat on a ruby red leather sofa, sipping wine at the exquisite coffee table. "Nice piece of wood," he said. "*Very* nice piece of wood!"

I sat in a browny green leather arm chair, one of a pair, on the other side of the table. Behind me were two glass cases, housing some of my more valuable and interesting books. "Yes, it's Amboyna Burl," I said. "So over here are my first editions," I gestured accordingly. "That section is books about books, and all that lot over there is on music." I'd been a book-dealer, then semi-pro guitarist for parts of my life, and Sandra, incredibly enough, had been quite adept on the bagpipes, much to my perturbation. The drone of the 'doodlesack' was most definitely *not* 'music to my ears.'

Dave murmured appreciatively. "What's those magazines in that glass case?"

A creature with its features set low in a huge round head glared at us, against an indigo background, full of what could have been bubbles or planets, reminiscent of the individual's head. Its face bore a frightened expression, as if it knew what we'd done.

"Oh, that's *Science Fiction Monthly*. It was published from 1974 to 1976. I've got the complete run, 28 issues!"

"I like science fiction," said Dave. "Russ Ballard and them other writers."

I rolled my eyes. "*J.G.* Ballard!"

The doorbell went.

"I'll go," said Dave.

A minute later he came back, ashen faced, accompanied by a lady. My jaw hit the floor.

"Well aren't you going to say hello," said Sandra.

"Y-yes, … of course," I said. "But er, where've you been?"

"Yes, sorry about that darling, I wanted to tell you, but you were off on your cruise thingy. I went to stay with Vanessa. Ronald's left her and she needed some support. I actually thought you were coming back next week. When I saw your car just now, I realized you must be back. I rang the bell. I didn't want to shock you, coming in unannounced!" She barked a laugh.

"Oh, it's … it's g-good to see you!"

"The books look very nice. Your fellow did a good job. Did he do that table too? It's lovely!"

"Yes, it's Amboyna Burl."

"By the way, darling, I had a lady in to measure up for curtains and carpets while we were both away. Has she been in touch? I haven't heard from her."

Brother, Oh Brother!

Other nights I'd have stayed in, watching the telly, or gone shopping at Tesco's, but tonight there was a play on at the village hall, *Brother, Oh, Brother!* a farce set in a monastery, of all places. Anyway, I thought a trip to the supermarket could wait till tomorrow. Why not have a laugh, instead of listening to a load of drab, sour-faced, overweight women arguing with the checkout operator?

So, I found myself seated on one of four rows of chairs, about half occupied. I looked round and nodded to people I recognised, embarrassed not to know their names when one or two greeted me by mine. But there, thank God, was old Jack Hargreaves, a bit of a bore about his bloody beehives, but at least a friendly, recognisable face. He came over.

"Hello, John, good to see you. Not seen you at one of these before."

"Oh, er, no, I was, … er, busy, the last time."

"I think you'll enjoy this one, the last one was written by the same guys. It was really funny. *The Great Village Bake Off!*" He chuckled at the memory. "Oh well, mustn't gas any more. If you'll excuse me, I'll sit with Fanny or I'll be in trouble." He winked and walked several chairs away to join his large, white-haired wife.

I took a seat next to a sallow-faced fellow of unshaven appearance. He smelt a bit too. I noticed a large holdall under his chair. I was debating whether to move, when lights came on above an area which had been converted into an imaginative stage, depicting a brewery-type scene. A rotund bald-headed man, dressed in a monk's habit, appeared. "Brother Paul, Brother Paul," he called.

Another monk appeared from behind a backdrop of a wall, composed of large pink monastery-type bricks. "Yes, Brother Derek?"

"Well, Brother Paul, I need some advice. Is it proper for a member of the brethren to use e-mail?"

Brother Paul smiled. "Yes, brother, as long as there are no attachments!"

The audience laughed politely. Outside, in the distance, I could hear sirens.

"I say, Brother Derek, do you have change for a ten-pound note?" asked Brother Paul.

Brother Derek shook his head solemnly. "Change comes from within, brother!"

More polite laughter. The sirens sounded louder and I noticed the fellow next to me was sweating profusely and fidgeting. Suddenly he jumped up, opened his holdall and pulled out a shotgun. "All right everybody, hands up, I'm taking you all hostage!"

I could see what looked like bundles of banknotes in the holdall. We all laughed. The two 'brothers' looked nonplussed.

"Up against the wall, the lot of you. NOW! You monkeys too!" He gestured towards the 'monks' with the shotgun, his finger itching on the trigger. I began to feel very nervous. Surely, this *couldn't* be part of the play?

There were flashing blue lights outside now and I acted instinctively, recognising the style of gun and noticing the safety catch was on. I grasped the barrel with both hands and his surprise was palpable. Beady narrow yellow eyes glared into mine with hatred. Then there was an ear-shattering explosion, the gun jerked in my hands, and a huge hole appeared in part of the 'monastery wall.'

The door burst open and the place was filled with yellow-jacketed officers. "Armed police, nobody move!"

The man dropped the discharged gun and raised his hands. He was quickly handcuffed and led away.

A tall, authoritative figure came forward. "I'm Inspector Andrews. I'm sorry ladies and gentleman, but the show must *not* go on." He smiled whimsically. "And you, sir," looking at my shaking hands, "that was brave and, if I may say so, extremely foolish!"

"Oh, yes, er, sorry."

He turned away, organising bustling officers. I guessed maybe I'd been wrong about the safety catch.

But Can You Hide?

To Whom It May Concern.

First, the good news. If you are reading this, you are still alive. Now, the bad news. In 24 hours' time you probably won't be!

You see, you took something that didn't belong to you. Oh yes, you likely thought, 'I'd better take this briefcase to lost property,' didn't you? But then curiosity got the better of you. 'I'll just take it home first, have a quick look inside, maybe I can find the owner's phone number. It'll be quicker that way.' Pull the other one!

Well, wherever you are. At home, in a seedy cafe, maybe in a dirty, smelly little toilet, there's something you need to know. YOU are now the target in an assassination game! You have 24 hours to hide or be killed, probably in quite a nasty way.

You see, the briefcase had a chemical powder on the handle. Nothing that'll harm you (much). You can't see the stain it made on your hand but it IS visible through special glasses. The ones worn by our agents. And by the way, it takes a few days to wash off!

The briefcase has a hidden camera. Ha, you didn't expect that, did you? A number of images have been taken of you and posted on secret websites. The ones used by our spies. Yes, there *are* such people and, furthermore, they need 'live' training exercises from time to time. Hence this little 'challenge.'

So, as you are reading this, you may feel a little frightened. 'Is this real?' you are asking. Or maybe you're thinking, 'Oh, this is one of those silly TV pranks. I'll be on the telly! Better brush my hair!' Sorry! It isn't. REALLY!

So, when you've finished reading this letter, you will have to start thinking and running. And by the way, just like the old TV program, this letter has a coating, which once exposed to air, will dissolve it within three minutes. Perhaps you'd better read a bit faster!

Well, maybe I shouldn't tell you this (it's all rather hush-hush), however I think it's only fair. But between you and me, there are twenty agents vying for a job. A very prestigious job, a bit like James Bond. They have your picture, your hand(s) will glow when seen through their special glasses and they know where the briefcase is right now. So 'they are coming to get you,' as they say in the old horror films!

Well, every other day for two weeks, a briefcase, just like the one you 'borrowed,' will be left on a train somewhere. The successful agent will be the one who accrues the most points over the fortnight. The agents get points for both their speed in locating the 'target' (people like yourself!) and the originality of his/her 'dispatch.'

For example, it could be a poisoned dart from a blowpipe (yes, we've borrowed a few ideas from our jungle 'cousins'!), it could be a 'crazed Japanese,' slashing you across the throat with a ceremonial sword, or perhaps a noose thrown over your head from a passing motorbike, before you are dragged to your death along the road. I know the agents are having fun with their ideas! They'll each have a partner on hand to film your demise!

Anyway, the clock is ticking so you'd better get moving. The good news. The hunt will be called off, and you'll be a free man (or woman) if you survive 24 hours! Good luck, you will (definitely) need it!

MI6

PS. I know what *I'd* do. But I'm not telling ;-)

Chateau Courdermaire

13th June 1952

Dearest Mama,

Well, we've all arrived safely and the chateau is lovely! Stephan drove us from Surrey in his motor car. We took the ferry from Portsmouth and the crossing was quite choppy. I'm afraid yours truly spent much of it leaning over the handrail! Anyway, after a couple of hours' drive from *Le Havre* we found the place, with some trouble actually. You see, it was dark, and the chateau, although most impressive from the front, is actually only one room deep, and is sideways on from the road, so not what we were looking out for at all! Anyway, we sought directions in *Ville de Courdermaire*, and the fellows there had a laugh at our expense. Apparently, we weren't the first to drive past *Chateau Courdermaire* without noticing it!

It has a sweeping gravel driveway and Stephan's motor car looks grand parked on it. I am taking lots of photographs!

Well, there are ten bedrooms on each of two floors. We selected rooms on the first floor as they are better appointed. I have a lovely four poster bed and an *en suite* bathroom, and I look out over sweeping lawns in front of the chateau. Imagine! Oh, I wish you could be with us mama, such a shame that your legs are bad.

Earlier, Jane came to me. 'Come and see what I've found, mother!' She was *so* excited. Well, down in the cellars there is a billiards table. You can imagine how Percy and Stephan took to that! They are down there now, as I write, showing Jane and Alexander the ropes!

The sun is sinking now, and I must start preparing supper. I am steaming a huge salmon and serving it with roasted vegetables from the village shop.

I will write again soon.

Much love,

Mary xx

25th June 1952

Dear Mrs. Henderson,

I write as the caretaker of *Chateau Courdermaire* to bring you news of a most awful incident, for which you have my deepest sympathy, madam. I hope the authorities will soon be in touch with you, but I wanted to let you know myself, as soon as I could. There is no telephone hereabouts and the only thing is to write, although the post can sometimes be quite unreliable, especially to England. But I know I will have done my duty in informing you to the best of my ability.

Well, I am so sorry to say that your daughter, Mary, was found in a disused ice house this morning. It lies at the edge of the front lawn and is ten feet deep, and mostly full of water. It appears she may have wandered at night, tripped and fallen in. It is low and the entrance is open. We believe she may have been sleepwalking.

A messenger was sent to the local *gendarmerie*. They attended post-haste and announced that your dear daughter had drowned through circumstances unknown.

Again madam, you have my deepest sympathies.

Sincerely,

Agathe Lemaire

23rd June 1952

Dearest Mama,

I write again. Things here are a little odd. I have encountered the owner, a grand old gentleman by the name of *Comte* Ducard. He called one evening to ask if we were happy with the facilities here – we are! He resides with his brother locally when guests are staying at the chateau.

Anyway, Stephan has been behaving strangely. He seems enervated and pale and has been taking to his bed in the daytime. He also complained about some insect bites on his neck and is now accustomed to wearing a cravat. I have urged him to see the local *medic*. But you know Stephan, 'No point in bothering the local quack, I'll see a proper doctor when I get back, if needs be!'

The chateau has a series of dilapidated attics and also a strange 'floor between floors,' only about two thirds of the normal height. That has just one door at either end of the landing, both locked and nothing to see through the key holes.

At night I have awoken to footsteps both above and below my room. I've called out, but no one answers and the footsteps stop. Most probably this isolated French chateau is stirring my fancies!

This morning the fellows at the *boulangerie* seemed quite agitated. They told me to lock my door at night and to hang garlic over it, even giving me some and refusing payment! Can you imagine? It seems superstition is still rife in the French *campagne*!

Well, today we were planning on driving to the coast, but once again, Stephan has taken to his bed, so we can't go. He does look very pale. I do think he should see a doctor.

Well, I hope you are well mama, and your legs aren't troubling you too badly.

I will write again soon.

Your loving daughter,

Mary.

P.S. I saw in the mirror just now that I have insect bites on *my* neck too. I cannot believe it is contagious. Perhaps it is the bedding? I will speak to the caretaker, Madame Lemaire, about it.

Circles and Stones

I

I was sitting on a wooden bench with my girlfriend, Daisy, in the graveyard of St. Mary's, in the village of Blackbarrow. My fingers traced random patterns on the warm, weathered wood, as I gazed over a sea of gravestones. Many were ancient, toppled at strange angles, worn illegible by centuries of summer heat and hostile, frigid winters. Why was there no system to put them upright again, I wondered?

"It's so peaceful here," said Daisy, squeezing my hand. "Thank you for coming."

I kissed her cheek, warm and soft. "That's OK, I like graveyards."

She sighed. "Two years. It seems like two months."

I noticed her eyes were wet. "I know, sweetheart, but they did everything they could." How many times had I said that?

She took a tissue from a brown leather shoulder bag and blew her nose. Then she reached back in and pulled out a thick paperback book.

"Christ, can't you give it a rest?"

"Look, I have to study. I have to pass my exams. One of us needs to earn some proper money."

The sky was cloudy but bright, the sun peeking through sporadically, and a pleasant warm breeze blew lightly, rippling the long grass. It looked well overdue for a cut. Pots of colourful flowers graced some gravestones, generally where the lettering was gilded and bright. Others held wilted, dry blooms, as if those who'd brought them had themselves died, unable to remove or replenish the desiccated ones.

I took some deep breaths, forcing myself to remain calm. I didn't want another row, not here. "What are you working on?"

She didn't look up. "As if you're interested."

I sighed and looked at my phone. There was too much glare on the screen to read it properly.

She turned and smiled, enthused. "Circles, as a matter of fact"

"Oh."

"There's so much to cover on the course."

"A circle's just a round thing isn't it?"

"Don't you believe it. There's Chromatic Circles, Archimedean Circles, Schoch circles, Woo circles, Ford circles, on and on."

"Sounds like some people had nothing better to do with their time."

She ignored my jibe. Honey-brown eyes twinkled in her pretty face. "Hey, if you draw a square around a circle, did you know the circle will contain 79% of the area of the square?"

II

I'm sitting in a circle, six women, two men. The room is lemon-yellow. At one end is a table with an intricate display of fresh flowers in a vase, surrounded by a picture frame, cleverly forming a three dimensional 'painting.' On the wall is a wooden plaque with black numbers on it, arranged vertically. 'Song' numbers, the word 'hymn' being avoided.

A small woman with white hair, leads us in a 'guided meditation.' "You are walking down a country road. The sun is shining and you feel its warmth on your bare skin."

How many times has she led one of these, I wonder, taking a quick peek at her wrinkled face. I imagine that when she started, mediumship was punishable under the witchcraft act.

"Then you spot an old pub and go inside. What do you see? What can you smell? You buy a drink. How does it taste?"

My mind quietens, and I visualize myself at the bar of my local pub. No, I don't want that. Try to think of somewhere different! Now I'm in a pub with dark wooden panels. In the corner an old man plays dominoes on his own, a cap pulled down, shielding his weather-beaten features. I imagine a hand pump, 'Heart of Stone Ale,' a picture of a heart-shaped stone on the shield attached to the pump. I take a sip, trying, not very successfully, to imagine a taste.

I'm in a circle designed to improve our psychic powers and our connection to 'spirit.' We meet weekly. I ask myself why I go? I don't know, I just want to.

Then we are guided onto a beach where we use a piece of driftwood to write any negative emotions we feel in the sand – bitterness, jealousy, guilt etc., knowing they'll be washed away by the waves.

"Now, just sit awhile and see who comes in." The circle leader turns on sound effects of waves and gulls.

To my surprise, it's Daisy. It's been a long time, over ten years. She's wearing a white dress with a red sash around the waist. Her blonde hair is long, blowing in the sea breeze. I imagine the scent of the ocean. "Hello sweetheart."

She smiles and sits down with me, on the sand at the edge of some grassy dunes.

I put an arm round her and imagine feeling the crinkled linen of her dress. I smell a perfume, sandalwood? Her soft lips touch mine.

Ten years, ten long difficult years since she went to study for a doctorate in mathematics in the USA, hooked up with her tutor, gave birth to twins, *our* twins, married him, and never came back.

"Now, it's time to come back to the room. Wriggle your fingers and toes. When you are ready, open your eyes."

III

There's a faint luminescence in the sky and Daisy and I are approaching ominous dark shapes, widely spaced. We'd left our small hotel early, to drive out to the stones, then a fifteen-minute walk over Scottish moorland by torchlight. It's June but it's chilly, although there is little wind.

We reach the first stone, and in the half light, marvel at its immensity, compared to our small, frail bodies. Perhaps twelve feet high and four feet wide, it towers towards the sky, its surfaces weathered by thousands of years of wind erosion.

To either side, perhaps ten metres away, is a similar stone, and beyond those in the gloom, we can just make out others, set to form a huge circle. Daisy looks at her watch. "Ten minutes."

"OK." I don't feel like talking. It's so quiet. There's no one else – thank God, no bird song, nor sheep even. I walk out into the circle. I can make out all the stones now. I turn around and around, in awe, gazing at the surrounding monoliths, all evenly spaced around a perfect circumference. How the hell ....?

A breeze blows on my face, gently rippling the grass at my feet. It's getting much brighter now. I head back to Daisy, who takes my hand.

"That's the stone we want," she says, pointing across the circle.

"Does it matter?"

"Yes, it's at the western point. We can watch the sun rise over the eastern stone."

She leads me over the moorland to the designated stone, saying nothing. We stand in silence, watching, waiting. Then an orange glow appears in the sky from the opposite side of the circle, gradually expanding. There is no sound, save an empty wind blowing amongst the ancient sentinels.

Suddenly the brilliant golden-orange disc of the sun starts to rise, casting huge shadows from the eastern stones. I stand transfixed until the dazzling light of the sun appears at the top of the stone. "Wow." I turn to look at Daisy and, to my astonishment find she has stripped naked. She doesn't speak, just pulls me towards the stone behind us. Her flesh looks so pale against its dark surface. I feel a vibration from the earth. It's in the air too, something magical. I feel an incredible sexual energy building in me, like nothing I've ever known.

Daisy is practically tearing my clothes off me and we're up against the stone. She reaches down and inserts my painfully-throbbing member into her. Then I'm thrusting into her, violently pounding her against the stone with an animal passion.

She is groaning, her eyes are white, the irises have almost disappeared behind her eyelids. I hear her shouting out in ecstasy, then I reach a shattering climax, aware of nothing else for what seems like an age.

Afterwards we dress in silence. She pulls a flask of coffee out of her bag and a packet of cigarettes. "God, I'm soaking. Inside!" She tucks a tissue into her panties and laughs, lighting a cigarette and handing it to me. "I'll probably have triplets now!" Then she hugs me and, before kissing my cheek, whispers in my ear, "we'll always be together, you and me."

Clarissa's Missives

I

There's a letter from Clarissa in the mail. The violet envelope stands out from its intimidating white neighbours. My heart beats a little faster. I deposit the others at the back of a drawer. I'll open them later. Maybe. I sit at my desk and open hers.

'Dear Stan.' That seems to be her 'pet name' for me, as my name's actually John. We'd only met once, briefly, colliding into each other in Tesco's. I hadn't bothered with a basket, clutching my shopping betwixt hand and chin when she, glued to her mobile, had rammed me with her trolley, sending noodles, bananas, butter, frozen fish and a jar of peanut butter flying. She'd helped me retrieve them although the peanut butter had met a sticky end.

I continued to read. 'Thank you for your e-mail, Helena printed it for me again.' Helena being her sister. Clarissa is by all accounts computer illiterate. She'd talked in a previous letter about 'downloading' my e-mail address and being unable to understand Google.

"Oh, I'm terribly sorry!" She'd looked so concerned it was hard to be cross. I'd noticed blond hair, tangled and somehow pinned back, big eyes that blinked furiously, deep green like an ocean swell, a smudge of lipstick on a neat white tooth.

She'd overseen the retrieval and replacement of my shopping and I'd also noticed she seemed quite attractive.

"Do you shop here often?" I'd asked, feeling somewhat foolish at the cliché.

"Oh, no, I've just moved here, this is the first time."

I saw her trolley contained several bottles of wine. "Are you having a party?" I'd asked.

She'd blushed. "Oh, not really…."

I hadn't pressed her.

"Look, here's my card." She'd given me a neat purple business card. It said 'Clarissa White – musician, composer and music coach.'

"Oh, that's interesting, I'm a guitar teacher!"

"Wow! Look, I've got to dash but let's keep in touch." She'd smiled and the green ocean swelled once more.

So that's how it had begun. I'd e-mail her and each time a violet envelope would arrive a couple of days later. Ornate purple script flowed, telling me she was recently divorced and staying with her sister locally.

I read Clarissa's latest news. She's got a new student, a girl of thirteen who's tone deaf. The girl can't tell if a note is higher or lower than the one next to it. Clarissa's beautiful cursive script belies its mundanity. Her cat has been sick on a kitchen surface.

Although I enjoy her letters, it's getting frustrating. In two of my messages I'd suggested meeting for coffee – with no response. I often gaze at the picture on her card, presumably taken a good few years earlier, where a glamorous woman leans over a keyboard, face concentrated and fingers splayed as if wrestling with Rachmaninov.

I read on, then *Eureka!* I stand and punch the air, hitting a low flying lampshade which makes my knuckles smart. No matter! I read 'Helena is away this Friday night, doing the Lyke Wake Walk. Why don't you come 'round and help me finish that wine off, say eight o'clock?'

I notice my breath is short and my hands shaking. *Calm down*, she probably just wants to chat.

I don't know what possesses people to tramp 42 miles across the North Yorkshire Moors in the middle of the night but I'm thankful Helena is one of them. Below the flowing signature, Clarissa has added, 'P.S. bring your guitar. We can make sweet music together!' Then she's drawn a little smiley face. Whatever her intentions, I can't wait!

I awoke. Had I heard a noise? Naked, I was snuggled up to Clarissa's equally naked back, one arm around her, my face up against her nest of blonde hair. Then the sound of clomping boots and laughter. My heart thudded. The bedroom door crashed open and someone turned the light on. "Oh, look. Your sister's got herself a new boyfriend!"

There stood Clarissa's sister, Helena, and three young men, all clad in walking gear and carrying rucksacks. "No prizes for guessing what they've been up to!" said Helena. They all roared with laughter. "Hey, he's no spring chicken is he!"

Bloody cheek. Had *she* looked in the mirror recently? I shook Clarissa's shoulder but she didn't move. "Clarissa, *Clarissa!*"

I jerked awake to find myself shaking a pillow. Light came through unfamiliar curtains. Where was I? Then memories began to filter back. Wine. Yes, I'd drunk several large glasses of wine, I remembered that.

Clarissa had shown me into a very large, comfortable lounge with a grand piano, then she'd gone to make some tea. We'd sat and chatted happily – her ex-pupils, my ex-pupils etc. Then she'd gone over to the piano. I'd listened, entranced as her fingers, long and slender, caressed the keys, drawing out mellifluous melodies and harmonies. "That's lovely, Clarissa."

She turned and smiled. "Oh, thank you, it's not hard actually. It's a Nocturne by Chopin."

I'd brought a guitar as she'd suggested, a Japanese classical guitar bought from Ivor Mairants' music centre in Soho, back in the dim and distant days of my youth.

She passed over some music. "I found some duets." Then, "I'm so pleased you could come over Stan, er, sorry, John."

"That's OK. Just call me Stan," I laughed.

She blushed. "Should we look at the first one?"

I examined it – 'Island Melody.' Suddenly I felt my confidence dwindling. "I'm not sure I can sight-read this," I said. "I think I'd need to look through it first."

"Oh, nonsense, you're a guitar teacher. Just have a go!"

The first page was a series of arpeggios, broken-chords as they're sometimes called. The first one looked like C. That went for a few bars. "Oh, OK, but can you go slowly please?"

She smiled. "Yes, don't worry!"

She counted us in, not especially slowly, and we began to play. Her part consisted of syncopated chords and a lilting melody. It sounded like she was no stranger to the piece.

My heart was pounding and my throat felt dry but I managed to keep the notes going, whether they were the right ones or not I wasn't sure.

She stopped. Had we reached the end of the page? "That was lovely John, er, Stan. It's a C9 chord in bars one to four. I think you played C major 7."

"Probably," I said. It was alright for her, she already knew the damned tune!

Suddenly the phone rang. Clarissa crossed the room. "Hello … oh, Helena … isn't there anyone who can fix it? … are you sure? … well, isn't there anywhere you can stay?"

She spoke for several minutes then turned to me, looking disappointed. Helena and her friends' 'support vehicle' had broken down and they'd deemed it too risky to undertake the forty-two mile 'Lyke Wake Walk' across the North Yorkshire Moors without it. Unsurprisingly.

"I'm so sorry, John!"

Ha, she got my name right!

"I'm going to have to go and pick Helena and her friends up. It's OK, you can stay. There's plenty of wine in the fridge and you can sleep in the guest room. It's just through there. Oh, can you take Boris and Henry out please?"

"Who?"

"Oh, they're my dogs. They're Anatolian Shepherd Dogs."

"What?"

"Oh, they're originally from Turkey, I think. They're a bit big. They're in the TV lounge at the minute. You'll have a chance to practice that music anyway!"

Memories of Boris and Henry came back. 'A bit big' was an understatement. They were *huge*. Hurriedly, Clarissa had shown

51

me their leads and directed me to a nearby park. In fact, they'd trotted along quite obediently, drawing admiring comments from the few passersby. By the time we got to the park I felt like an authority on Anatolian Shepherd Dogs.

With embarrassment I remembered Boris squatting to deposit a huge steaming turd on a path. *What to do?* Well, it was growing dark and who would know it was 'my' dogs? Suddenly a woman dressed in green tweed and grey leggings appeared. She was about sixty, had grey hair and waved a stick in my general direction. "Hello young man, I hope you're not thinking of leaving that dog poo there!"

"Oh, of course not," I replied, "it's just I don't have anything to pick it up with."

"Well you could always use your hands!" she exclaimed.

"No, I meant those little plastic bags people carry."

Evidently a self-appointed dog poo warden, she reached into a pocket and pulled out a bundle. Under her stern gaze I was forced to put my hand in a bag, and put it over the hot, squishy, stinking 'poo'. It felt like it was in direct contact with my hand.

"Now pick it up!" she exclaimed.

I did so, noticing a little left on the pavement. I hoped her eyesight wasn't too keen. I turned the bag inside out, tying it with the special tie, feeling quite proud of my 'capture.'

"Now put it in the bin!" She waved her stick in my face and then pointed with it to a red bin about 10 metres away. Obediently I went over and deposited Boris's 'doings.' I smelt my hand. *Hmm.* It didn't *seem* to smell. Even so I couldn't wait to get back to Clarissa's to give my hands a good scrub.

Now as I lay in bed, I could hear a loud whining sound from somewhere. No doubt Boris and/or Henry expressing their desire to head to the park for another titanic 'poo.' Reluctantly I got up. But surely Clarissa would be back by now? I headed for the lounge and saw a flashing light on the answerphone.

"Hello John, it's me, Clarissa. The weather's been awful up here. They'd managed to find a guesthouse after all, so I stayed too. I don't think I'll be back until midday. Can you take the dogs out again please darling? I'll phone again later. Thank you so much!"

Darling! Well maybe I would take those hulking great hounds out just one more time after all, although armed with some 'dog poop bags' this time.

III

It was almost 2 p.m. by the time they got back. I'd taken the dogs to the park for a run and a 'poo,' poop-bag at the ready, but the grey-haired lady wasn't on self-appointed duty today. Still, I did my bit, now knowing the ropes.

Henry was the more affectionate of the two, trying to stand on his hind legs, with his front legs on my shoulders, to lick my face, but his head was so far above mine he could only lick my hair, not that I was sorry. He weighed a ton too.

I'd discovered that Helena had quite a large garden – a long rectangular lawn, and a further sizeable grassy area with mature shrubs down both sides. Beyond that lay some steps down to a small stream and an area planted with ferns and bamboo. The whole was overhung by low trees, and there were two iron benches. Numerous Arum lilies graced the area, displaying their large scented white flowers. A pleasant place to sit in summer, I imagined.

There was new wire mesh across the stream at both ends of Helena's property, so I imagined the dogs were allowed down there, although I wasn't sure the mesh would hold those two hulking brutes if they felt determined to 'explore.' They seemed happy enough to sleep in the TV room for now though, where there were two enormous baskets, so why tempt fate?

I practised the music I'd looked at with Clarissa. In the cold light of day and no pressure of a talented pianist breathing down my neck, it wasn't so hard. I found a pencil and marked some fingering in for future reference.

Then I had a little 'wander.' I looked in Clarissa's bedroom. A large double bed stood by a huge bay window that went up to a high ceiling. The house was old and solid, likely Victorian I surmised. Clothes were strewn around the room and I saw some panties on the floor by the bed. I felt a sudden urge to pick them up and sniff them, but instead turned to a dresser, covered with spectacle cases and contact lens solution bottles, along with a pack of her violet stationery.

I had a peek in a medicine cabinet, grinning at myself in the mirror. *Esomeprazole, Montelukast, Prednisolone, Seratide, Salamol, Beconase* and the ubiquitous *Ibuprofen*, among other boxes and packets, haphazardly stacked. Looked like she had a few health issues! A small pink packet contained *Zyprexa* – hmm, where had I come across that before? Suddenly feeling guilty, I closed the cabinet, carefully wiping a thumbprint off the mirror. I wouldn't want her to think I was nosy.

I made a sandwich for lunch, and some extra for the girls, and afterwards began to feel like a spare part. I was just thinking about going home when I heard the doorbell ring.

I answered it, relieved to see Clarissa and, presumably, Helena, her sister, laden down with rucksacks and other gear. Clarissa looked old and tired, her blonde hair rumpled and out of place. She managed a weak smile. "Hello, John, I was hoping you'd still be here. I thought it'd save looking for the key if I rang. This is Helena, my sister."

By contrast, Helena looked ten years younger, was about a foot taller and had short, bright-red dyed hair. She smiled brightly at me with even, porcelain-white teeth. "Hello, John, Clarissa's told me all about you!"

I wondered *what* precisely, seeing as I barely knew Clarissa. "I made some sandwiches," I ventured. "Ham, cheese and tomato."

"Lovely!" exclaimed Helena, "We're starving!'

After they'd eaten and tidied themselves up we all sat in a comfortable conservatory that gave onto some variegated shrubs in the lower part of the garden.

Helena looked at me. "You've got a good man here, Clarissa dear. His aura is very blue!"

"Pardon?" I said.

She turned her chair to face me directly and her eyes took on a faraway expression. I noticed they were large and pale blue, with wide pupils. "Yes, John, I see a room, a room in your house. There are some guitars, four or five, on stands."

"She's training to be a clairvoyant," explained Clarissa, looking slightly embarrassed.

"Yes, there *are* some guitars on stands," I affirmed. Clarissa had no doubt told her I was a guitar teacher!

Helena continued. "And is there a … a cello?"

"No, sorry," I said.

"It's just that I see those funny little holes that cellos have."

Then the penny dropped. "Actually, I do have a jazz guitar, it has the same type of holes, 'f-holes' they're called."

Helena smiled. "Now, your father, he's in spirit, is that right?"

"What?"

"She means, has he passed over, died?" explained Clarissa, whose interest had perked up.

"Yes, that's right, seven years ago."

"He's here with you now. I'm hearing the name Jim, or is it Joe? Yes, Joe I think."

I looked around. No sign of the old man! "That *was* his name," I affirmed.

Helena stood up and started lurching around the room in an odd manner. "I'm feeling no movement down my right side. Did he suffer a stroke?"

"Yes, he did," I said, feeling a chill run down my spine.

She turned to me. "He wants you to know that he's OK now, he's well again."

"Oh, that's good." I didn't know what else to say.

"He says you've been offered a job, at a private school, but you're not sure. It seems like there won't be enough hours teaching for the travelling involved. Is that right?"

I was gobsmacked. That was absolutely spot on and I hadn't told a soul either!

"He says to take it, it will lead to greater opportunities."

"All right, I will!" I said and smiled. Well that was a turn up for the books, I'd been wondering what to do about it!

Just then, the 'reading' was shattered by a loud howl as Henry burst into the room. He began to bark loudly.

"Henry, stop it!" shouted Clarissa, but, looking from me to Helena and back, he continued his ear-shattering noise.

"Henry, shut up!" Helena shouted repeatedly, to no avail.

Then Clarissa clapped her hands. "Henry, play dead!" Henry dropped to the ground and rolled onto his side, occupying most of the conservatory floor, and becoming completely still and quiet.

Clarissa laughed, suddenly looking years younger. "I taught him that when he was a tiny puppy!"

Henry got up and sat with his head on Clarissa's lap, making an odd whimpering sound. "Don't worry Henry, the spirits have gone now," said Clarissa, soothingly.

"I'm going to show John round," said Helena.

"OK." Clarissa lay back in the chair and closed her eyes, one hand stroking Henry's head.

Helena took me round the house. It was much bigger than I'd realized on my little 'inspection.' The kitchen was large and modern with oak units and extensive black slate surfaces. It looked expensive. A small staircase led upstairs. "That goes to an annexe," she said. "There's a guest bedroom, a bathroom and an office space, but we don't use them right now. The main staircase is on the other side of the lounge."

"Uh-huh," I said, nonchalantly.

We passed through a chilly pantry, shelves covered with jars and packets, and down to the stream-side area. Helena gestured for me to take a seat. "Look, I like you, John, and I know Clarissa does too. But go easy with her. She took a nasty knock when Stan, er, her last husband left her."

"Stan?" I said, surprised.

"Yes, he ran off with an ex-pupil, thirty years younger than him, can you believe!"

"Wow!"

"Anyway, poor Clarissa almost had a nervous breakdown, what with the press interest."

"What happened with them?"

"Oh, they're still together. Got three little kids now too!"

We heard a door close up at the house. "Shh," said Helena.

"Hello!" Clarissa appeared with a piece of paper in her hand, Boris and Henry at her heels, almost up to her shoulders. The dogs lay down by the side of the stream and Clarissa handed it over.

'The Lucknow Centre presents Circus Skills with The Joules Mangier Troupe – unicycle, juggling, tumbling, clown workshop, acrobatics and more!'

"It's on Wednesday evenings, six to nine, starting next week," said Clarissa excitedly. "I've always wanted to juggle!"

"Me too," said Helena, "and I'd just die to go on a unicycle!" She stood up and motioned her hips backwards and forwards, as if balancing on one, laughing.

"John, say you'll come!" exclaimed Clarissa, an earnest expression on her face.

I looked from Clarissa's wide emerald eyes to Helena's pale blue ones and back. I wasn't sure what I was letting myself in for, but I felt at home here. I'd have to rearrange four students, but, what the hell, 'in for a penny ....' I laughed. "I always wanted to run away and join the circus!"

Cruising Down the River

"Come on Pete, wakey-wakey!" Julie shook her boyfriend's shoulder, looking with affection at his unshaven face. She wore just a shirt, lemon yellow with white stripes, and her shoulder-length blonde hair was tipped over her face.

Peter's closed eyes blinked half-open. "Huh, wha' the time?"

"It's gone ten thirty. Come on, you said we could go to the park. We can get coffee at the kiosk."

"I was dreaming of walking Lexie."

"I've got her lead ready. Come on sweetheart, get up!"

Just then, three things happened. Someone started shouting down in the street below, a siren sounded somewhere and the phone rang.

"What's that siren about? It's weird." Julie snatched up the phone.

Her sister Josephine sounded anxious, afraid. "Jules, have you seen the news?"

"No."

"Well, you'd better put the TV on! The Navy fired a cruise missile at a terrorist warship. They've hacked it, turned it round towards the City of London. We're getting out now!" Josephine hung up and turned to Alan, her husband, a good-humoured black man in his thirties. Now his face was so pale it didn't look so different from hers. "I told Jules. They're on their own now. Come on!"

With a shoulder-bag each of clothing, books and toiletries hurriedly thrown in, they left and Alan locked the door, wondering what, if anything, would be left of their house.

The street was almost empty but three doors away he could see Malcolm raising his hands in frustration, shouting to Sally and the kids. "Come on, we've got to go now. NOW!"

Alan waved. "Hurry up!" he yelled.

Malcolm checked his watch. 11.15. What the flying fuck were they up to? He went back inside. Ted was fussing over two guinea pigs in a cage; he turned, his face streaked with tears. "It's not fair, I don't want them to die!"

"OK, OK, bring their cage. We've got to go now, and I mean NOW."

Sally came running down the stairs, her black bob of hair bouncing. She was wearing red shorts and sandals.

"For Christ's sake, don't you have any shoes?"

"Yes, they're in my case. How long have we got?"

"Twenty minutes. Before we get fried! Come on!"

Sally, Jake 11, Daniel, nine, and Ted, seven, toting his guinea pigs, ran out of the house and bundled into the car.

Two blocks away they hit a traffic jam. There'd been an accident at a cross roads, two vehicles crashing head on. Horns were hooting, people anxiously getting out of their cars, yelling, gesticulating.

"What's going on Dad, we don't have time to stop, do we?" said Jake.

Malcolm jammed his hand on the horn. *Jesus Christ!*

Captain Charles Hester looked down on the gridlocked cars from the high cabin of his fire engine. He glanced at his companion, Edgar Tierney. Tierney's face was white, his hands shaking. "I hope to God, Jude and the kids got out in time," Tierney said.

Hester looked at his watch. Fifteen minutes to go. "They'll be fine!" He felt his stomach lurch. *I have to do this.* He slammed his foot down on the accelerator and the car in front buckled up, swinging out of the way and smashing into another vehicle. Someone inside was shrieking hysterically. With his foot still hard on the accelerator, his ears closed to shouting and screaming, the fire engine bulldozed cars aside until it reached the accident spot. He could see blood over one windscreen and people in the back of the other car, motionless. He kept his foot down, the unstoppable force meeting the immovable object syndrome, he reflected grimly. What happens? The unstoppable force stops and the immovable object moves. With the engine roaring like a beast possessed, the now-wrecked front of his vehicle ploughed the mangled cars off the intersection, leaving a channel behind, into which those still undamaged enough to drive, sped through.

One of them was Alexa Rogers, an attractive barrister in her late twenties. Popular and wealthy she wasn't hanging around for anyone. She'd not spent seven years studying, not to mention being the butt of sexual innuendo, assault even, on occasion, to get burned alive in her car! No, she was heading for the hills. Well, Lavender Hill to be precise. To her surprise the roads were running freely all the way there, the traffic going just one way – away from the financial district. A few hundred others must have had the same idea as her, she realised, as she hit congestion at the bottom of the hill.

She managed to park, then half-walked, half-ran up the hill, passing anxious families with crying children in tow. She kept her eyes fixed towards the trees at the top, signifying the park entrance. She wasn't stopping to reassure anyone. She checked her phone. Ten minutes to go.

A crowd was gathered on the heath at the top to watch the spectacle from a safe distance, several miles away. Samantha Lacey hugged her husband, Tom. She spoke anxiously. "They're saying it'll be here in five minutes." They looked down on the panorama below. Neat rows of red-roofed Victorian houses, then the wide silver ribbon of the river Thames, and in the far distance to their left, barely visible, the grey line of London Bridge. Beyond that, almost invisible brown dots, lay the Houses of Parliament and Big Ben.

She pointed. "Oh my God, look!"

A gasp went up as a silver pencil-like object flew from their right, low above the river, engines screaming. Everyone watched, transfixed, as it disappeared out of sight to the left. Samantha gripped Tom's hand tightly. She noticed his was wet with sweat. Then a distant deep echoing thud and ... nothing.

The crowd stood, silent and expectant. Thirty seconds. One minute. Two minutes. Tension evaporated. It was a dud, Tom realised. After all that, the terrorists' hacking skills had turned back a dud! The news went around the crowd. He hugged Samantha and they laughed for the first time that morning. "We can all go home!"

Suddenly, nothing existed but brilliant, blinding light. Instinctively, they put their hands over their eyes and flung themselves to the ground. There was a tremendous ear-shattering roar that seemed would never stop, the earth vibrated against their bodies and Tom felt the intense heat of a fireball howling over their heads. Samantha was whimpering like a scalded puppy. After a while he cautiously took his hands away from his eyes. There were some white spots swimming around in front of him but his vision seemed otherwise unaffected. *Thank God, I can see!* "Are you OK Sam?"

She nodded affirmation, her face white and streaked with dirt and tears, and her fair hair now a blackened mop.

Behind them, cars parked on the heath were on fire. Below, they could see a wall of smoke and flames rising from the houses, and in the distance, beyond London Bridge, a red flame burned with the intensity of a firework. Above it, a huge pall of black smoke was forming into something they'd all hoped they would never see. "Fucking hell, they never said it was carrying a nuke. Why didn't they tell us!"

Cars were exploding like firecrackers behind them. They walked the other way, down to the lake, following the crowds. They passed a burning kiosk, turning away from two charred corpses on the ground. Then Tom spotted something close by the stick-like charcoal arms of something that had once been a man. He picked it up, a metal disc with burned leather attached. He wiped soot off it. *Lexie.* What was that about?

Samantha tugged his arm. "Come on Tom. Let's find help."

He tossed the disc back onto the corpse. "OK. Poor sods."

Comic Tragedy

Monastic life had its ups and downs. At first it had been quite exciting, rising at 4.30 in the old Abbey in the summer, seeing mist covering the expansive lawns, whilst a golden glow on the horizon diffused over the orchard.

Opening a window with its ancient leaded panes and breathing in *that* air, the air of creation. Taking it deep, deep into the lungs, holding it, thanking God for this life, and exhaling with gratitude.

As the months went past and summer turned to autumn and autumn turned to winter, it wasn't quite so exciting. The attraction of getting out of a warm bed onto stone cold flags, seeing your breath misting in the candlelight, not so appealing. Then a trip down a dimly lit corridor to fetch a jug of hot water for washing and shaving. Today, there was something wrong, the water was freezing cold, an ordeal to do my ablutions.

Then out into the cold wind of the cloisters to the church and *Vigils*, the first service of the day. Brother Cecil greeted me, his double chin wobbling beneath his round pink face. "Having a lie-in Brother Paul?"

"No, the water wasn't heated, it took me longer."

Brother Cecil's laugh sounded like a dog barking. "When I was a novice the water was *never* heated!"

I looked at his fat smirking face with disdain, then mentally asked God to forgive my uncharitable thoughts.

The day proceeded as usual, 6.15, a bowl of tea, bread, butter and marmalade, then *Lauds*, half an hour of praising God. My thoughts had changed over the last months. Surely a supreme being who designed the universe didn't need to be adulated? It was rather like making a *vivarium* for an ant colony. Yes, you'd like to observe them busying themselves with making tunnels, attending to the queen, and doing whatever in God's name ants do, but you'd hardly need them to be singing hymns and worshiping you!

Anyway, after *Lectio Divina, Terce,* and Mass, I felt zombified due to lack of sleep. I'd prayed for God's help, but he was obviously off on a mission somewhere else today. I felt truly knackered.

"Come along Brother Paul, no more slacking today!" the dulcet tones of Brother Cecil rang out. "Cellar duty for you!"

My four-letter reply stayed in my mind, the Lord be praised! I looked at a clock on the wall, 10.05, three hours to go, until after dinner I'd be able to retreat to my chamber and 'crash out' for half an hour before *None*, the fifth service of the day.

"Come along, come along, Brother Maurice is down there already!"

Down in the cellar, it was my and Brother Maurice's task to brush mould off an area of wall with heavy wire brushes. Then to paint the area with limewash. Cold, damp and unpleasant work.

"Good Lord!" I heard Brother Maurice exclaim.

"What's up?" I went over to where he was working to find a brick had become loose, revealing a cavity. "Is there anything in there?"

He removed the brick and fished around, pulling out a small book, some candles and a wide cardboard tube about a foot long. "It's a diary, written in Latin," he said, examining the book. "It talks about Father Jeremiah. That was before the war!"

I took the tube, and prised off the cap. There was something inside. I extracted it to find a roll of some kind of waxed paper. I unrolled it on a nearby table. "Look at this!" Inside was a copy of the *Beano*!

We both stared at it. Why on Earth would anyone have secreted a comic behind a wall! Brother Maurice smoothed out the curled, but still brightly coloured paper. It showed the antics of an ostrich and a monkey in six frames. A red oval contained white lettering, BIG EGGO. "Good Lord, this is number one!"

The cover advertised a 'Whoopee' mask. He shook the comic and a thin black cloth mask with two elastic loops to go behind the ears tumbled out.

"Brother Maurice, Brother Paul!" called a familiar voice. The staircase creaked under the fat, brown-robed form of Brother Cecil.

We exchanged glances. There wasn't time to hide the comic.

Later, after 1 p.m. *Sext*, a short hymn and some prayers, I proceeded to Dinner. Today mutton stew, served with chips, roast parsnips, and whole-wheat rolls and butter – a most welcome repast!

"Brother Paul, Brother Paul!" It was Brother Maurice.

"What?"

He led me to one side. "That comic we found. It's worth … it's worth …. He was visibly shaking.

"What? How much?"

"Twenty to thirty thousand pounds … with that mask!"

"What! Look we'd better find out what Brother Cecil did with it."

"No need!" Brother Cecil's booming voice interrupted as his rotund form came into view. "I was intending to speak to Father Abbot, I thought it might be worth a pound or two and suitable for our Christmas auction, but just then I heard that Brother David had a bad case of diarrhoea, and there was a severe shortage of toilet paper. Brother Cedric had just gone for a supply. That, er, comic was an excellent substitute!" He looked at our ashen faces with surprise. "Apparently there wasn't quite enough, unfortunately, so he had to use that mask thingy to 'finish off.' Praise be to God that you found it!"

Death by DVD

Horncastle Suicides, a special report by Genevieve Messier for the Horncastle Times. January 2018.

Horncastle, a small Roman town dating from the ninth century, and situated in the Lincolnshire Wolds, an Area of Outstanding Natural Beauty, lies at the confluence of three waterways – the river Bain, the river Waring and the Horncastle canal. Today, many of the old wharf buildings lining the canal and the river Bain, once traversed by barges laden with grain, timber, and coal, have been converted into smart, desirable apartments and town houses.

Horncastle boasts a plethora of antique shops, from the smartest emporia of expensive furniture and rare porcelain, to a converted church, shared by a number of dealers, with a myriad illuminated cases displaying bright, enticing jewellery and knick-knacks, to the chaotic and mind-boggling maze of bric-a-brac and junk that is Archer's.

But this picturesque town and its surrounding villages hold a dark secret. In the past two years, since January 2016, there have been 12 suicides, predominantly of young people under the age of 21. An astonishing SIX times the national average.

Genevieve Messier spoke to Mary Todd.

Mary, your son, Saul, was just seventeen years old when he died. He was a pupil at the local grammar school. Are you able to tell me about it?

Yes, it was in February 2016, nearly two years ago. He'd gone to school, normal like, he didn't seem upset or anything. When he didn't come home, I thought he'd gone to Wayne's. That's his best mate. About eight o'clock I phoned Wayne's mum, Karen. She said Wayne was there but Saul wasn't and that Wayne hadn't seen Saul at school neither.

That's when I got worried. I texted him, then later I phoned his mobile but he never answered, so I called the police. I spent a sleepless night, as well you can imagine. Then the next morning they came to tell me they'd found him in the woods, down the river just past Tesco's. He'd hanged himself with his school tie.

I'm so sorry Mary. Did he leave a note?

Yeah, he did. It was under a pillow. It said he realised there was too much evil on Earth and that on 'the other side' it was just light and love, and that he wanted to join his friends there.

It was several months later that a rumour about a 'suicide DVD' began to emerge. The police have denied any knowledge of it, but Genevieve Messier spoke to Susan Brown (not her real name), a pupil at the local Grammar school, where it is understood five students have taken their own lives in the past two years.

Susan, what do you know of this 'suicide DVD'?

Well, some say these kids killed themselves cos there's nothing to do round here and no work, or else cos their parents wouldn't let them go into Lincoln of a weekend. But what others are saying is that there's a DVD. You watch it and you just want to kill yourself afterwards. But you have to write a suicide note about how it's horrible on Earth and lovely in Heaven, and how you just want to go there, now rather than later. Then you have to pass the DVD on to someone else, before you ... top yourself. And that person is sworn to secrecy.

Have you seen this DVD?

No, I haven't! But a mate did. Kelly Ann.

What did she say?

Well, she said once the DVD starts, you can't pause it, so she kept going out of the room and looking in from time to time. Anyway, it starts off showing all these horrible scenes from concentration camps, and the music's really sad. Makes you want to cry, y'know. Then there's film of these people disfigured by the nuclear bombs, and then these kids with awful injuries and mutations from gas attacks. Modern ones, y'know.

She could've turned the DVD player off though?

No, she said she wanted to see what happened. Anyway, after about twenty minutes, there's all these coloured lights flashing on the screen, and this weird pulsing music. It's really hard to look away, she said. Then it finishes off with instructions about how to hang yourself, how to do the knots and all that. Or if you don't want to hang, they tell you about what pills to take, and how many.

Why didn't Kelly Ann take it to the police?

Well, she'd been sworn to secrecy, y'know, so she had to pass it to a friend, Saul, his name was.

How did she feel when she heard he'd killed himself?

I dunno. She'd committed suicide herself by then.

Thank you, Susan.

Just a fortnight ago, another young man, nineteen-year-old Jake Tyler, was found hanged in woodland by a disused quarry on Tetford Hill. The police are continuing to investigate this mysterious outbreak of suicides and would ask anyone with information to contact them.

For confidential support call the Samaritans on 08457 90 90 90 or visit a local Samaritans branch – see www.samaritans.org for details

Doing Time

"Mr. Donovan Jones, the court has heard how you, as Jaspar Harding-Heath, did on the fourth of November 1833, together with accomplices, Ned Barret and Harold Mutton, ambush the evening coach from Lincoln to Great Wenlock, and in the process of robbing the travellers therein did cause the death of Lady Sylvia Rossington, namely by slitting her throat with a Bowie knife.

"You were later recognised by the deceased's travelling companions and also identified by your accomplices, under interrogation. How do you plead?"

"Not guilty, Your Honour."

"Do you have anything to add before I send the jury out?"

"Yes, Your Honour. This is the year 2018. The robbery was one hundred and eighty-five years ago."

The nightmare had begun twelve months earlier. I'd had an overwhelming feeling of guilt since childhood. No one could explain it. I'd had therapy of different kinds over the years but I was guilty of nothing worse than stealing a bag of sweets from a sweetshop at the age of seven. Hardly a crime to cause a lifetime of remorse. Then a friend had suggested I try a 'past life' hypnotic session. Well, it was incredible. Within a short time, I was reliving scenes that seemed completely real, but that I had no conscious memory of.

I'd learned that I'd been a highwayman in a previous life. As a member of the 'Witham Gang,' we'd had rich pickings along the roads into Lincoln, especially from ecclesiastical folk and rich pilgrims. Apparently, I'd thought of myself as a kind of 'cavalier-thief' and my comrades and I, with our faces well-powdered, would wear black cloaks, broad-rimmed Manilla hats with an abundance of coloured ribbons, satin neck-cloths and masks over our eyes. We would also adorn ourselves with brooches and rings, the pickings of previous robberies.

Well, there'd been a change of government and a case where a ninety-year-old was hanged for killing her brother, aged seven, when she was just twelve years old, something she insisted she had absolutely no memory of whatsoever. A touch of dementia hadn't helped either. There was good forensic evidence however.

Following that, it was argued that it was only a small step to look into crimes that had gone unpunished in previous lives. It was now the duty of all regressive hypnotherapists to report relevant cases to the respective police department. Unfortunately, I must have missed that on the news and the therapist hadn't mentioned it either. However, 'ignorance is no defence' as my lawyer told me.

Because it was in a previous life, they'd decided not to give the death penalty, but here I was, doing ten years in 'stir' in Lincoln prison for something I'd had no control over – that's how I looked at it anyway. It didn't seem right.

But my lawyer, one Henry Barrowclough, thought we had grounds for appeal. "Hello, Mr. Jones, how are we today?" he said, one bright sunny morning.

"Well, I've stayed in better hotels, what've you got?"

He laughed, sat down and opened his briefcase. "Look, I think we've got a line on this matter of identification."

"Yes?"

"Your – that is to say, Jaspar's – companions in crime identified you under duress – torture most likely, so we could argue that the only real identification came from the travelling companions of Lady Sylvia."

"Yes?"

"Well, you were wearing a mask. How could they have recognised you for certain?"

I tapped a small oval birthmark high on my right cheek. "This."

"What you mean Jaspar had the same birthmark?"

I sighed. "I believe so. If you go through the transcripts of the trial, you'll find it."

"But …."

"The hypnotist who regressed me to Jaspar explained it. He said birthmarks are often signs of wounds from previous lives."

"Really?"

"Yes, they've researched it, found correlations. Anyway, seems I was stabbed in the face."

"I thought you said they were signs from previous lives?"

"Yes, he took me back further. I didn't mention it before. Seems I was one William Widrington in the Civil War. I got the wound at the Battle of Winceby in 1643."

Dreams on Board

"'Clothes horses,' that's what she calls 'em."

"Uh huh."

"That's all they do, walk up and down the deck, flaunting themselves."

"Uh huh. That a problem, sir?"

"Who, me? No … no, it's just that she … that's my wife, Josie, doesn't like me looking at them. Says I shouldn't 'gawp at other women's anatomy'!"

The bartender wiped a glass, smiling wryly. "Well, you have to admit, sir, they're lookers."

"They sure are. Those crazy long legs, long blonde hair, low cleavage showing their ripe mangos! What are they, dancers in the shows or something? I never see 'em during the day, just the evening, 'bout seven, I guess. Up and down, up and down they walk, eyes straight ahead. Till about eight."

"D'you ever get to speak to one?"

"No, no, I mean, well they look too, er, haughty, I guess you'd say."

"Well, you're wrong there, sir, it's not such a big deal. Say hello, pay 'em a compliment. You'll get a great big smile. And she'll be happy to chew the fat with you!"

"Really? Well, I guess I'd like to, but there's Josie you see, she wouldn't like it. Can't say as I'd blame her."

The bartender put down the glass he was polishing, took another one from a shelf and poured a large shot of bourbon into each. "Here you are, sir, on the house!"

"Why, that's kind of you!"

"You're welcome, sir." The bartender took a sip. "Look sir, I'll let you in on a little secret." He winked.

"Yes?"

"Those gals, they ain't human."

"What! Whaddya mean, they aren't human?"

"They're robots. They're goddam robots!"

"Come on, you don't expect me to believe that!"

The bartenders smile vanished. "God's honest truth. Cross my heart."

71

"That's amazing. They seem so … real!"

"Oh, they're human-looking all right, right down to their sweet little beavers. And you can try 'em out too, although it don't come cheap!"

"So, what, … I mean, why?"

"It's the company. They don't advertise it, but word gets around. Come on these cruises, ogle the women, parading their wares every night. Have a few beers and back to your cabin with one, or two if you've got the dough, and they'll do anything you want. And I mean *anything*!"

"Wow!"

"No one gets hurt, the gals make it clear that they're there just for customers' entertainment, nothing more."

"But, I mean, don't guys realise the girls aren't … well, human?"

"They aren't told, but if for any reason they find out, they keep it to themselves, or … no more pussy on these cruises! No one'd believe 'em anyway … Well, lookee here!"

A tall, slim woman with curly red hair, prominent breasts and a glossy smile walked into the bar.

"Oh, that's Josie," said the man.

The bartender's jaw dropped.

Josie joined her husband at the bar. "A large white wine, a large Bud and whatever you're drinking," addressing the bartender, "You look like you could use one!"

"Oh, thank you ma'am," He busied himself behind the bar, shaking his head.

She flashed him a gleaming smile, revealing ample cleavage as she leaned forward to take her wine. "Thanks, hun." She blew him a kiss, then headed to a table in a corner.

The man grinned at the bartender. "Yes, guess I'll stick to good old flesh and blood!"

"Of course, sir. I don't blame you. By the way, the company's just decided to do a half-price cruise in a couple of months' time. Quite a few of the, er, 'extras' will be half price too … if you get my drift." He winked, producing a flyer and putting it on the counter.

The man quickly perused the brochure, paying special attention to the price list. He glanced over at his wife, busy with her phone, then folded it carefully and put it in a back pocket. He nodded to the bartender and, smiling to himself, went to join her.

Don't Dig for Bombs!

Tweed Newsboy cap perched jauntily on my head, I pulled into a small car park and turned the engine off. The place was deserted, shabby even, with broken tarmac in places. I took my cap off, pleased to see in the mirror that my hair was still in place, and put the convertible's soft top back up. I got out and took a long, deep breath, expecting to inhale the scent of the ocean. But the air seemed disappointingly normal, despite the grass-covered dunes surrounding the car park.

I walked over to a board, a map of the Skendlethorp nature reserve. Odd, it showed the sea as coming almost to the car park. I walked along a path, up a nearby dune, and gazed out, not onto the vast ocean, but onto a sea of purple flowers, stretching perhaps half a mile. Beyond was sand and in the far distance, the dark blue ribbon of the ocean. No wonder I couldn't smell it!

The weather was hot, the sky a clear, bright blue and the sun a burning orange disc. Most unusual for the English East-Midlands! I'd decided to take a drive out to the coast, having lived within striking distance of it for a couple of years, but whenever I'd previously thought of it, the weather had been cold and wet, the climate we normally endured.

Now, it was as perfect as it was ever going to be. But the sea looked such a long, long way away. Hmm. I walked back to a nearby caravan park, proudly boasting its very own fish and chip shop, the English coastal obsession. The owner was friendly enough. "Oh, the sea comes well in, even up to the top of the dunes, just beyond the car park."

"Well, why isn't it there now?"

Apparently, it was the wrong season, tide, and/or year. I sat and ate my over-salted fish and chips on one of two benches, the totality of Skendlethorp's visitor amenities, along with a rubbish bin, looking out to the distant sea.

In the foreground was a huge sign warning of buried World War Two bombs and missiles in the currently-desiccated marshland that stretched out ahead. It stated that no reward would be given by the Ministry of Defence to anyone finding one. Well, that kind of made sense, they wouldn't want to encourage idiots digging for unexploded bombs!

It was six o'clock in the evening, but still very warm after an oppressively hot day. I deposited my chip wrappings in the Skendlethorp bin and slowly started to cross the purple-flowered salt flats, the soil cracked by lack of rain into a crazy paving-like landscape. I followed a well-worn sandy track, presumably bomb and missile-free, until after ten minutes, I reached the beach.

I rested on a nearby sand dune as a few families, fat, and spouting one vulgarism after another – "Wayne, wai' for me, you cun', I wanna get some fuckn' chips" – came the other way.

"Balthazar, here Balthazar!" A small white dog scampered past my dune, pausing just long enough to spray a stream of foul-smelling urine onto the sand near my feet.

What a stupid name for a dog! Maybe it was trained to find myrrh, whatever that was!

It ran back to join an approaching woman, presumably its owner, fat and red-faced. As she passed, she looked right through me as if I didn't exist. My cheery greeting stalled in my throat.

I felt tired and the sea still looked a long way off. But when would I come here again? I began to trek across the sand, noticing hundreds of sea shells, mainly pod razors, *Ensis siliqua.* I picked one up, marvelling at its hardness and lightness and the way the two halves were hinged together. I wondered about the little creature that had created such a miraculous artefact and for whom it was home. Where had it gone and had he/she had a good life?

With child-like pleasure I began to assemble a small hoard of shells and flotsam. Here, a purple-tinged scallop, there, a piece of jet – charcoal-black, fossilised wood. Then, the pride of my 'collection,' a small, paperweight-sized rock filled with tiny bubble-like air pockets. Volcanic, I presumed.

Ten minutes later I stood at the edge of the sea. I looked back towards the land. The rise where I'd eaten my food on the bench was barely visible. I took out my binoculars and looked out to sea. There were several large tankers off in the remote haze. Another world on board I couldn't even imagine. Then I looked up and down the beach. In one direction two people at the sea edge in the far distance. In the other direction, no one.

The sun, still hot, bore down on me. I reckoned I could see five miles in either direction and the sandy beach was a good half mile wide. A quick calculation told me that I was one of three people on probably five to ten square miles of sand. How different to the crowded resorts not far down the coast where people flocked in droves for fish, chips, and bingo!

I rolled up my trouser legs and ventured into the water, to my surprise wonderfully warm and shallow. I waded out a few feet, watching the waves gently rolling past and feeling the soft sand beneath my feet. How lovely. Suddenly, something black and round emerged briefly from the sea, perhaps twenty metres out. My first thought was a dolphin. How nice to tell my friends. Then it popped up again, but this time remained with its dog-like head out of the water. Through the binoculars I could see a dark muzzle, big black eyes and long whiskers. A grey seal. I wondered if it would swim closer, just as another one popped its head up nearer to the shore. Then there was another, and another.

Soon there were about a dozen of them, bobbing up and down, keeping a wary eye on me it appeared. I wondered if seals would ever come out of the water and attack? I doubted it, only in the mating season, perhaps. I didn't know when that was, but remembered a seal-breeding ground, *Donna Nook*, just up the coast, a tourist attraction. Hmm. Well, I felt fairly confident of out-running a seal! I didn't remember reading about people being attacked in the water by them, though, or even swimming with them.

Would I go in the sea if I'd had my bathing gear with me? Given their powerful bodies, sharp teeth and the isolated location, despite the glorious weather, I decided … probably not. Discretion is the better part of valour, after all.

Just then, there was a loud thud from behind me and a distant scream. I turned to see a pall of black smoke above the purple-clad marshland about half a mile away. I looked through my binoculars in time to see something small and white hit the ground. It looked like Balthazar had been digging where he shouldn't have been!

Earthbound

Windsor Great Park was my destination, somewhere I'd never been before. I drove my little silver *Toyota* through the busy streets of Windsor, noticing in the distance a red flag flying above the famous Round Tower of 'the oldest and largest occupied castle in the world,' signifying that the Queen was in residence.

I followed the signs and found myself on less manic roads, finally pulling up at an impressive lodge, beyond which lay green fields and trees. A manservant in an antiquated purple robe came out. "Hello, Madam, may I help you?"

"I'm Sylvia Williamson, I've come to look at your ghost."

His aged face betrayed no surprise. "Ah, yes, come this way please." He led me into the sumptuously furnished building and along corridors, where faces of unrecognisable royal personages glared at me through the cracked glaze of ancient oil paintings, mounted in enormous gilded frames.

"This is Mrs. Sad-ov-ski." He enunciated the syllables pompously, as a middle-aged lady, dressed in an olive-green trouser suit, came to greet us.

She smiled. "Good day, Mrs. Williamson. That'll be all, Sidebottom, thank you." The purple-clad manservant disappeared and she led me out through a door and along a path to an old cottage. "Thank you for coming, Mrs. Williamson. We spoke on the phone ...."

"Call me Sylvia, please. Yes, I'm pleased to meet you."

She led me into a surprisingly spacious lounge with comfortable, modern furniture. She gestured towards a brown leather sofa. "Please take a seat."

"So, where's the haunting?" I asked, getting to the point.

Mrs. Sadowski looked embarrassed, coughed, and waved an arm. "Right here is the worst, but everywhere in the cottage really."

"OK, can you leave me alone for fifteen minutes please?"

I'd received a phone call out of the blue. A lady had heard of my reputation at getting rid of unwelcome spirits. People would be reluctant to admit, even to themselves, that their house was haunted. But after months of things being moved around, bumps in the night, footsteps in empty corridors, you name it, they usually decided to admit, albeit reluctantly, that it *was* the case. Then my telephone would ring.

So here I was. I closed my eyes and tuned into the 'world beyond the veil.' Soon I became aware of an aged woman in a long black dress with a white apron, seated opposite me. She regarded me with large brown eyes and I noticed I could see through her to the material of her armchair.

Telepathically, I received her story. She'd had a harsh mistress in a large house nearby. The only person she had loved was the mistress's young son, Alex, who had drowned in a local pond. For years she'd served, until the mistress's death. Since then she'd happily lived alone in her cottage, without being at the mistress's beck and call. In her own confused way, she believed Mrs. Sadowski to be her lodger.

"Don't you have any family?" I asked.

"No."

"What about friends?"

"I ain't got no one." The vulgarism fell naturally from her lips. She continued, "This cottage'll last me out, it's enough for me."

"Last you out, what about when you die?"

"Die?" The old woman snorted. "That's the end of you, ain't it?"

"What about Heaven … and Hell?" I asked.

"Stuff and nonsense. I don't believe in 'em! Having this cottage to myself is all the heaven I want!"

"But what about Mrs. Sadowski, she lives here now?"

The old woman became confused. "I don't know, I see her about, she … she's my lodger, ain't she?"

I had an idea. "Yes, she is. But she's not well. I'd like you to call her a doctor."

"A doctor, well, I don't know … I ain't seen one for years. I … I don't see folk much these days."

"Well, I'd like you to call one for her please, I'll come back tomorrow to make sure you've done so."

I returned the following day. Again Mrs. Sadowski left me alone in the lounge. Soon I made contact with the old lady, whose name I'd discovered was Agatha.

"Did you find a doctor for Mrs. Sadowski?" I asked.

"No, no, I never. Truth be told, I ... I couldn't find the village." She sounded confused.

"Listen, Agatha, don't you have any friends or relations who've passed over?"

"No, there was just little Alex, the lad who drowned. Look, I know what you're getting at. Don't tell me I'm dead. Please. I love my little cottage too much." She began to cry. "I ain't going, I tell you."

I suddenly felt desperately sorry for her. "Look, there *is* a better life." I said and called on my spirit guide for help. He'd told me he would be ready and able to assist.

Agatha's sobbing suddenly stopped. "Why, there's ... there's little Alexander!"

"Follow him into the light."

Suddenly, the apparition vanished and the oppressive atmosphere lifted. I knew Agatha had done as I'd requested.

Mrs. Sadowski appeared. "Has she gone?"

I smiled. "Yes, she'll be with loved ones and friends now. Even though she thought she didn't have any."

EC Was Here

Profundity of expression wasn't Brad's strong point. "I don't care if you don't *fucking* believe me. Eric Clapton's my mate and if I asked him to come and play here, he'd fucking come and play here!"

Fred, the landlord of The Black Swan, coughed diplomatically. "Well, I expect he's a busy man."

Brad ran a hand through his greasy, swept back grey-blond hair. "He'd still come and play – if I asked him to."

"Bollocks!" said Billy, a large bald-headed man with tattoos down both muscled arms.

Brad looked daggers at Billy. I'd never noticed how much Brad looked like Dracula before. Give him a cape and the fangs and that look would have killed.

"All right, how much?" said Billy.

"What?"

"How much d'you wanna bet? I say you can't get him. Five hundred?"

"I don't want your fucking money!" snapped Brad.

"You bloody liar, you don't know him at all!" laughed Billy.

"All right then, you're on. I'll give Fred five hundred quid tomorrow to look after. You do the same, OK?"

"All right," said Billy. I'll give you three months, till September. Eric Clapton to perform in this bar! Never!"

"I shouldn't really allow betting," said Fred.

"No-one'll know if you don't tell 'em," said Brad.

"All right," said Fred, "just this once, as it's Eric Clapton!" His eyes lit up at the thought of an interest free 'loan' of a thousand pounds.

So, the weeks passed. There was a blackboard with the name of the musician or band playing that week. So far, the letters 'E.C.' had been conspicuous by their absence. It was a touchy subject. Mention it to Brad and he was liable to fly off the handle or, at the least, return abuse. He'd been in the pop business for many years, once a kind of 'pop star,' now, long forgotten and unmissed, but a 'mate' of EC? The idea seemed preposterous.

Brad's 'squeeze,' Jilly, likewise acted schtum. "I'm not saying anything. You'll find out by the end of September," she'd say, with an enigmatic smile and a shake of her curly red locks.

The second week of September I called in on Tuesday for the weekly pool match, on this occasion a home match against the 'Tigresses,' a ladies' team from the curiously named *Coach and Tiger* in Thaxleby, an 'easy' match – in theory. With embarrassment I remembered our last meeting when the motley crew of elderly ladies had emerged victorious, their near eighty-year-old captain, Ada, winning the final game with a gloating expression on her wrinkled face, "Hard luck boys!"

Then my jaw dropped. The blackboard for the music that Friday indicated 'Special Guest.'

Fred appeared. "D'you want a drink?"

"Is that who I think it is?"

"Well, all I know is it's Brad's friend." He raised his eyebrows.

Friday came and, burning with anticipation, I called in just before eight, surprised to find a meagre handful of patrons chatting and listening to an old man wearing a fedora, singing 'I Walk the Line' to an out-of-tune guitar. Lizzy, the barmaid smiled at me. "That's Eric Clapton," she said whilst pulling me a pint of *Old Gravedigger.*

"You're joking!" I said.

"No, honestly, he showed everyone his birth certificate and driving licence, his name really *is* Eric Clapton!"

"Bloody Hell, what a swizz!"

"Just then Billy walked in. He took one look, then turned to Lizzy. "Get Fred in here, I'll have my five hundred back!"

Brad appeared, having returned from the toilet. "I didn't say it was *the* Eric Clapton, did I?" he laughed. Jilly came over and hugged him. She turned to Billy. "No, he never. He won that money fair and square!"

Brad and Billy stood a few feet apart, sizing each other up. 'Eric' had stopped playing and the bar was ominously quiet.

Fred appeared. "Calm down everyone. I've got someone else in to play."

There was a gasp of amazement as a familiar figure strode through the door, carrying a worn hard-shell guitar case and an amplifier. He put them on a table, adjusted his round glasses and ran a hand over his stubbly grey beard. "Hello everyone, just give me five minutes to set up. Fred's asked me to start with *Layla*, I hope that's OK?"

There was a cheer and more customers came through from the restaurant area. I turned to Fred. "I don't believe it!"

He laughed, "It's amazing who you can book for a thousand quid!"

Evil Versus Evil

Justice of the rough variety was the order of the day at my old school.

"Hey, Johnny, Billy Stone's going to get you after school."
It was Tony 'Smiffy' Smith.

"What?"

"Says you've been messing about with his sister and he's going to give you a fat lip."

I felt a sudden queasiness in the pit of my stomach. "I talked to her at the bus stop. That's all." Susan Stone was pretty, intelligent and friendly, everything her brother wasn't. I often wondered if they had the same parents.

"Says he's going to knock your teeth so far down your throat you'll have to stick a toothbrush up your arse to clean them."

"Hah. Let him try!"

"Oh, you think you can take him on, do you?" Smiffy laughed. "He'll pulverise you!"

I sat in the toilet, literally shitting myself. There'd been this kid, Denis someone. Rumour had it that Billy Stone had taken a dislike to him. True, Denis was pale, spotty, wore thick-lensed glasses and had a high, annoying voice, but live and let live was what my parents had taught me. They said Billy had accused Denis of bumping into him at the bus stop. Apparently, Billy then punched Denis in the gut. When Denis bent over, gasping for breath, Billy had kneed him in the face, busting his nose. Denis had gone down and for good measure, Billy had kicked him 'where it hurts,' leaving Denis howling in agony and blubbering like a baby. It was all over in ten seconds. To add insult to injury, Alex Rawlinson, one of Billy's gang, was said to have held Denis's school bag open whilst Billy urinated into it.

To avoid a further beating, Denis had sworn he'd tripped and fallen over onto his face. He'd left the school shortly afterwards.

Then there'd been a playground fight with Ginger Tomkins. Ginger wasn't a pushover like Denis, but I'd witnessed it myself. Surrounded by a mob of baying schoolkids, Ginger had managed to trade a few punches before Billy had headbutted him in the face. Ginger had gone down as if poleaxed, leaving Billy to 'put the boot in,' as was his custom.

Ginger had subsequently spent an agonising week, bandaged-up in a hospital bed. When questioned by the teachers, though, he swore he'd 'fallen down the stairs.' Billy evaded punishment once more.

That night I took a totally different route home, planning on telling mum I was coming down with flu and hoping that a few days off would give Billy a chance to pick on someone else.

I borrowed a mate's bicycle and rode to a nearby railway station, a bare platform with a small waiting room and a toilet. It was totally deserted. I looked at my watch. The train wasn't due for ten minutes so I elected to leave the bike and use the toilet. When I came back my heart sank to my ankles. Sitting on the bicycle was Billy Stone! I turned, thinking to run across the track but marching over it towards me, grim-faced and determined, were Smiffy and Alex.

Billy slipped something silver and metallic over his fingers. "Come on Johnny, let's see what you're made of. Smiffy says you ain't scared of me!" He gave a harsh laugh, punching the knuckleduster into his other, cupped, hand.

I was in the direst of dire straits.

"Listen John, there's some advice I want to give you. You're young but it's as well to know the score. There are evil people in this world and sometimes you have to fight evil with evil."

I was eight years old, standing in my grandfather's study. Books lined one wall. Many were ancient, leather-bound tomes. My grandfather selected one, opening it at a diagram of a pentagram in a circle. The circle enclosed many bewildering concentric circles, and the page was covered in strange symbols and hieroglyphics. "I got this book from a great magician. His name was Aleister, a *real* magician. Know what that is, John?"

"No."

"Someone who can summon beings not of this Earth – angels, demons, and other, er, lesser entities, to do his bidding."

"Oh." I didn't really know what he was talking about.

So, I'd been given half a page of Latin to learn, a call to the demon, Valefar, a spirit said to bring protection and retribution. I'd been scared, but grandad said not to be. If I said the verse right, angels would control the demon. "And make sure you keep this to yourself, Johnny. If you tell anyone, anyone at all, mind, it'll weaken the magic, understand?"

Now in desperation, I recalled those Latin phrases and recited them furiously under my breath, whilst Billy circled, a cruel lopsided grin on his face. Suddenly I thought I saw something behind him, a dark shadow flitting past, then with a raucous screech a huge black bird came from nowhere, swooping down on him and latching on to his head where it pecked repeatedly at his face. 'Get it off, get it off!" he screamed, whilst Alex tried to swat the bird with his satchel. He made contact and it flew off, leaving Billy clutching his face, blood streaming through his fingers. "I can't see! I can't see!"

I retrieved the bicycle and rode away, grinning like a Cheshire cat. I'd take the scenic route home. Justice had been served!

Femme Fatal

Eighteen hundred hours. OK, *go, go, go!*

Ten metres away across the dark, moonless sand, a lone sentry stood. Behind me, black parachutes, like water holes in the desert.

Orders were 'no shooting' – ours not to reason why!

Running softly, knife at the ready, I ran the few paces. At the last moment the sentry turned, revealing a strikingly pretty face. I hesitated. Somehow, she launched a flare.

"Bitch!" I stabbed her through the heart and her shirt turned black.

Behind, someone screamed as shrapnel ripped their guts out.

In the now-lighted scene she lay, wearing a smile of triumph.

For She Had Eyes ….

I could hear she was quite young, nervous at meeting me, wanting to make a good impression on her first day, but afraid of my disability.

"Andy'll show you the ropes," said Sheila, my boss's secretary. "Andy, this is Sonya."

"Hello Sonya," I said, and smiled.

"Hello, Andy," said a girl's voice.

I continued, "Well, this is where it all happens." I ran an audio and video library for a big HR department. "I do the audio, and you'll be my eyes for the video!"

She laughed self-consciously.

Once alone together, I said, "Look, I know you probably don't want to talk about me being blind, but let's get it out of the way."

Her voice showed relief. "That's fine, if you want to talk about it."

"Take a seat."

We both sat on comfortable black leather office chairs. "Look, I'm really not much different to anyone else. I've lost a sense, but I've made up for it in many ways."

"Oh."

"Well, I know you're wearing mascara, I hear the clicking of your eyelashes."

"Yes, I do." She laughed, and it was genuine this time, surprised, interested.

"And you have shoulder length hair, I hear it brushing against a jacket. It doesn't catch, so it's not so long."

"Wow, that's right. Can you tell what colour?"

"May I?" I put a hand out towards her.

"Yes."

I felt her hair. It was fine, soft, shampooed and conditioned this morning. I wanted to smell it up close, but that would be going too far. "It's auburn I think."

"That's incredible!"

I smiled, no need to tell her that Sue in accounts had told me that. "From your voice, I'd say you were, er, 27 or 28."

She laughed. "29 actually. By two months!"

"I must be slipping!" No one had told me that, but the timbre and manner of her speech had. "Look, close your eyes."

"OK. now what?"

"Imagine you've just sharpened a pencil with one of those sharpeners with a holder for the shavings. Now you unscrew it and smell the shavings."

"Wow, I can a bit!"

"Now, imagine a burning match. Then you blow it out. Can you smell the smoke?"

"Sort of." She laughed.

"And that's just with your imagination! So, us, er, blind people, we can do most any jobs nowadays, especially with all the technology we have now. It can read the screens, make the letters huge, change the colour of the fonts on command. All that kind of stuff."

"What do *you* see Andy, if you don't mind me asking?"

"I don't see anything, Sonya, just light and dark. I can tell if it's day or night!"

"That's a shame."

"They found I had glaucoma twelve years ago. It left me blind in my right eye, but I still had some vision in the left. That's gone now, but I've got over it. It's not such a problem. I've got a dog, Sasha, and a white stick. Most people are helpful."

"Thanks for telling me all that," she said, and I could tell she meant it.

Over the next three months, we worked together quite closely and I found her to be friendly, cooperative and efficient. I didn't pry but she told me about her life. A difficult childhood with alcoholic parents, a chance to go to university. A guy, Chris, there. Then a life with an itinerant musician, Al, who found a kind of fame, and moved on to other pastures, and other women. She'd been on her own for a year and a half now. That surprised me. I didn't need anyone to tell me that she was attractive.

Christmas came and she sat with me at the works' Christmas dinner. "It's OK Sonya, you don't have to," I said.

"I want to. Here!" She handed me one end of a cracker. We pulled it and it exploded, hurling something plastic into my face. We burst out laughing and I could hear her retrieving it.

"What is it?"

"Oh, it's, it's …." Her voice trailed off.

I laughed. "A magnifying glass!"

"You're amazing! How …."

"From the sound when it hit the floor … and your embarrassment."

She didn't say anything.

"*You* have it, you never know. It might come in handy!"

She laughed. "Are you coming to the party tonight, Andy?"

"I don't know, I'm not really a party animal."

"It'd be good to see you. I'm bringing a friend."

"Oh." I felt desperately disappointed, imagining a strapping rugby-player type.

That evening I'd spruced myself up and called a cab. I didn't really want to go but felt I ought to show my face. The thought of Sonya being there tipped the balance. I used my stick, having given Sasha a break from her duties, and took the lift up to the entertainment suite on my own. The doors opened onto a noisy, crowded scene. Music was playing loudly, *Merry Christmas Everyone,* and glasses were clinking over the hubbub of speech.

"Andy!" It was Desmond, my boss. "Really pleased you could make it. Look, I want you to meet someone." He escorted me across the crowded room to a secluded alcove. Several familiar voices greeted me on the way. They sounded genuinely pleased to see me, although their pleasure was doubtless fuelled by alcohol.

Someone handed me a beer and I was introduced to Paul, an information science graduate, who wanted to discuss reorganizing the sales training material. After about fifteen minutes, I'd had enough. Were Sonya and her friend here yet? I wondered. "Excuse me, Paul, perhaps we could continue our discussion in the New Year?"

He was good enough to take the hint. "Of course, Andy, sorry, let's get you another drink." He escorted me back through the throng to the bar. Suddenly I felt a hand on my arm.

"Andy!" It was Sonya. "Let me get you a drink, what would you like?"

I felt in need of something strong. "Oh, could I have a large glass of white wine please?"

I could hear the tinkling sound of it being poured.

"Oh, and this is my friend, Erica."

I felt a soft feminine hand in mine and shook it, feeling relief it was Erica not Eric.

"It's nice to meet you, Erica," I said.

Sonya spoke close to my ear. "She can't hear you. She's deaf!"

I stood, bewildered. For once I didn't know what to say or do.

Then they both laughed. "Sorry, bad joke!" said Sonya.

I laughed with relief.

"Look, do you know what's hanging above our heads," asked Sonya.

"What?"

She put a hand on my arm and I felt the warmth of her face, smelt a faint, lavender perfume and wine on her breath. Then her lips on mine, hot, pressing, lingering, a touch of a flickering tongue. We embraced and I heard a cheer go up around us. I felt embarrassed but I didn't care.

"Look, you two go and dance, I'll catch up with you later," said Erica.

"I'm not very good at dancing," I said.

"Don't be silly," said Sonya. She laughed and kissed me again, this time on the cheek. "Merry Christmas!" then led me towards the dance floor.

Golden Tips

Head Cook and Bottle Washer was the name of the quaint little cafe I'd discovered. It looked empty, but I'd fancied a change from the noisy, greasy clientele, and the even greasier sausage rolls of Kell's.

"Here you are, sir." A girl placed a silver tray onto the blue chequered tablecloth in front of me and transferred a white porcelain tea pot and cup onto it, followed by a white plate with a pink rose motif. On it sat a large scone, dotted with dried mixed fruit. Then a small bowl containing butter, and diverse jugs of milk and hot water.

"I'm impressed!"

Her large green eyes looked into mine with a sincerity that made me feel slightly embarrassed. "Is there anything else I can help you with, sir?"

"No, … no, that's fine thank you."

"Thank you, sir." She smiled and walked away. I noticed she wore a smart brown uniform with a white apron and matching white headpiece. This cafe might be small but they didn't do things by halves!

I poured some tea out, noticing it looked good and strong, just how I liked it. I took out my phone. There was a message from Laura. Could I collect Shaun from school? She had a migraine. I looked at my watch, only 2 p.m. No problem. I buttered the scone and took a bite, starting to text a reply. Suddenly I stopped. This scone was gorgeous! Rich, fine-textured, and the dried fruit – sultanas, raisins, cherries, and others, more mysterious yet – were sweet and deliciously spiced. Why waste attention on a stupid text message!

I looked around. There weren't many tables, perhaps ten, mainly arranged along a kind of corridor, with three at the front of the cafe and three behind me at the rear. Only two were taken. A mother, father, and two small children, mouths full of cake rendering them temporarily silent, sat at the front, and behind me an old couple, whispering secretively, as if discussing a terrible family secret.

The girl stood at a counter looking attentive. "Was everything all right for you, sir?"

"Actually, it was delicious!"

"We bake our Scottish Lardy Cakes fresh every morning."

"Well it was lovely!"

She smiled, as if genuinely pleased I'd enjoyed it.

"And the tea was lovely too!"

"Oh, yes, we import it from India, it's our own blend." She gestured to some small orange boxes on a shelf, high on the wall behind her – *Head Cook & Bottle Washer Golden Tips*.

I handed over the surprisingly reasonable price for my tea. "I'll probably get some next time."

"Yes, it's very popular."

That had been Thursday. So enamoured had I been with the place and remembering an enticing array of cakes in a lighted compartment under the counter, I returned on Monday afternoon, having finished work early, to find it was closed. I felt a stab of disappointment and looked at the opening hours. Monday to Tuesday 09.00 to 12.00, Wednesday to Thursday Closed, Friday to Saturday 09.00 – 16.00. Sunday Closed. Hmm. They didn't seem to open much.

I peered through the window. The cakes were gone but the tablecloths were in place, and the little orange tea boxes stood to attention neatly on the shelf. But with the lights off and no sign of life it all looked rather forlorn.

"Look Jilly, you must come to this fabulous little cafe I've found!"

"Where is it?"

"It's behind the market place, down the little alleyway opposite the Cats Protection charity shop. They do this divine Lardy Cake!"

"Oh, I don't usually go down there."

"I don't think many people know about it – yet! They do their own special brand of tea, imported from India, can you believe!"

"Wow! OK, that'd be lovely. Meet me from work at one on Friday and we'll go down together."

Friday came and at 1.10 p.m. precisely, we both stood, staring into the cafe window. A sign said, 'Sorry, closed due to illness.'

I felt deflated, embarrassed, although it was hardly my fault. "Look, that's their special blend of tea." I pointed to the little orange boxes on the shelf behind the empty counter.

Jilly was fine about it. "It's OK. Don't worry. Look, we'll come next Friday, give him, or her, a chance to recover!"

I took a break from work on Tuesday morning. I told my partner I wanted to check I'd locked my car properly. The cafe was sombre, unlit, the staff presumably still unwell. Still, they'd be well again in another three days, surely?

Friday came and I was ravenous. I'd skipped breakfast, looking forward to a fuller repast there, and Jilly accompanied me, dressed in a fetching grey suit, her blonde hair in a pony tail, and swinging a smart red handbag.

We stood, gazing into an empty window. Tables and chairs were piled up. The tablecloths and till were gone. There were no cakes behind the glass under the counter, now unlit and forbidding, and the shelf on the wall was bereft of the orange tea boxes. The place looked dead, desolate, abandoned.

"Look," said Jilly, pointing to a small handwritten sign in the door. 'Closed. Opening soon under new management.'

I stared in utter disbelief. I could taste the Lardy cake, smell the fragrant brown tea pouring from the white porcelain teapot. See the girl's pleasant smile and her large green eyes looking into mine, seeking approval. I wondered what could have happened? "Oh, that's a shame. Sorry to have dragged you here again." Why hadn't I bought one of their little orange boxes of tea when I had the chance?

Jilly sighed. "Should we go to Kell's? I'm hungry."

The thought of their greasy sausage rolls made me feel sick, and they didn't use butter in their sandwiches either, just a flavourless pale-yellow spread. "Oh, all right." The coffee wasn't so bad.

Gravity Hill

"Not wishing to doubt you Sue, but cars can't coast uphill, get real!" So said Spencer Schneider, generally regarded as the class 'nerd.'

"Come on Spence, she says it happened. You calling her a liar?" Johnny Serpa's tone was hostile.

"No." There was a hesitation in Spencer's voice. "I'm just saying there has to be a scientific explanation."

"Scientific explanation my arse!" retorted Johnny.

"Come on boys, cool it. There's a simple way to find out. We'll just drive out there tonight," said my sister, Sue. Six years older than me, she was infinitely more sensible than Johnny, good friend that he was. I was inclined to believe her, whatever the explanation.

"On whose wheels?" I asked pragmatically.

"Jojo'll drive us," said Sue, speaking of her boyfriend.

"Have you asked him then?" asked Johnny.

She smiled enigmatically. "No, but I'll … make it worth his while."

We didn't enquire further.

So that evening Jojo pulled up at the house to pick me and Sue up.

"Don't you ever wash your car," Sue exclaimed. "It's filthy!"

"Look, d'you want a lift, or don't you?" he snapped.

We collected Spencer and Johnny, then, as we set off, Spencer asked, "What exactly happened Sue?"

"Well, I was with my friend Olivia. She was driving us back from friends in Manchester and our normal route was closed for roadworks. We had to take a detour. Well we were going up this hill and the engine just cut out, it was really weird. She put the car into neutral and it just started moving of its own accord!"

"I've heard of this," Spencer replied, "it's an urban legend, supposedly the ghosts of a bunch of school kids are supposed to push the car up the hill."

"What in Hell's name are you on about?" exclaimed Jojo.

"Well, at the top of the hill there's a junction." Sue took over. "A bus full of kids crashed into a petrol tanker. It went up in flames and most of them got burnt alive. They were the lucky ones."

We all fell silent, horrified.

Then Johnny laughed, "It's rubbish, a bullshit story made up to scare kids!"

Spencer continued. "Some people say there's a magnetic deposit that attracts the vehicles up the hill, but it's not. It's just an optical illusion. It looks like you're going uphill but you're actually going downhill!"

"That don't make sense!" retorted Johnny.

"Look, let's just wait and see, shall we?" said Sue. "It's just off the road to Redcliffe. I have the co-ordinates from Olivia's satnav."

Jojo pulled into the side of the road and programmed in the co-ordinates. "Clever stuff, nowadays!" he remarked.

Presently the satnav directed us onto a smaller forest road. The sun was sinking and it was growing dark.

"You have reached your destination," said the satnav, as we arrived at the foot of a gradual hill.

"Is this it?" asked Jojo.

"Yeah, I think so," said Sue excitedly, I remember that funny little bridge we just came over."

Jojo turned the satnav off and stopped the car. "Are you sure?"

Sue continued, "Yeah, I'm pretty sure. At the top we join a bigger road. There's a 'Stop' sign."

"Shame the kids' bus driver didn't see it then!" laughed Johnny.

No one else felt like laughing. We all got out. It sure seemed like any normal hill.

"Come on, let's go," said Jojo.

We all got back into the car and Jojo started up the hill. Suddenly the engine conked out.

"Jesus Christ!" Jojo exclaimed.

"Just a coincidence … probably," said Spencer.

Jojo put the car into neutral and it began to roll uphill.

"There, I told you!" Sue laughed.

"Hang on, I think I know what's happening," said Spencer. "It's an illusion. The trees aren't straight. We're actually going downhill."

"What the Hell are you on about, man?" snapped Jojo.

"There was a meteorite strike hereabouts. It bent all the trees."

We reached the Stop sign. The main road was empty. Jojo stopped the car again and we all got out. Looking back the way we came it was hard to tell if it was uphill or downhill if you screened the trees out of your view.

"Look, we'll come back tomorrow and test it out properly," said Jojo.

He put a CD on and we relaxed, listening to Steely Dan's *Aja*. After a few miles there was a petrol station. Jojo pulled in. "We're running low on petrol."

I got out to go and buy some M&Ms. I craved chocolate for some reason. The others got out to stretch their legs. Suddenly there was a scream. "Oh my God, look at this!" Sue stood pointing, her hand shaking. In the bright station lights, we could see little handprints all over the dirt on the boot.

Green and Pink

Lawrence from IT had always seemed so quiet. We tried hard not to stare when he arrived one morning with two black eyes, a bandaged ear, and his hair dyed green. He avoided eye contact with us and sat at his desk, turning on his computer and staring at the display as if it were showing the latest Oscar winner.

My phone rang. I answered. "Hello, Julie Dawson, accounts."

"Jules, where are the sales figures? They were supposed to be on my desk by nine!"

I suddenly remembered there was a big sales meeting at twelve. My mouth went dry and my stomach felt hollow. Due to problems with my family and trying to find the rent, I'd totally forgotten the urgency of this week's figures. "Sorry Janet, I ... I'd forgotten you needed them earlier. I ... I haven't quite finished."

"Well, I need them by eleven at the latest!"

"I'll have them finished by then, they're ... they're almost done." Not exactly true but hopefully it'd keep her sweet.

"Another thing, Julie. The printer here's playing up. Print them out and bring them to my office. Before eleven!" She hung up.

I kept my head down, working solidly on the figures, vaguely aware of the green head opposite peering around from time to time. Once I looked up and found myself in eye contact with Lawrence. I blushed furiously and returned to my task.

I looked at the clock. Ten fifteen. Then at the spreadsheet I was working on. I felt a hot flush sweeping over me. Sweating profusely, I became aware of someone standing before me. I looked up at Lawrence.

"Julie, don't ask. But you look stressed. Can I help?"

"Jan wants the sales figures by eleven or I'm in the shit. I'm only up to week two."

"E-mail me the raw data for week four. I'll compile the figures for you. That help?"

"That'd be fantastic, Lawrence. I owe you one."

"It's fine, Julie, don't worry about it" He smiled, exuding friendliness and camaraderie, such that I quite forgot his appearance. I admitted to myself that I'd always rather fancied him, but he was engaged – to Maureen in shipping.

The clock showed ten thirty and I was ready to print out my three weeks' worth of figures. Hopefully Lawrence had done his one week. Then my heart sank. Two police officers had entered the office, down at the far end and appeared to be making a bee line for him. Without me being able to check his progress, he was escorted to a side office and now appeared to be locked into an interview.

I went over to Lawrence's computer and found the file he'd been working on. Bless him, there was only one column of data left to be analysed. It'd take me no more than five minutes. The phone rang on my desk. I deliberated, then walked across and answered.

"Jules, I know I said eleven but I've had old man Kowalski on the blower, chewing my ear off. He wants to look those figures over pronto, before the big guns get together. Where are you with them?"

"Ten minutes max, Janet, I've just got a couple of columns left, then all ready to print."

"OK, don't be late!" She hung up.

Trying to stall a rising panic I went over to Lawrence's desk to find a blank screen. I hit a button and, to my horror, a log-in screen came up. Oh, my God what was his bloody password? I tried a few likely ones, then started to ransack his desk, looking everywhere in vain for a list of password hints. The clock showed ten thirty-five. Nothing for it. I ran to the office where he was being interviewed, knocked on the door and entered without waiting for a reply. "I'm sorry to interrupt but I need Lawrence – Mr. Marsh's – password. It's urgent."

The officers looked nonplussed. "Er, sorry, madam, this is an official interview …."

Lawrence interrupted, red-faced. It's 'paper lace,' all one word, but 'fours' instead of 'a's. Paper is uppercase, lace is lowercase."

"Paper lace. That was a crummy pop group in the seventies!"
He looked sheepish. "Well, my mum liked them …."

A few minutes later, back at my desk, I hit the print button, wiped the sweat off my face with a tissue and took three deep breaths. I'd made it! With my hands still shaking I went into a side room where the printer lived and, instead of the sizeable pile of sheets I'd expected, was dismayed to see a flashing 'out of paper' light. *Shit!*

I went to a nearby stationery cupboard. There were normally two or three boxes of paper, ten reams per box. But today there was none. I raced out of the door to the next office and crashed into Janet.

"For God's sake, Julie, look where you're going! She glared at me. Where's that report?"

"The machine's out of paper, I just need to get some more."

A phone went in Janet's hand. "Hello … yes, Greg … yes, I'm getting it now … yes, I know you did … yes, I know, sorry … yes, five minutes, Greg, sorry." She turned to me. "I don't want excuses, Julie, you're on a warning. One more and you'll be picking up your papers. Understand?"

I'd been sent to help out in the copy room till lunchtime, photocopying mind-bogglingly-boring reports with Freda, the company gasbag, a lady with nothing good to say about anyone. I was so glad to get out of there at lunchtime I headed into the high street, giving the canteen a miss. I eyed O'Neill's bar longingly. But I daren't go back intoxicated, even slightly, unless I wanted to pick up my papers at five o'clock!

"Hello Julie. It was Lawrence."

"Oh, hi. Thanks for your help. Got there in the end, but that old cow, Janet, gave me a sodding warning!"

"Snap!"

"What d'you mean?"

"After the police left, she called me in and said I'd been seen fighting and bringing the company into disrepute!"

"Were you?"

"No! Well, yes, in a way. Two young black guys on bikes were trying to steal a girl's mobile. I tried to stop them." He smiled wryly. "I came off worse. But they didn't get her phone."

"Sounds like you should be getting a medal, not a warning!"

"That's life, I suppose. Fancy a drink?" He gestured towards O'Neill's.

"Aren't you having lunch with Maureen?"

"Haven't you heard? She's ditched me for Roy."

"Oh." Roy was the shipping manager, a portly bachelor and arrogant man-about-town sort. But wealthy. My heart skipped a beat. "Oh, all right, why not?" What the hell, I'd just have a small pink gin, I could sober up in an hour. "You can tell me how you got your green hair!"

Lawrence laughed. "OK, but you won't believe me!"

How to Eat a Peanut

"Become one with the peanut!"

I looked at a small salted peanut sitting on a blue china saucer before me. "How exactly do I do that?" I asked Shinzen, my 'guru.'

"Imagine it growing underground, in the dark, from a tiny seed, forming in a shell with its companion."

"I thought they grew on trees, like spaghetti!"

Shinzen ignored my attempt at humour. "Now imagine it grown, being pulled from its hiding place and exposed to the sun and the air. Feeling the warmth of the sun for the first time in its life, seeing the sunlight penetrating through its thin shell."

"Peanuts can't see!"

"You must imagine!" he said, adjusting his round, silver-rimmed spectacles and brushing a hand over his bald pate, as if trying to remember what hair felt like. "Now, after drying in the sun for a few days, it is harvested. See it being spun in huge drums, the shells splintering and the nuts dropping down onto conveyor belts."

"I didn't know they did that. I thought it was starving kids, allergic to peanuts, who de-shelled them."

Shinzen sighed. "Be serious now Stephen, imagine YOU are that peanut!"

That was kind of difficult to do but I didn't want to spoil his fun, so I kept schtum.

"Now imagine huge ovens roasting mountains of peanuts. Can you smell that smell?"

I closed my eyes and visualised enormous ovens, tended by black men in straw hats. I had no idea why. But I could smell roasting peanuts, an earthy, pungent, oily odour. Then the nuts on conveyor belts, salt sprinkling onto them from chutes, pouring into boxes. More men in straw hats loading the boxes into trucks. The vehicles roaring off down sandy roads, throwing up clouds of dust. I heard them shouting. "Hey Pablo, how's Maria?"

"She's fine man, another one on the way!"

"Another one man, you should have that operation!" Raucous laughter, the men slapping each other on their faded blue denim backs.

Shinzen brought me back to the room. "Now examine the peanut. Look at every line on its surface, see the tiny grains of salt clinging to it. Regard its shape. Except for the little nub on the end, almost perfectly oval."

I did so, feeling a new respect for the humble nut.

"When you are ready, eat it!"

I looked at the peanut closely for a while, then, eyes closed, reverently put in my mouth, feeling its shape and size and weight with my tongue. The salt tasted tangier than I ever remembered. Finally, I crunched down and my senses were overwhelmed with earthy, wooden, plasticky, oily flavours. I chewed and chewed like a man possessed as it turned into mush and I swallowed it bit by bit. Finally, I opened my eyes. "Wow!"

Shinzen beamed. "Now wasn't that the best peanut you've ever eaten!"

I laughed. "YES!" I didn't have the heart to tell him that I'd done the exact same exercise with a raisin five years earlier.

I Dream of Diwana

I

"Impressive, isn't it?" I smile.

"Oh gosh, have I got to eat everything?" says my wife, Laura.

In front of each of us lies a circular metal tray, in the centre of which stands a bowl of steaming rice. The grains are tiny, some coloured red, yellow or green. Surrounding it are small metal pots containing vegetables – some plain, some battered and fried, in a variety of sauces. One pot contains chopped tomato, cucumber and raw onion, sprinkled with finely diced coriander leaves, and another, plain yoghurt. The restaurant is full of the aroma of curry and I'm salivating like crazy.

"Would you like anything to drink sir?" smiles a young Indian girl with deep brown eyes, darker than her dusky skin.

"Can I have *Cobra* please?" I say. Laura asks for mineral water.

I laugh, indicating a pot, half full of a thick yellow paste, inconspicuous amongst the others. "I remember the first time I came here I ate the *shrikhand* with my curry. I didn't realise it was a sweet!"

I serve myself a portion of rice, some curried cauliflower, and some small pieces of potato in a thin greasy-looking sauce. "Wow, this is hot!" I exclaim. They'd not spared the chilli! I spoon a generous portion of yoghurt on top. It's delicious, my taste buds overwhelmed by the fiery, aromatic experience.

It's September 1987, the seventh year of my marriage to Laura, and I'm definitely feeling like scratching the seven-year itch. The first years had been wonderful, although marred by frequent fights, but isn't that usually the way? Her long dark hair still looks glamorous, but the pretty face has grown rounder and the pounds have piled on. Health problems abound with increasing frequency. Still, 'Till death do us part …' as they say.

Laura stands, long black hair cascading over her black coat. She's stood against the polished blue tiles of Regent's Park tube station. She hasn't noticed me approaching through the thin crowd yet. I linger and watch her. She's looking straight ahead, blinking and touching her hair, glancing at her watch. She looks in a red leather handbag, pulls out a tissue and dabs her forehead, cheeks and nose. I approach and her face breaks into a wide, pink-lipsticked smile. She hurriedly stuffs the tissue back into her handbag. "Hello." Her eyes are wide and dark. She's wearing mascara and some face powder.

I put an arm on her sleeve and kiss her mouth. There's a faint odour of floral perfume. Her lips are cool but tingling with electricity. "Hello, sorry I'm a bit late." We walk up the steps, out into the bright autumn air, and the bustling pavement.

There's the usual newspaper kiosk. Three rows of colourful magazines below a shelf with more magazines and newspapers on it. There's a rack of chewing gum, one of the worst inventions ever, how I hate the stuff! At the back there are more racks of magazines. The top row shows enticing glimpses of pink, brown and grey female flesh. To the left of the kiosk is a stand of international newspapers. *EL PAIS, Süddeutsche Zeitung, La Tribune* .... They're dated October 1980.

Presumably there's a human being lurking within this newsprint and glossy cave? I try to imagine someone actually designing the kiosk. And factories making them. Then I try to envisage all the people writing and designing this seemingly endless number of newspapers and magazines. There must be thousands, tens of thousands even? Massive machines printing millions of copies. I fail miserably.

"Should we go for coffee," says Laura.

Can this gorgeous creature really be with me? "Yeah, that'd be good."

She looks at the stand. "I just want to buy some gum."

I start to say something, then change my mind. "Good idea."

105

II

"Impressive, isn't it?" I smile.

"We have bigger *thalis* in Gangtok!" says my partner, Lhamo.

"You always have to go one better don't you?"

She laughs, shaking her red-brown bob, her hooded cat-like eyes twinkling. It's September 1997 and once again I'm in *Diwanas*. I haven't been here for ten years, but it's like a time warp, everything seems exactly the same, even the waitress.

Lhamo isn't eating a *thali*. Instead, she has a *dosa*, a long, rolled pancake, fried and filled with spiced potato, lentils and onion.

The restaurant's packed, as always. A small queue stands by the door, resignedly waiting for a vacant table.

Lhamo looks apprehensive. "I need to tell you something."

I know what's coming. I've heard it often enough. "What?"

"I'm leaving, going back to Rasheb."

I could save my breath. "Why?"

"I miss Ahmed. He needs me." Her eyes mist over.

I take a mouthful of *Cobra*, close my eyes, and swill it round my tongue with my mouth slightly open. The light hoppy flavour mingles with those of butterscotch and dandelion. It's amazing what you can find when you *really* focus on something! *Back to reality.* "Please don't go." And I mean it. Despite all the problems with her estranged husband and her collusion with him, I really love her.

We'd met at a theatre group in our small town. There were a handful of good actors, the rest of us weren't any great shakes. To my astonishment she'd taken a shine to me, saying I reminded her of Robert Redford, and it was only weeks before she'd moved in, leaving her fifteen-year-old son and husband gnashing their teeth. Soon that slim brown body and her willingness to please had made every bedtime an exquisite experience.

"Thank you for the lift," I say. Lhamo has just dropped me off after theatre rehearsal – a pretentious 'farce,' written by our director, Maurice, entitled *You Don't Know My Mother!* – saving me a bus fare. She'd seemed very friendly, smiling whenever I'd looked at her, until I'd felt a bit embarrassed. At the break she'd come and sat with me at the small theatre bar, drinking tea together.

"Where do you live, John?" she asked. I noticed how white and straight her teeth were. Her skin is brown with a few light wrinkles. She's not so young but still attractive.

"Oh, opposite the town centre. In one of those white flat-roofed houses. King's Crescent. Do you know it?"

She smiled and her dark slanted eyes shone. "No, but I can give you a lift. I go that way." She looked at me expectantly.

"All right."

To my surprise, after dropping me off, she gets out of the car and walks along the path to my house with me. We don't speak. We reach the front door. "Er, do you want to come in?" I ask, hoping she'll say no. She seems a bit 'odd.'

"No, I have to get back. I have to help Ahmed with his homework before bed."

"Who's Ahmed?"

"Ahmed, he's my youngest son." She pulls a photograph from her handbag and shows me a young Asian face, handsome even in the orange street light.

I make suitable noises. Then, "Thank you very much for the lift, I really appreciate it. I'll see you next week then?"

She doesn't speak, taking my arm and reaching up to kiss me quickly on the lips. Then she turns and walks back down the pathway without looking back, leaving me confused and wondering.

Six weeks later and I'm standing outside a staff entrance door at the back of a huge hospital complex. The year is 1996 and it's late in the evening and dark, although there's a street light nearby, casting an even white light. I feel nervous, wondering if I'm on camera. Then the door opens and Lhamo appears in a white coat, smiling and tossing her bob of chestnut-coloured hair. I relax and smile. It's good to see her. She guides me through the door and down empty, echoing corridors. There are signs to departments I've never heard of – Nephrology, Oncology, Urology. Finally, we arrive at a tea room. A lady, dressed in a similar white coat looks up. Her name badge says Ann. She looks knowingly at Lhamo, then turns to me. "Hello, you must be John."

I feel embarrassed but smile. "How did you guess?"

She laughs. "Lhamo said she was having someone to keep her company tonight. She said a few things about you …."

Ann and Lhamo discuss work for a few minutes. They're 'on call,' running any blood tests required overnight. They can sleep when there aren't any. Tonight, a baby is very ill and needs blood analysis. The nurses had a problem extracting any blood, then the machine doing the analysis went wrong. Operator error, I surmise. They both look tired. They're debating who's going to phone the nurses to apologise and ask for fresh blood.

Finally, Lhamo leads me through a sizeable laboratory, leaving Ann to smooth the ruffled feathers of the nursing staff. Surfaces are covered with test tubes and glass vessels of all shapes and sizes. Here and there stand large, strange machines. I'd like to ask her about them but she hurries ahead. Finally, we come to an area with a sign, 'On Call Suite,' a grand name for a number of small rooms with an external kitchenette, shower and toilet.

Lhamo unlocks a door and leads me into her room. It's small, cosy, like a room in a cheap hotel. There's a single bed with a light on a bedside table. She turns it on and the room is illuminated with a warm yellow-white light. She faces me and takes off her white coat. I'm surprised. Underneath is nothing but soft, brown, yearning flesh.

III

"Impressive, isn't it, sir?" The Indian holds out the huge aubergine I'd been eying up outside his shop. "Only seventy-five pence sir!"

I laugh, not wanting to lug vegetables around London, and tell him so.

108

"We're open till 10 p.m. sir. You pick it up later!"

"Maybe." I smile.

It's September 2017, and I'm back in Drummond Street, just around the corner from Euston Station, inhaling the wonderful smell of curry that always envelopes the area. I pass other greengrocers, admiring the colourful displays of unrecognisable vegetables outside. Curious, I look at something resembling a bent white courgette, about 18 inches long. I wonder what it's called and what strange land it comes from?

Passing two Indian restaurants I reach the Ambala Sweet Centre. I remember how Laura and I would buy boxes of delicious sweets there – made from condensed milk, coconut and suchlike, flavoured with spices. My mouth waters at the thought of *gulab jamun*, small cardamom syrup-soaked doughnuts. I ask myself why Indians aren't enormously fat?

I walk a little further to *Diwana Bhel Poori House*. As usual, it's packed, even though it's only 7 p.m. I'd like to go in. But not on my own. I gaze through the window at the crowded tables where I'd sat with Laura and Lhamo. A waitress is serving plates of steaming *dosas*. A car drives past playing Michael Jackson on the radio – *Bad*.

Suddenly it seems like yesterday. I wonder where they are and what they are doing right now. I feel an ache in my guts, of nostalgia and loneliness.

I think of what might have been. Laura hadn't wanted children, in fact had gone to quite extraordinary lengths not to have them. My mind refuses to go there. They'd be in their thirties now, doctors, architects perhaps? Incredible! Lhamo on the other hand longed for a daughter. I'd been more than happy to do my bit, but she hadn't become pregnant. So, no beautiful little coffee coloured girls running around our house in bright dresses, giggling and laughing. They'd be teenagers now, glued to their iPhones. More than likely rowing with us over 'unsuitable' boyfriends.

Maybe it's better this way? I walk back down the road again. Thankfully my mood lifts. Never mind Laura, Lhamo and the rest of those damned women, I'm going to buy that aubergine!

109

Incident on Putney Bridge

Impressive! A glance at his TomTom runner's watch showed it had taken him just fifteen minutes to reach the kiosk. Smiling inwardly, he anticipated uploading the GPS data to Strava, and satisfaction at the thought of his running mate, Eric's face when he saw it. Ha! Who's the better runner now?

It was early, just gone 7.30 a.m., the pavements of the City of London still sparsely populated. Suited young men and women scurried to offices like robots, perhaps hoping to arrive early enough to impress the boss.

Towering buildings, beacons of opulence, homes to banking headquarters and financial institutions, dominated the area. Within their hallowed myriad offices, computers communicated thousands of impenetrable transactions a second with similar institutions in unimaginable places.

The sun was bright, the air fresh and Orlando felt good. He'd gone to bed early after a glass of expensive *chianti*, and slept a dreamless sleep, waking to the alarm at six a.m. He'd taken a shower, then performed some stretching exercises in his small neat garden, Victorian red brick walls protecting him from prying neighbours' eyes. He thanked God for those barriers, high enough to keep the neighbours' wretched cats out. He didn't want those damned creatures scratching at his flowerbeds. His mind recalled a forbidden memory. A black cat digging in a rose bed in his previous garden. Taking a spade, he'd .... *Don't go there!*

He'd taken the morning off, then later today, in his role as a top investment banker, he would be advising a Middle Eastern conglomerate. That was seriously big money, even for Hyland's. He smiled at the thought of his commission, more than many 'plebs' earned in a lifetime!

Hot and sweaty, he stopped and paused his watch. A woman was deliberating over her coffee order. Hurry up, you silly cow, just buy a bloody *cappuccino*! Orlando bought an *espresso doble*, so plenty of room left in the large cardboard beaker for running with it. He pressed the lid on, gave a curt 'thank you,' restarted the watch and began to run again. He'd stop at the park for the coffee.

He reached Putney Bridge, feeling a spring in his step after the short break at the kiosk. Then a stab of annoyance. What was her name? Sally! Two hundred metres away, strutting along the sunlit pavement as if she owned it, just on the edge of the long shadow cast by the parapet. Sunlight sparkled on the river, a pretty sight, but he felt too perturbed to appreciate its beauty. What the hell was she doing here? She worked on the other side of the city. Unless she'd changed jobs?

Traffic roared past as he approached. She was mouthing something, looking at him with anger etched on her face.

Orlando was almost upon her. 'All's fair in love and war.' What was her problem? He determined to run past and ignore her.

"You bastard, I'm pregnant!" she shouted.

Without knowing why, perhaps fuelled by the adrenalin of running, he swerved into her, turning to give her a hard push with his right hand. Her face showed a mixture of surprise and belligerence. In that split second, off balance, she lost her footing. With his left hand holding the coffee cup clear, he pushed her again as she toppled. Thank God the lid stayed on. He didn't want to go back to the kiosk again! He carried on without stopping, conscious that she had fallen right over. *Good!*

After a few seconds he became aware that there was no traffic passing him. He felt panic in his guts. Had she fallen into the road? *Don't look back!*

As he passed the far end of the bridge, a multitude of disturbing thoughts competing in his mind, the running began to calm him down. They'd visited hotels booked under his alter ego, Robin Jackson, and she only knew his special 'dating' number. She didn't know where he worked, or where he lived. Would the police trace him? Nothing to do but take the chance. Bluff it out if necessary. He reached the park and smiled. Exactly ten minutes from the kiosk. Despite losing a second or two on the bridge, a personal best!

Is There Anybody There?

Melt the ice, that was the name of the game. I'd done it myself in guitar classes. Go around the circle, getting everyone in turn to say why they wanted to learn the guitar and what they hoped to achieve. This was a bit different though. We had to say why we wanted to develop mediumship. Talking to the dead, in other words.

My real reason, if I was honest, was Uncle Cyril, an outwardly rich investment banker. He'd died intestate, unexpectedly, with no sign of the wealth we'd all supposed he had. Auntie Irene, his sister, had eventually been appointed trustee and had gained access to his bank accounts. Frequent large cash withdrawals were discovered, and a butler was currently under suspicion.

I'd always been Cyril's favourite, and I knew he must have carefully sequestered his savings, he was a financial expert after all. But he'd died suddenly, fallen off a horse awkwardly whilst hunting, and broken his neck, leaving no clue to the whereabouts of his supposed riches. Otherwise I was sure I'd have figured prominently in any will.

So, the thought of being able to contact Uncle's spirit was mighty appealing. True, I could have gone to an existing medium, but it would be rather embarrassing. "Ask him what he did with his money and how I can get my hands on it," wasn't very 'spiritual.' Easier to 'do it yourself,' as it were.

Now I sat in a circle, a motley crew of mainly aged, grey-haired, overweight females, plain-looking, to put it kindly. We were told to breathe deeply and imagine a silver chord from our hearts extending down to the Earth's core, then a beam of golden light extending upwards from our hearts, out across the universe. Then Sylvia, the medium, a young, conspicuously attractive woman with long silver hair, announced we were going to play 'Spirit Hokey Cokey.' The mind boggled!

We mentally invited 'spirit' in (for some annoying reason the singular was used), noting sensations, then asked 'spirit' to 'step back,' noting any difference. She prompted us to do this several times. The poor old spirits must have been getting pretty fed up.

To my surprise, I found a pressure on my right eyeball that was there when they were asked to 'step in,' but which vanished when asked to 'step back.'

Sylvia spoke about the different mental states, Beta, Alpha, Theta and Delta, and how, even though the brainwaves were slower, the mind vibrated at a higher frequency in order to contact 'spirit.' Or so she said.

Apparently 'spirit people' had to likewise attune their minds to lower vibrations to contact those on Earth. I imagined a similar group of frumpy women gathered together in a room in 'Heaven.' "Ooh, I just had a picture of Wayne in my mind, you know, Sharon's youngest."

"Very good dear, now concentrate on sending him love."

Back on the physical plane, we were now told to form five small groups to examine the different 'clairs.' Observing our blank faces, Sylvia explained that there were five ways to receive 'impressions' from spirits: *clairvoyance*, *clairaudience*, *clairsentience*, *clairessence*, and *clairgustance*, corresponding to 'clear seeing,' 'clear hearing,' 'clear sensing,' 'clear smelling,' and 'clear tasting.'

She elucidated, "*clairvoyance* is receiving mental images, pictures, shapes, colours, symbols etc., even seeing spirits directly."

I wondered if Uncle Cyril would look like Uncle Cyril, or just a white luminescent 'blob'? The other *clairs* were as expected.

Our group was assigned *clairgustance* and whilst the other groups were excitedly chattering about hearing otherworldly voices and seeing unexplained lights, we sat staring blankly at each other.

"I thought I could taste garlic once," said Trudy, a lady with short spiky blonde hair. "I thought it was grandma, she was French you see, then it turned out it was our Daryl, he'd been using the chopping board to cut up garlic to rub on his acne. Course, when I cut myself a slice of cake it tasted a bit funny so I thought grandma was trying to get in touch."

Next Sylvia placed a chair in the centre of the circle and asked for a volunteer. She looked around, then pointed at me. "Andy!"

Well, that wasn't my idea of volunteering but I forced a smile.

"Now, Andy, I want you to think of someone, someone who's passed over, and imagine them on this chair."

Hang on a minute, this might be useful! I visualized Uncle Cyril seated there. Curly black hair, not tall, face a little like a Toby Jug. He wore a Barbour jacket and had a springer spaniel called Nelly. I pictured her lying on the floor beside him.

A huge woman with long grey hair plonked herself down on the chair, which creaked ominously.

Sylvia continued, "Now, Ruth, I want you to get impressions from the spirit Andy has just called to be with us."

I did?

Ruth closed her eyes, breathing deeply, her stomach and breasts meeting sporadically.

"Yes, I see a man. Black hair. Not handsome. Quite short."

"That's right!" I said.

"I see a dog, some sort of … spaniel?"

You could tell Ruth had done this before.

Sylvia spoke. "Where do you see this man?"

With her eyes closed, Ruth continued. "I see a lot of people, um, it's very noisy, there's a table with one of those … what d'you call 'em … wheels, roulette wheels, that's it."

That sounded ominous. "I'm not sure about that," I said.

"No, he doesn't want people to know, that's the impression I'm getting."

"Anything else?" asked Sylvia. "Does he have a wife, girlfriend?"

"Wait a minute." Ruth's breathing became more rapid. "He's in a room. There are three women, all naked! They're putting something on a mirror. Powder. Yes, a white powder …. He says he's sorry."

Great. My hopes were dashed. In the words of George Best – or was it W C Fields? – it sounded like Uncle Cyril had spent his money on gambling, drugs and prostitutes … and wasted the rest.

Just the Ticket

"Servant? well it's, er, someone who performs duties for someone else, like someone who used to work in a big house in the old days, like a butler or a maid."

"Did they get paid?" asked Elsa, my eight-year-old granddaughter, a pretty little thing with blonde hair.

I laughed. "Yes! Otherwise they'd be a slave. Not a lot though, I don't think. Anyway, I was a *Civil* Servant, a government pen pusher!"

We were headed into a green tunnel. On both sides of the path, stretching back many yards, was a wall of burgeoning saplings, mature trees, bracken, vines, beds of nettles – a mass of lush verdant vegetation, flourishing in chaos. Dappled sunlight filtered through the greenery, here and there turning patches of leaves a variegated yellow.

Elsa pointed ahead to a row of low concrete columns that seemed to stretch forever along the left-hand side of the path. "What's this granddad?"

"Ha, this was a platform. That's the edge. Trains used to stop here."

"But it's covered in all these trees and things!"

My daughter Mary was visiting. She was separated from my son-in-law, Martin, and they'd been living apart these past six months. It was 'Till death do us part' in my day, but what could I do? My well-meant advice fell on deaf ears and just led to bad feelings. It was heart-breaking for me but I'd learned to stay schtum and just play the part of the doting grandfather. I'd left Mary on the phone to her solicitor and taken Elsa to the shops along an old railway line, now converted into a cycle path. "Well, the trains stopped running in 1965. That's over fifty years ago!"

"That's a long time. Before mummy was born even."

There wasn't a single square foot on the whole platform that was free of vegetation. "Look, see how the roots have buried down through the concrete and broken it up." Hundreds of young elder trees had sprung up along the edge of the platform and the path itself was encroached by nettles and grass. The council penny-pinching as usual. "This path was the railway line!"

"What happened to it?"

"Oh, the council took it up in the 1980's."

"Why, granddad?"

"I don't know. For scrap iron I suppose."

Elsa's wide blue eyes met mine but she remained silent, walking along, swinging her arms and gazing at what had once, incredibly, been a bustling railway platform.

I envisioned an army officer waiting on the platform – tall, slim, dressed in khaki, with a leather dispatch bag over his shoulder. Next to him a shorter fellow, destined for a bank with his charcoal suit, polished black shoes and Homburg hat, puffing on a pipe.

It was 1952 and I'd get out of the train here with my workmates to walk to the nearby aircraft factory. I still remembered the clanking carriages; large metal boxes with worn, faded, chequered cloth on the seating that always smelt musty, even when new, and how we'd wait to go home along this line again in the evening, tired, nails blackened after a day in the machine shop, but in good humour, laughing and joking with each other.

Then we'd hear the distant puff-puff rhythm of an engine and a cumbersome steam train would suddenly appear, coming over a long-vanished bridge and pulling into the station, smoke belching out, blackening the sky.

"Granddad, granddad, I can hear a train coming! We've got to get out of the way!"

I smiled. "OK, we can go down those stairs." I pointed to a short flight of steps with a handrail, twenty yards away. They led through woodland to our right, down to some houses.

"Quick, granddad, we'd better hurry!"

"OK." I bustled along as fast as my old legs would carry me, Elsa's slim young legs hurtling ahead.

"Come on granddad, hurry up!"

Out of breath, I reached the 'sanctuary' of the stairs and we both retreated a few steps down. I laughed. "Just made it!"

Elsa didn't say anything, just looking from left to right and back, and gripping my hand tightly. "The train's so noisy, and all that steam!" she shouted.

Finally, she let go of my hand. "It's gone off over the bridge now, it's OK."

Funny, I didn't remember saying anything about a bridge.

Elsa spoke excitedly, "A man waved to me and threw something out of a window. I saw it land just over there." She pointed to the left.

"Oh, OK, but we need to get to the shops. Your mum asked me to get some things for lunch."

"*Please!*" said Elsa, looking at me anxiously.

"OK, be quick." I stood and looked up and down the path as she scampered off. Some houses just visible to the left beyond the far end of the platform were almost unchanged from the thirties, maybe new windows and roof tiles, and perhaps a new chimney, but the railway, the trains, the fences, the ticket collector – all gone.

Elsa returned, holding out a small piece of yellow paper. "Look!"

I took it and gazed in astonishment. "Good Lord, this looks new!"

The thick oblong paper had clear blue print. 'L.N.E.R. Available for three days, including day of issue. Nast Hyde Halt to Hill End. Fare THIRD, Class C.' and the price, '5d.' It was undated.

"Five pence, when there were 240 of them in a pound!" I laughed.

Elsa looked up at me earnestly, "The man threw it to me, I told you!"

I smiled at her. Suddenly a strong gust of wind snatched the ticket out of my hand and it flew high up into the air. Helplessly we watched it sail into the impenetrable 'jungle' on the old platform.

Elsa looked horrified. "Granddad, we'll never get it back!"

"Never mind, maybe we'll find another. Best be getting on our way." But my heart felt heavy. I hadn't held one of those for sixty-five years.

Keeping It in the Family

"Hard to imagine he'll get away with it," said my sister, Donna.

"Well, he says if we both stick to the story, they can't prove anything."

Donna looked thin and pale, not surprising, considering the strain we'd all been living under. "I still can't believe it, that poor woman!"

"Look, I know it's awful, but nothing we can say or do's going to bring her back is it?"

Donna sighed. "I suppose not. But it's not justice is it?"

"What's justice at the end of the day? Just someone's opinion over someone else's. Where's the sense in him spending years in prison. He'd lose everything, and it'd destroy mum."

Donna turned away, saying nothing, busying herself with preparing lunch. I collapsed into an old armchair.

My brother Matthew and I had gone to see a play. Donna was coming too, but had cancelled, feeling too ill after a minor dental procedure. On the way home, with Matt driving, a woman had walked out onto a zebra crossing, just as we were coming out of town on the main high street. Matt had been pontificating about the main female role, in his view the only one who could really act, never mind that she was a pretty blonde thing with large breasts. He wasn't concentrating and the car ploughed into the woman with a loud thud, sending her flying. We got out and stood in horrified silence, looking down at the attractive face, blood now leaking over it from a crack in her head where it had hit the road. In the orange street light, the vital fluid began to resemble a black veil.

"Listen Sarah, she ran out in front of us, I didn't have time to stop," said Matt, staring into my eyes.

"What!"

"You heard."

We looked around. It was gone eleven and the streets were deserted in the quiet town. There was no other traffic.

Then a window opened above a shop by the zebra crossing. A woman looked down. "Oh my God!"

Matt whispered, "She ran out in front of us, remember!"

Reluctantly, I nodded, just as a door opened to the right of the shop and a middle-aged woman clutching a mobile phone rushed out in slippers and a coat, hurriedly thrown over a nightie. "I'm a nurse," she said, then bent to test the woman's pulse. "She's still breathing!" She phoned for an ambulance.

Later, we'd heard that the woman, 33-year-old Sylvia Barnes, had died on the way to hospital. I'd felt totally gutted and mad at Matt. He'd said he was sorry, but he'd always had a ruthless streak and seemed to be taking the whole shocking affair in his stride. I'd needed to confide in someone, so I'd told Donna. I could trust her to keep it in the family.

We'd been taken to the police station and breathalysed. Fortunately, Matt had only drunk Coke at the interval. I'd had a large glass of Pinot Grigio. The car was in Matt's name and I wasn't insured to drive it, so they'd believed him when he said *he* was driving.

Then we'd both been interviewed the next day. I'd been asked the same question in twenty different ways. What *exactly* had I seen? My answer: "Nothing." I'd been looking in my handbag for my mobile phone and just been aware of a crash and being restrained by my seat belt as I jerked forward under the impact. In the end I'd come to believe it myself.

The police had appealed for witnesses but no one had come forward, and there was no CCTV, thank God! It had all come down to Matt's word against the suspicions of the police and Sylvia's family.

Then yesterday had come a bombshell. I'd read that Sylvia had recently given birth to her first child, a girl they'd named Emma. I hadn't known. A thought came into my mind, 'It's never too late to do the right thing.'

"What are you thinking?" asked Donna, putting a plate of ham and tomato sandwiches on the table.

I took one, and opened it, looking at the juicy thick-cut local ham. "Oh, just wondering if there's any mustard."

Midnight Train to Marylebone

Princes Risborough, that was good news. The train slowed down as we passed through the deserted and desolate station, small oases of luminosity above the station signs the only indicators of civilisation. The town lies at the north end of a pass through the Chiltern hills and the railway links the affluent Buckinghamshire settlement with Birmingham and London, my destination.

A kiosk stood, black and shuttered, looking like a relic from World War Two. Hard to imagine people queuing, a young woman smiling as she handed over *cappuccinos* in cardboard beakers with plastic lids. Guaranteed to spill burning coffee over you if you tried to drink it once the train was moving.

Once through the station, we began to pick up speed and my small, dimly lit carriage began to sway, as a hubbub of rattling and clanking permeated the compartment once more. I looked at my watch. 1.30 a.m. I should be in London for 2.00 a.m. Though quite who or what would be waiting for me I was unsure.

I wound the window down and let a stream of warm summer air blast over my face. Heating was on in the carriage and despite the late hour it was growing sultry. Now we were headed around a bend and I looked along the train at the elongated chain of freight that curved down and out of sight, wagon after wagon, perhaps thirty of them. Some resembled cement mixers, others, square containers with huge letters denoting alien products and companies, a world totally unbeknown to me. Ahead was another small carriage and beyond that, thundering ever onwards, the huge metallic leviathan pulling thousands of tons. My phone beeped.

'Hi darling, I'll be at Marylebone in ten minutes. What's your ETA? xx'.

Thank God! Fiona had got my text and was coming to pick me up.

The carriage was shaking and rattling, too noisy to make a voice call. I noticed the battery was almost flat too and rebuked myself for forgetting to charge it. I sat down on the ancient, worn seat, pale green with a barely decipherable floral design, and musty-smelling. How many thousands of people must have sat there? Briefly, I tried to imagine the lives of that inconceivable weight of humanity. I wondered if any murderers had sat here, right where I was sitting? I sent off a reply. 'Half an hour with luck. Love you. xxx'.

I thought of the incredible good fortune I'd had. Toting a small suitcase, I'd gone to Drierley station about 11 p.m., a lonely halt in South Warwickshire, hoping I could get to London. There'd been a couple of lights on the single platform but there were no timetables anywhere, just an antiquated ticket machine that simply asked for my destination and gave a corresponding price.

I'd tried to phone Fiona, my fiancé, to get her to check train times, but there was no answer. After hanging around on the ominous, lonely platform for twenty minutes, I'd mooted returning to my guest house, no doubt to a disgruntled landlady, when the rail sang with an approaching train. Hope had burned in my heart, then was dashed as I saw it was pulling freight. But as the train grew closer, it slowed, groaning and creaking, finally pulling up at the end of the platform with a momentous sigh. Its waggons stretched the whole length of the platform and far beyond. Suddenly all was completely silent.

A huge man in a black uniform and cap lowered himself gingerly onto the platform from the cab and waddled towards me. I felt embarrassed, as if I had no right to be there.

"'Ello, squire, all the trains 'ave gone. Didn't you realise?" He called.

"Actually no, there aren't any timetables."

Coming up to me, he laughed, "No, they don't bother with 'em anymore. People can look train times up online. Saves 'em a packet." He was very overweight, with a round, friendly face and small, widely spaced eyes that twinkled in the sparse light.

"Oh."

"Look, I need to take a leak … where are you off to?"

"Well, I wanted to go to Marylebone."

He laughed, his double chin wobbling. "Ha, it's your lucky day, squire, that's where I'm headed, and I've got a couple of carriages in tow!" He gestured to two antiquated boxes, tucked just behind the engine.

"How much?" I asked.

"Well, I shouldn't really take passengers but I'll write you out a ticket, don't worry. We'll sort it out later. That OK?"

Well, that was more than OK. Here I was, just half an hour from meeting my sweetheart, against all the odds. True, I only had myself to blame for not checking the journey times or getting ready on time, but, well, that was in the past now. Everything had worked out fine in the end.

I wondered about paying the fare. Maybe I could go and see the driver now? Perhaps he might even welcome some company? It must be lonely driving freight trains on your own at night.

I exited the carriage and went down the corridor, balancing against the movement of the train. Then, warily, into the next compartment, over the shaking, clanking join between carriages. The next one was dark, just a small yellow light in the ceiling showing all seats unoccupied. I reached a cream-painted door beyond. 'Strictly no admittance,' it said, in a forbidding font. I knocked on it.

No reply. I knocked louder, my knuckles smarting with the impact on the metal. "Can I come in?" I shouted. Again, no reply. I turned the handle and was surprised to find the door unlocked. It swung open to reveal the gargantuan form of the driver slumped over the controls. One look at the anguish etched on his greyish-blue face was enough to tell me he was dead. Presumably a heart attack.

OK, what to do? I tried to suppress a rising panic. These trains had a 'dead man's handle' didn't they? He would be pressing something with his hand or foot. When it was removed the train would slow and stop. Permutations rattled around in my mind. But then another train might crash into it. But then the braking would send a signal to some control centre somewhere, surely?

With difficulty I shifted his bulk enough to determine, to my horror, that there was nothing resembling one. *Stay calm!* I took my phone out and typed a text to Fiona. She'd be at Marylebone by now and could tell the staff. They'd know what to do. Perhaps they could even stop the train remotely? 'Train driver is dead. SERIOUSLY. Train still running. HELP!!'

It seemed like an age as, sick with trepidation, I watched the trees hurtling past in the powerful headlights to the body-numbing throbbing of the engine. Finally, my phone beeped. Thank God! I read the message. 'You have insufficient funds. Please top up and try again.'

I looked at the huge corpse, propped in awkward, permanent repose. Why had he chosen this time to die? I didn't want to join him; my real life was only just beginning. I felt fear and cursed a vengeful God.

In Dulci Jubilo

The morning sun streamed in through the landing window and onto the red breakfast tray I was holding, reflecting off its gold rim and almost blinding me, as I knocked softly on my daughter's bedroom door. On the tray sat Clare's favourite breakfast – scrambled eggs with button mushrooms, fresh, not tinned, wholemeal granary toast, and hot strong milky coffee, laden with four spoonfuls of sugar.

I went in and saw she was awake, sitting up in bed, looking at her phone. "Morning, mum." She turned and smiled weakly, and I noticed her face, framed by her long straw-coloured hair, pale and drawn, even more so than normal. Thirteen, going on seventy. I pushed the morbid thoughts away. "Hello, sweetheart, I've done your favourite."

She sat up and I placed the tray on her lap, kissing her on the cheek. It felt so cold. The phone rang on the landing. I went out and answered, my heart almost thudding out of my body as it always did whenever the phone rang. "Hello, Rosalind Kennedy." I listened and a cold calmness swept over me. "Can you repeat that please … yes, please … yes, OK, thank you." The phone hung up at the other end and I went into Clare's room where her fork was held poised at her mouth, laden with scrambled egg and toast. "Don't eat!"

She turned, her green eyes wide open and a look of total astonishment on her face. I stepped forward and knocked the fork out of her hand. "That was the hospital. They've got a heart and lungs for you. A car will be here within an hour. Get ready!"

"OK." Calmly she got out of bed and headed for the shower.

One hour later we were streaking along the outside lane of the motorway, blue light flashing, heading towards Humberside airport. In the car were my ex-husband, Cyril, and my other daughter, Penelope, three years older than Clare. I sat in front with the driver. I glanced at the speedometer and turned back to Cyril. "You said Skodas were no bloody good. This is doing a hundred and ten!"

126

He didn't reply. I knew he would never admit he was wrong, but I could tell he was impressed by the speed and efficiency of the Transplant Services Team, a nationwide network of paramedics, ambulances, specially-equipped cars, helicopters and planes, on twenty-four-hour alert and ready to go at the drop of a hat.

I went through a checklist in my mind. Enough food for our animals – two dogs and three cats, everyone who mattered notified we could be away for up to a week, and the house left reasonably tidy. No dirty knickers left on the floor anyway. My neighbour, Sally would take care of things.

After two years of waiting and imagining this scene it was hard to believe it was actually happening. Clare had been ill since the age of three. She'd had high blood pressure and difficulty breathing at times, but it had taken two years to diagnose pulmonary hypertension, a one-in-a-million terminal disease. The only 'cure' was a complete transplant of heart and lungs. She'd been accepted onto the transplant list at the age of eleven.

A passenger jet roared low over our heads and I knew the airport must be close. We arrived there beneath a bright blue sky and in brilliant sunshine. We were whisked through the airport by helpful, friendly staff, and onto a small private jet, piloted, to my surprise, by two young women, dressed in the dark-green uniforms of the Transplant Services Team. The co-pilot, Trudy, an attractive brunette, turned and smiled. "There's a hamper in the back."

Cyril opened the lid of the huge basket to find cling-film-wrapped sandwiches, chicken legs, quiches, sausage rolls, Scotch eggs, even plastic glasses of wine. He and Penelope looked at each other, then at me and then at Clare. He hesitated, then dropped the lid. I turned to the co-pilot. "Thanks, but no thanks."

Ten a.m. and we were airborne, heading for London. "Look, that's Market Rasen racecourse," Trudy gestured to a small green oval far below us. As we neared London, twenty minutes later, the pilots indicated further landmarks – Windsor Castle, the Houses of Parliament, the Tower of London. Then we were landing at a small private airfield at the edge of the city. We all clambered into an ambulance and were soon speeding towards the Royal Children's Hospital. It was a Sunday and the streets were curiously quiet, almost as if people had kept away to give us safe passage. Clare was totally calm and sat, sucking her thumb, and reaching out to hold the ear of a paramedic who accompanied us.

"Don't worry. She likes to hold people's ears!" I said. He reminded me of Sid Vicious with his black hair cut in a punk style.

He laughed, "No problem. You see it all in this job!"

He escorted us into intensive care where we expected to put on gowns and 'scrub up,' ready to visit Clare in theatre. To my surprise, Olive, Clare's transplant co-ordinator, stood waiting for us, dressed in normal clothes. My heart sank to my knees as I looked at her expression.

"I'm so sorry. The organs weren't suitable. They were damaged. We can't use them."

"Oh." I didn't know what to say. My daughter's one hope of living past her fifteenth birthday had just been dashed. I felt sick to my stomach.

"Do you have any questions?" she asked.

"Yes," Clare said, "Can I have something to eat? I'm bloody starving!"

And that was that. We waited again, and waited and waited. I tried to live a normal life, although I couldn't really remember what that was. Since she'd been three, we'd gone to the Royal Children's Hospital every three months for a check-up, but more and more frequently as time had gone by and Clare's condition had grown worse. Often, we'd have to stay for up to a week in special accommodation. That had grown a lot harder since I'd discovered Cyril had been having an affair with Margaret, a woman at his golf club. He said it was due to the stress of worrying about Clare's health, but he was unapologetic and unwilling to give it up. The last thing I needed was my husband shagging some other woman four nights a week, and, after a massive row one night, when I went as far as throwing the television at him, he packed some bags and left.

Now, when he stayed in the hospital flats with me, we'd sleep in separate beds, and the 'elephant in the room,' Margaret, was never mentioned. When Clare was with us, I would sleep with her, hugging her close in my single bed, or else I would sleep on the floor or on a bench in a bay window.

One night in mid-December, eighteen months after the aborted transplant, there was a big party in the village, just over the road from my house. Everyone was there – except me, I was always ready for a call from the hospital – and everyone was pissed, judging by the loud music and shouting, still going strong at one a.m. I sat in the kitchen, watching one of my favourite films, *Groundhog Day*, on DVD – with my dear old black cat, Muffin, on my lap.

I was jerked awake by the sound of the telephone. The film must have finished and the screen was blank. I looked at the clock. Two thirty a.m. All was silent. My heart skipped a beat. Transplant calls were usually at night. There were more accidents then. I ran to the phone. "Hello, Ros Kennedy. Who's that?"

"Hello, Ros, it's Olive from the Royal Children's Hospital. We have a heart and lungs for your daughter. Would you like them?"

"Yes please!"

"A car will be with you in within an hour. Please be ready." She hung up.

I felt suddenly calm, hope once more burned in my breast, and my mind went into overdrive. I grabbed the ever-ready bags from under the stairs – spare sets of clothing, underwear, toiletry and cosmetics, and put them by the door. Then I raced upstairs and into Clare's room. I flicked the light on and my world came crashing down. Brown straggly hair lay across the pillow and sleepy eyes blinked open. "What's up?" It was my god-daughter, Francis.

It all came back to me. Her parents were at the party and wanted her to stay with a friend whilst they partied till the early hours. I was to run her home sometime in the morning. Clare was at her dad's. "It's OK, Frankie, go back to sleep. Everything's fine."

I phoned Cyril. The phone rang briefly, then an answerphone cut in. I left an irate message. "Cyril, the hospital called. They've got organs for Clare. Get your arse out of bed and get round here now, and I mean NOW." I rang twice more in the hope that the brief ringing would disturb him, always assuming he was there, of course.

I ran around the house making sure everything was turned off. Sally, my neighbour, would have to be woken and told. She'd take care of Francis and the animals. I phoned Penelope. She answered, thank God, sounding sleepy. "Who's that?"

"Penny, it's me, I need dad. They've got organs for Clare. I can't get hold of him."

"I'll go round to his house." She suddenly sounded energised and awake. "Give me fifteen minutes."

I went and made some coffee, trying not to look at the clock. Whenever I did, the minute hand seemed to be in the same place. Finally, fifteen minutes were up … then twenty. I phoned Penny's mobile. No reply. It went to voicemail. "Penny, what the fuck is happening? Call me." A further five minutes crawled past. I began to sweat. The transplant car would be here soon.

I phoned my neighbour, Sally, who answered, fortunately. She was on alert, same as I was, for a call from the hospital. I went through some practicalities quickly with her. I needed a home delivery cancelled and my car taken in for its MOT. She was a named driver in case she needed to use it in my absence.

The phone rang. I looked at the clock. Ten past three. It was Penelope.

"Hello, mum, I've got dad and Clare. Dad was pissed, he'd been to a dinner party. We're on our way."

"Put your foot down, Penny, but be careful!" I didn't want to lose two daughters.

A car screeched to a halt outside. I looked out to see a flashing blue light. Shit! I opened the door to a man dressed in Transplant Team garb. The cold December air hit me and I shivered.

There was no one else in the car that I could see. "She's not here. She should be, any minute, with her dad. You're alone?"

"Yes. But there's oxygen if she needs it."

"Where are we going?"

"I'm driving you down to London. The roads will be quiet."

"I thought there'd be a paramedic."

"I can call one to meet us if necessary. We need to go very soon."

I looked down the darkened lane. I felt sick. Where the hell were they?

The driver's radio went and he walked several yards away to take the call. I could hear him speaking quietly, but couldn't catch the conversation. It wasn't hard to imagine what they were discussing.

My phone rang. It was Clare!

"We're almost home mum. Penny says about three minutes."

"OK, love. How are you feeling?"

"I'm OK. I'll see you." She hung up.

We were in London in two hours. The driver told us he was an ex-racing driver. It showed. But the car was powerful and I always felt safe, watching the street lights and houses flash past as we sped down the empty roads at over a hundred miles an hour. Somehow, the other three managed to doze. I kept my mouth shut about Cyril not being ready. As Clare's father he was needed at the hospital to sign consent forms. He had a responsibility to be available twenty-four hours a day. He'd let me and, more importantly, Clare down. Let it go, I told myself, it doesn't matter now.

It was still dark as we drove more slowly through the familiar streets of central London, sporadically lit by gaudy Christmas illuminations. The flashing lights on top of the car cleared a way for us through the thin traffic like magic. Then we were pulling into the hospital and my heart was in my mouth. This was it. I whispered a prayer. Please God, let the organs be OK this time.

Olive was there to greet us, this time in a theatre gown. She explained that the organs were from the north and were being flown down shortly. We could all scrub up and join Clare in the theatre before the preliminary work was done. But first we could go to the cafeteria for some breakfast. All except poor Clare, of course.

Cyril, Penelope and I sat by the windows in the large spacious canteen, feeling the feeble warmth of the early morning December sun through the glass whilst we ate warm croissants and poached eggs on toast, and drank cup after cup of *cappuccino*. A Christmas tree stood in one corner with a stack of gift-wrapped presents beneath. There were streamers and other decorations hung from the ceiling. We didn't talk much. There really wasn't a whole lot to say.

Cyril and I put on green gowns and facemasks and stood, facing mirrors, scrubbing our forearms, hands and fingers with a strange pink liquid, whilst an odd, medicinal smell pervaded the room. I hardly recognised the gaunt face staring back at me. My hair looked greasy and I was glad to cover it. My face was badly in need of makeup but there was nothing I could do about it there and then.

We proceeded through to a room where Olive stood with Clare. She addressed Cyril. "We need you to sign the consent form for the transplants to proceed."

He looked nonplussed. "Can't Rosalind sign?"

Olive looked surprised, "Er, yes, she can. Is that OK, Rosalind?"

I gave Cyril a withering look. "Do you have a pen please?"

We said our goodbyes. Cyril kissed Clare on her cheeks and gave her a brief hug. I held her, feeling her warmth through my gown, knowing it could well be the last time I would ever do that. I wondered how many times I'd hugged her over the years. A thousand. Ten thousand? The thought that this could be the final time broke my heart. She hugged me harder back. "Bye mum, it'll be OK."

I drew back, my eyes wet with tears. "I know it will, sweetheart." I had to stay strong, for Clare's sake. I kissed her one last time and Cyril and I left the room without looking back.

Olive was waiting outside. She smiled. "We'll give you a call about one thirty when she's out of theatre and in intensive care. In the meantime, don't worry. She's in the best of hands."

I wondered how often she had reassured parents like that, when their children had never come back. I forced a smile. "Thanks Olive. I'll feel more optimistic when I've had some sleep. I'm shattered."

The telephone rang in our transplant flat. I was awake in an instant. The bedside clock said ten thirty. What the hell? I snatched it up. "Hello?"

"Rosalind?"

"Yes."

"Hello, it's Dr. Khan. I'm phoning from the transplant unit. We need to see you. It's urgent."

My heart almost stopped. "Why? What's happened? Is Clare OK?"

"Everything's fine. There's a little problem. I can't explain over the phone. Please hurry."

I got dressed, resisting the urge to smear on some makeup. My hair looked a mess. Cyril came through from another bedroom. We'd got a bigger flat this time. He was unshaven and looked ill. "They need us at the hospital?"

"Yes, they didn't say why, just that it's urgent. Come on, get dressed."

We half-jogged, half-ran the few hundred metres from the flats to the hospital and went in through a side entrance, past a Peter Pan statue, set among flowerbeds and shrubs, a mass of green and colour, even in December. The character was portrayed in a crouching position, one hand reaching out to touch the fairy, Tinkerbell, who hovered just above it. Nearby was a small fountain where the water droplets sparkled like jewels in the cold winter light.

Shortly, we stood, facing a man, short of stature and slim. He had neat ginger hair, parted to one side, and wore silver-rimmed glasses and a green theatre gown.

"Mr. and Mrs. Kennedy, I'm sorry, there's a problem. I'm Mr. Levin. I'll be leading Clare's surgery team."

Cyril and I exchanged glances. It wasn't usual to meet the surgeons who were doing the operation.

"Clare has been prepped but the organs haven't arrived. They're flying them down from Manchester but they can't get the plane door to shut."

We looked at each other, hardly able to believe what we were hearing.

"The organs are from a younger child. We can't be a hundred percent sure they'll be suitable."

"Well ... what?" Cyril got out.

"Look, time is of the essence. If we start to prepare her for the operation when the organs get here it'll be too late. They won't be usable. We need your permission to take her into theatre and open her up ready."

"Can't they use another plane?"

"No, I'm sorry, they only have one at their disposal."

"Well, you will be able to sew her up if the organs aren't any good?"

"I'm sorry. That's just it. We can't reverse the process. She would die on the operating table."

Cyril's face turned grey. "I'm sorry, I can't handle this." He left the room.

"Sorry, he's fucking useless, pardon my language. Look, I'm a fitness instructor. You couldn't tell me how to do my job and I can't tell you how to do yours. What would *you* do?"

He looked me in the eyes. His were light blue, the colour of a summer sky. "I know what it's like to lose a child, Mrs. Kennedy. I lost a son. He was twenty-one."

"I'm sorry. What happened?"

"He hung himself, whilst I was here, operating."

My heart went out to the man. This wonderful, skilled man who put children's bodies back together, and yet who had suffered unexpected loss first hand. "That's really awful. I'm so sorry."

He forced a smile. "The priority is the living now. If I was in your place I would go ahead."

"OK, where do I sign?"

I left the hospital with Cyril. To this day I don't remember where we went or what we did. We were in a daze. I guess we must have gone back to the flat and smartened ourselves up. An hour later we were back in the hospital and being taken into theatre, scrubbed and gowned.

"Good Lord," Cyril exclaimed. He took my hand and I squeezed his. Clare was connected up to so many machines it was unbelievable. I couldn't count the number of tubes coming out of her.

Olive was with us. "She's had some pre-meds. She probably won't recognise you."

I stood and looked down at Clare, wondering if it would be the last time I'd ever see her alive. Her eyes opened and a half-smile played on her lips. Then her eyes closed again.

Olive smiled. "Go and get some rest. They got the plane door to close and the organs are on the way."

I looked out of the transplant flat window onto a paved area at the corner of a park. There were people selling flowers and fruit. Behind them were old black iron railings, marking the park's perimeter, and inside the park, someone stood with a little boy in a wheelchair. He was throwing food to a group of squirrels. I'd heard that at night foxes would come and rummage through the bins there. All around the park stood huge Victorian houses, beautifully preserved. A world away from the drama that happened daily on their doorsteps.

I watched as an ambulance came around a corner, lights flashing. I felt a stab in my guts and I knew, I just knew, that inside that vehicle was an icebox, and inside that icebox were the organs of a little girl. A little girl who had died so that my own daughter could have a chance at life. My heart reached out to the mother of that small child, likely suffering inconsolable grief at that very moment, just as I was feeling a kind of elation. I felt guilty at feeling like that. But maybe it was God's plan? I'd never believed in God or religion, but now the possibility flitted through my mind. I lay down and that was my last thought until the phone rang in the mid-afternoon.

"Hello, Ros. It's Olive. Clare's operation was a success. She has a new heart and lungs! She's out of theatre, in intensive care. You can come and see her."

There she was. Sitting up in bed, looking at her phone. Christmas music was playing quietly over hospital radio. *In Dulci Jubilo.* 'In sweet rejoicing.' How appropriate! She was plugged into some instruments. Displays and numbers flickered. Several tubes were fed into her from drips, but she didn't look so bad. She smiled and her pale face lit up. "Hello mum, hello dad. Look." She held up some Christmas cards. "From the nurses. Isn't that nice?" She held up the biggest one. "This is from Olive." The picture showed Santa standing in the snow with a bag of presents and a shocked look on his face. The caption was 'Santa saw your Facebook pictures. You're getting a dictionary and clothes for Christmas'!

It took my aged brain a minute to get it, then I laughed out loud. "That's you to a tee!"

Olive appeared. "You're a special girl. There's not many that get a new heart and lungs for Christmas!" She turned to us. "We'll keep her in for about ten days but she should be able to go home for Christmas Eve. Take it easy now, relax and get some sleep. It's all over."

She turned back to Clare. "Are you OK, Clare, is there anything you need?"

"I'm sure she's fine," said Cyril, smiling at his daughter.

"No, I'm not, dad. There's no bloody TV!"

Olive laughed. "I'm sure we can rustle one up for you."

"Yeah, there's loads of Christmas films and stuff I wanna watch."

I smiled. My daughter sounded like she was already on the road to recovery.

Five long, difficult, years later, I was back at the Royal Children's Hospital. My best friend's daughter had asked me to take part in a survey about the transition from junior to senior hospitals. I'd been invited to London and was staying at a hotel, all expenses paid, nearby.

Well, I had plenty to say about it. The situation was that at the age of sixteen a child became an adult – in the eyes of the law, at least regarding medical care – and the responsibility was taken away from the parents. From that age, doctors phoning for Clare would no longer speak to me. They wanted to speak directly to her.

Her care had been transferred to a different hospital and after my life revolving around her since she was born – collecting her medicines, taking her for endless tests, doing everything for her – I was out of the loop. My ex-husband took Clare to appointments now and no doubt derived a sadistic pleasure from it. I no longer had any say in the matter.

After the operation, things hadn't been so rosy. She'd been ill for two years and often in a lot of pain due to infections. Unusually, her body hadn't tried to reject the new organs though, like everybody else's seemed to.

Because of the time delay in bringing the organs for the transplant, a bit of the lower part of one lung had been damaged. Like a piece of meat left out on the side for too long and going dark, some of the tissue had died.

So, fluid would build up in that lung and would have to be drained off. She'd have to do special exercises too. Some days, the pain was so bad, I was horrified to find myself thinking that she looked like an animal needing to be put to sleep.

As a child she'd been wonderful – kind, loving and adorable. For the first two years after her operation nothing changed in that respect and I would often sleep with her, hugging her to help ease the pain. Then her personality completely and utterly changed. At the age of sixteen she became a different person entirely. Rude, uncooperative and abusive towards me. Nothing I could do or say seemed to make any difference. Then on her seventeenth birthday I'd gone shopping to get her a special present – a beautiful red dress that I knew would match her light blonde hair and that she'd look wonderful in – and returned home to find no one at home and a letter for me on the kitchen table. With tears streaming down my cheeks, I read that she'd gone to live with Cyril.

He and Margaret had subsequently married and so Margaret had become a stepmother to Clare, and had doubtless replaced me in her affections.

All the above was running through my mind as I went through the hospital doors for the first time in years. No one took any notice of me as I walked along the corridors and through wards, noticing that they'd been modernised and painted in bright colours. I didn't recognise any of the staff. I could have been in a completely different hospital.

I came to the Caterpillar Ward, where Clare had stayed so often. An Indian nurse approached me. "Can I help?"

"Yes, my daughter had a transplant operation here, five years ago. Heart and lungs."

"Oh. What was her name?"

"It was Clare, Clare Kennedy."

She hesitated, pulling a brown earlobe as she tried to remember. "I'm sorry, that must have been before I came here. But feel free to look around. There are some of the old staff here still."

I wandered around, noticing all the beds looked new and were in different places from how I remembered them. There'd been some building work done and a new wall constructed and others removed. I couldn't even be sure where Clare's old bed had been. Eventually I found Nurse Alvares, a Portuguese lady who had often brought food for my daughter. She made me some tea and tried to cheer me up, bless her.

Afterwards I went to the park but there was a 'No Admittance' sign and I could see the paved area was being taken up and replaced. There was no one working there at the time though.

I walked back down the street to the Peter Pan statue, passing the little side road where ambulances took organs in for transplant, and sat on a nearby bench. I watched the water sparkling in the fountain and suddenly the tension and pain of the last fifteen years hit me like a sledgehammer. My eyes filled with tears and my body was wracked with sobs. I felt in my handbag for tissues but there weren't any. I wiped my eyes with my hands, smearing my face with wetness. I don't know how long I cried, it could have been one minute, it could have been ten. Suddenly I felt an arm round my shoulders and a hand offered me a welcome bunch of tissues.

"Rosalind, don't cry, it's me, Olive."

I hugged her and sobbed my heart out, whilst she patted my back and tried to sooth me. Eventually I calmed down. "I'm sorry Olive, my life's been shit these last few years. Clare left and went to live with her dad."

"Children grow up. People change."

"I know, but after all we went through …."

"She'll come round. It happens. You're not the first." She smiled and wiped my eyes. "Look, come and have some coffee with me. We can chat about old times."

I'd gone with Olive and talking with her had been the therapy I'd needed. Three years later, things *had* changed. Penelope had emigrated to South Africa and Clare and I were back on speaking terms. Maybe Penny leaving had helped change Clare's mind? Things could never be the same, but she was twenty-two now, and more mature in outlook.

We sat in my kitchen, where I handed Clare one pill after another, from a handful which she had to take morning and night. She insisted on taking them separately, swallowing each one with a gulp of water. She'd had her hair cut and coloured auburn; she wore it in a neat bob now. The child had gone for good. She was a young woman, and good-looking too. She'd got a boyfriend – Allan. They'd been together for a year.

"Why don't you swallow a few at a time?" I asked.

"The doctors tell me I should drink more water."

I laughed. "Oh, that's one way, I suppose."

She smiled. "I'm sorry I was so horrible, mum. You know …." She looked away, embarrassed.

"You've got a life, thanks to that operation. We don't know how long it will be. Just try and make the most of it, sweetheart."

She turned and her eyes were wet. "I will, mum, I promise."

Monasticity

Monastic-style beers were her favourite. Heavy, sweet, and above all, high alcohol! She peered through the small opaque panes of *Oliver's Beer and Books.* No sign of anyone in the small cafe behind the faded yellow door. She pushed it open and a bell rang.

Inside was a counter, and behind, shelves upon which stood perhaps twenty dusty brown bottles. Bold fonts on cream and blue labels displayed odd foreign names – *Zundert, Achel, Gregorius, Westmalle,* all ones that she was now familiar with. Perhaps too familiar? A coffee machine, all shiny bright steel and red levers, stood at one end of the counter. The enticing odour of coffee was noticeable by its absence.

A tall thin man in a green apron appeared. Oliver perhaps? He had short grey hair, with matching beard and moustache. He wore thin-rimmed silver spectacles. He looked like a university lecturer, or what she imagined one to look like. She sighed. *She'd* had to leave school at sixteen.

"Hello, Mrs. Fuhring, the usual?"

She averted her eyes and nodded, saying nothing.

The man busied himself behind the counter, taking a round, unlabelled brown bottle from a fridge.

She wondered why Oliver, if it were he, didn't dust the bottles on the shelves. It would only take five minutes! And where exactly did he go when he wasn't serving?

He opened the bottle and brought it over with a matching glass, a large shallow goblet with *Monasticity* printed on it in gothic red script.

She poured out a cloudy orange liquid, admiring the miraculous white fluffy head, and inhaling yeasty orange aromas. She waited for the man to leave, pretending to look at her phone. As if anyone would call or message her! She thought of her husband, Eric. He'd said he was going to get a new blade for the lawnmower, but from the shine in his eyes and the smell of aftershave she knew where he was really going. She'd caught him bang to rights recently, a packet of condoms in his jacket pocket. He'd said he'd 'found' them on the pavement and was 'going to give them to a friend.' As if!

Presently he'd be with his teenaged 'lover,' Christine. Knowing him, right now they'd probably be having a 'sixty-nine.' Yuk, the thought made her feel sick.

Once alone, she closed her eyes and took a large mouthful of beer, feeling the foamy head tickle her nose. She swirled it around her mouth and tongue with her pink-lipsticked lips slightly open. What could she taste? Honey, raisins, banana, leather perhaps? and the bite of pure alcohol. Wonderful! Her head swam and she felt better.

Mrs. Fuhring ran her fingers over a piece of coloured paper stuck to the front of a large, olive-green, hardback book, old but in very good condition. Looking closely, she saw it was a painting. Lighted cabins at the front of a sailing ship against stylised, unrealistic grey-blue waves. On the deck were a group of what looked like elves, and looking down from the upper cabin, three young figures, one of whom sported a pair of wings. Fairies, she presumed.

She traced her nails over the gilded title above the 'pictorial onlay,' as she knew it to be properly called. *The Children's Golden Treasure Book.* And beneath the onlay, the words, 'Brimful of Joyous Entertainment.' Hah, if only she could feel joyous!

Inside, on the thick cream paper were stories of schoolchildren, witches, fairies, goblins and elves, and there were numerous illustrations of all kinds. From rough pencil sketches, through more sophisticated engravings, to colour plates. An enchanted world, now vanished, replaced by Xboxes, and PlayStations, she reflected with disdain.

She admired the endpapers, brightly coloured figures from the tales, no doubt. Hideous witches confronted a handsome prince in a green cloak, a knight rode on a white charger, and a yellow sailing ship displayed a flag, *The Golden Vanitee.*

Mrs. Fuhring had passed through narrow corridors lined with old Penguins, more modern paperbacks, and cloth-covered volumes from the past, 'when books were books,' as she thought. Then down a spiral staircase into her 'special place,' a circular room filled with nothing but books and two armchairs, covered in worn red-brown leather.

She looked at the price, £12. She didn't really want to spend so much, maybe she could offer £10? The thought of doing so made her stomach queasy, she wasn't one for bartering.

She plucked out a short thick black hardback – *The Answer Book*. Interesting! She read the back cover. 'Concentrate on your problem for sixty seconds, with your right-hand palm on the front cover, then open at a random page and the solution will be given.' She had a quick peek and saw that every other page had a short sentence on it.

All right! She did as instructed, closing her eyes and thinking of Eric, his thinning hair and beer belly, and how thirty years of marriage had worn them both down. Then of silly, plain-looking Christine, sitting, bored, at her menial library job. She was nevertheless well proportioned, and, no doubt Eric took pleasure in her eager, young body, Mrs. Fuhring admitted. Mind you, Christine hadn't had to bear three kids!

A minute must be up, surely! She opened the book and stood shocked. The 'answer' was 'Laugh about it.' Well it was hardly a laughing matter, your husband 'playing away' with a young 'floozie'! Suddenly, she envisioned Eric's spotty fat bottom riding up and down on top of Christine's sweaty white body. She smiled. Surely Christine couldn't really enjoy it. She was just after the perks – meals, concerts, hotel rooms. She felt a bit better. Well, two could play at that game. There was a young lad at *Tesco's* who was always friendly towards her. In fact, more than friendly on occasion. Probably sex starved. Well maybe she might just put him out of his misery! She looked at her watch. Just time for another bottle of *Monasticity* first!

Myrtle Shaw Investigates

Myrtle Shaw sat on a well-cushioned, folding chair, sipping champagne. It was six o'clock in the evening but the sun was still quite high, casting a comforting summer warmth over the thin crowd of spectators. To her back was a wall of the ancient stone church, St. Mary's, and in front of her, white-costumed figures stood, ran, and enacted their roles on the smooth grass.

"Ooh, this champagne's going to my head."

"That's the idea!" laughed Major D'Arcy-Smith, her erstwhile companion and ever-hopeful suitor. "Would you like some more?" He took a heavy green bottle, glistening with water droplets, from an ice-bucket.

Myrtle was in her seventies, but sprightly, her skin well-toned, and her brown hair still its original colour, untinged by chemical potions. Her eyes were green and she only wore glasses for reading, and, of course, for examining clues. "Just a drop, Tom."

A cheer went up as a young man from the home side threw himself along the ground to catch a ball.

"By Jove, Myrtle, did you see that? Young Bill Smethurst made a magnificent catch!"

Just then, the peaceful summer's evening at Saltby St. Mary's cricket pitch was shattered by a scream, as Millicent Dawson appeared from the church. Her face was red and her eyes were wet. "Oh my God, Myrtle. Reverend Hughes has just been … just been murdered!" She began to sob.

'Carpe Diem,' thought Myrtle jumping to her feet. The champagne effect cleared instantly. "Tom, look after Milly, will you?" She put down her glass and headed through a gate in the wall, past rows of haphazardly-leaning and undecipherable gravestones, and through the vestibule into the cool, silent depths of St. Mary's.

Coloured light, filtering through the stained-glass windows above the altar, played on the upturned face of the Reverend Nicholas Hughes. She felt for a pulse and lifted an eyelid. No sign of life. Blood still seeped through his cassock, forming a sticky red pool on the ancient stone floor. He appeared to have been stabbed. She searched his clothes. Nothing out of the ordinary and no sign of a weapon anywhere.

She heard the door open, and heavy footsteps.

"Hello Myrtle." It was Inspector Jack Johnson from Thicksby. "I was just passing when I got a call on the radio. Quite fortunate as it happens … He hasn't been dead long, by the looks of things."

"No more than half an hour, I'd say," replied Myrtle.

"Murder weapon?"

"Probably a kitchen knife, but no sign of it."

"I see, how many ways into the church are there?"

"Well, unless someone climbed over the wall, and it's about five feet high all the way round, there are just the two gates, and I've been sitting by one for the last hour. I don't recall anyone going past me, just Milly coming out, but then I was watching the cricket. Some of the time, anyway." She smiled wryly, barely disguising her lack of enthusiasm for the game.

"The crime boys will be here in a minute. They'll seal everything off."

The next day, Inspector Johnson stood in Myrtle Shaw's drawing room. Antique furniture graced an emerald-green Axminster carpet. A bookcase stood against one wall, whilst Regency windows looked out onto manicured lawns.

Johnson perused the bookcase. There were several shelves of detective stories. Agatha Christie, Phoebe Atwood Taylor, Ngaio Marsh. Why was it always damned women who wrote detective stories? "We've taken statements from everyone there. Three people are reported to have entered the church in the previous forty-five minutes."

"Uh-huh. Who?"

"Well, Johnny Hughes – the reverend's son, your friend, Millicent, and an unidentified chap, middle-aged, unshaven and of scruffy appearance, apparently. All three were seen entering through the gate by the road. The men left the same way."

"I see, and have you interviewed them?"

"Yes, Millicent said she'd gone to see the reverend to discuss the music for the flower festival, she's the organist there as you know. Johnny had gone to ask his dad for money. He was quite upset. Apparently, he hadn't seen his father for three years, but says he's fallen on hard times. Reverend Hughes didn't see eye to eye with him, though, and wasn't forthcoming with any cash."

"Hmm. Not very Christian!"

"No, so he had a motive, of sorts. They're searching his house today."

"Mm. What about this 'unidentified' chap?"

He was reported by Milly's sister, Doris. She'd been waiting for a bus, saw the chap go in and come out a few minutes later. She thought he seemed in a bit of a hurry. Walked down to the Green Man car park, got in a car and drove off."

"Description of the car?"

"Red."

"Is that all?"

"She thinks!"

Myrtle had arisen at eight, somewhat late for her, and after tea, toast and marmalade, her unskipable morning routine, she sat in the study, feeling the warm sun through the windows on her arms as she wrestled with the Times' crossword. Seven across. 'All flats are available on such a scale.' Nine letters, second letter H, penultimate letter I. *Hmm.* She chewed her pencil. *Ah-ha*! The answer came to her practised mind. She filled it in with satisfaction. Then a thought took hold, a thought that grew and grew, until it would not go away.

"Good morning Madam, I'm afraid no one's allowed in the church. That's why there's all this tape around it," the policeman said, barely suppressing his sarcasm.

"Yes, I'm perfectly well aware of that, constable, but I'm a friend of Inspector Johnson, and I'm sure he won't mind me taking a peek. I'm Myrtle Shaw."

The constable's demeanour changed instantly. "Oh, in that case madam, I think it could be permitted. But be sure not to touch anything. Please," he added, obsequiously.

146

"Of course not," said Myrtle, intending to do just as she pleased.

Once inside the quiet, cool interior of the church, she approached the organ and turned it on. She began a chromatic scale, playing every note on the higher of the two keyboards. Up and down. Then the lower keyboard. Almost immediately, she smiled. She continued to the highest note, then back down to the lowest note, nodding to herself in approval.

Just then the door opened. "Hello Myrtle, I just had a call to say you were here." It was Inspector Johnson. "I heard you playing. Not very tuneful, if I may say so!"

"Hello, Jack, actually it wasn't supposed to be."

"Well, we're no nearer to solving the crime. We can't trace the man Doris claimed she saw, and the reverend's son is sticking to his story. We've found nothing to implicate him from a forensic point of view. What about you, Myrtle, I don't suppose you've had any ideas?"

Myrtle smiled. "Well, actually, Jack, I remembered seeing the reverend taking tea with Dora, the lady who does the church flowers, last week at Meryl's Cafe. They were holding hands under the table. I thought it most improper! Then I realised that Millicent Dawson had been spending an inordinate amount of 'practice time' here in the church, allegedly working on Saint-Saëns' *Organ Symphony,* for a performance later this year."

The inspector looked perplexed. "All very good, Myrtle, but where exactly is this leading us?"

Myrtle reached out to the keyboard and played a low E flat. Along with the sonorous note there came a slight, almost imperceptible rattling sound. She smiled. "It was a crime of passion, Inspector. My friend, Milly ... Millicent, and the reverend, they were, er .... Anyway, I think you'll find this organ pipe worth looking into!" She held down the note once more until a metallic rattle became quite audible, then launched into Bach's *Cantata and Fugue in D minor.*

The inspector gasped. "Myrtle, you never cease to amaze me!"

147

No Gold Pavements

Well, there are no black curtains, but it's a white room I'm standing in. Quite large, I'd say about twenty-foot square, and the ceiling's high too. I can't jump and touch it. The walls are luminescent, so there's a fuzzy white-blue light in the room. I snap into reality. *Where the Hell am I!*

You know when you've been dreaming because you know you've awakened. That's how I'm feeling right now. I'm sure I'm *not* dreaming, everything feels normal. Well, as normal as it feels to wake up in your PJs in a strange white room with no doors or windows!

I try to rationalize the situation. I *do* remember going to bed. I'd been drinking Gallo chardonnay and ordering books on Amazon until gone midnight, then a DVD – *Communion*. I remember checking the newspaper headlines for today. Something about Prince Harry's girlfriend – Meghan someone, Brexit, earthquakes, and hurricanes. Then listening to some music in bed. *The Best of Cream.*

But now I start to feel seriously worried. I *feel* awake. What are the tests for dreaming? Oh, yes. Jump in the air. I do so and immediately land back on the ground. Try to remember the sequence of events of the last few minutes. Well, I woke up, found myself in this room, tried to remember what I'd been dreaming. Remembered what I did before bed. Yes, a linear sequence of events. What else? Oh, yes. Look at some writing, look away, look back and see if it's changed. Well there isn't any writing, just snow-white walls and floor.

Wait a minute, there *is* some writing! I don't remember seeing *that* before! I cross to a small printed sign. It says, 'Do you want to exit this room?' *Ha, yes!* I look away for a few seconds, look back and the writing *has* changed! 'Are you *sure* you want to exit this room?' So, I *must* be dreaming! On impulse, I shout, "YES!" Then, "YES, I'M SURE I WANT TO EXIT THIS FUCKING ROOM!"

I shout repeatedly, feeling a little crazy and expecting to snap awake at any moment. My voice reverberates harshly around the bare walls. Suddenly, silently, part of the wall dissolves, leaving an arch-shaped doorway about eight feet high. *Thank God!* With relief I pass through it to find myself in a white corridor. Opposite is a door with a fluted glass window. There's something blue and pink moving behind it.

I stand, nervous and expectant as a man emerges. To my amazement, it's my neighbour, Alan, wearing a royal blue robe. "Hello John," he says. "They got you too then?"

"What d'you mean? Where are we?"

A woman with long blonde hair follows him, closing the door after her. She wears no makeup and her face is pale, unsmiling. "Hello John." It's Alan's wife, Sandra. She wears a pale green robe.

"Hello Sandy, what's going on, where are we?"

"I'm sorry, it's bad news I'm afraid."

A white shape appears behind the fluted glass. It's tall, higher than the window. Twice it moves away, then back again. Finally, the door opens. I shudder. It's dressed in a white robe and has a large oval head with two huge black eyes. The mouth is small and thin-lipped. It doesn't have a nose, just two small holes.

It doesn't speak but I hear its voice. 'Welcome to our ship … John. We will return you to your home presently. But first we need to run some … tests.' It reaches into the robe and pulls out a hypodermic syringe. The needle is three inches long.

Nine Miles to the Silent Woman

I was sitting at a bar with Tom, my ex-husband. He was being pleasant, that's why I should've known it was a dream.

"I think Toni should go back to art school," he was saying, as an alarm shattered the illusion. I fumbled for my phone under the pillow as the clouds of sleep reluctantly rolled away.

Any messages? Just one, a destination alert. '9 miles to The Silent Woman.' What the hell? My mind began to clear. *The Silent Woman* was the name of an old liner, moored out at Saltfleetham, converted into a museum and restaurant. Ironically, Tom and I had once gone there. I remembered the evening. Warm, a gentle sea breeze blowing through the open windows. Enchanting, tinkling piano from the resident pianist, and Tom on his best behaviour, all smiles and charm. And all the time he was seeing Nicholl, the bastard!

Anyway, that was three years ago. Why on Earth should I get a destination alert for that now?

I wasn't working today, so I'd set the alarm for 9.30. Best get up. Suddenly, I heard the sound of a door closing downstairs. I froze. There was no one in the house, just me.

I reached into a bedside cabinet and took out a kitchen knife. I quickly pulled on my underwear, some jeans and a sweater, then, with shaking hands, I crept down the stairs, startled at the loudness of my breath, and the thumping of my heart. On the second last step it creaked and I heard a noise from the kitchen. Adrenaline pumping, I threw the door open, brandishing the knife. There, on a worksurface, was Cudgel, my neighbour's ginger cat. Caught in the act, pulling open a cupboard door in search of food, he turned and meowed, then sat and started to lick a paw, as if to protest innocence. I noticed the window was ajar. It can't have been closed properly, and the cat must have opened it further. Suddenly, Cudgel looked up, his ears flattened and he hissed at something behind me. I whirled round. Tom!

His handsome face wore an evil grin and he grasped the wrist of my hand holding the knife.

"Ow, you're hurting me!"

"Waving a knife at me isn't a very nice welcome!"

He turned my wrist around, squeezing harder, so that the knife was now pointing at my stomach. He was strong, something I'd always admired in him, but now he seemed to possess superhuman strength.

'Stop it, Tom!'

I felt the knife tip puncturing my skin as it pressed through my sweater. Then something began to beep, the kitchen faded and I found myself in bed, dripping with sweat. 9.40. I must have pressed the 'snooze' button.

Later, I gunned my little *Toyota* into sixth gear and put my foot down on the last five miles of road out to Saltfleetham, a straight stretch, where the endless brown marshes reach out interminably on either side. On the horizon I could just make out the dark blue ribbon of the North Sea, set against a pale blue sky, the colour of the birds' eggs I remembered collecting as a child. I'd fancied taking a run out to *The Silent Woman*, assuming it was still there. I hadn't bothered to check. Let that be part of the mystery!

As I drove down the coast road my jaw dropped. It *was* still there but it looked rusty, derelict even. I pulled off into an area of low dunes and took my shoes off. I walked across the beach, listening to the waves breaking, feeling the sand between my toes and smelling a scent of wet seaweed in the air.

There lay *The Silent Woman*, dark blue at the bottom of the hull, but now its white sides were streaked with vertical swathes of rust. The once gleaming-white bridge covered with large brown patches and its windows broken.

There was a gangplank. I ignored a chain and warning sign and trod the boards gingerly until I entered a strange world. Endless empty corridors, echoing to the sound of the waves, and strewn with rubbish. I passed dilapidated cabins, a ballroom where sunlight reflecting from the sea swirled over the high ceiling, and bars where the stools were covered in mould and the shelves bereft of bottles.

Then I heard something that froze my blood, the sound of a piano. A single note played repeatedly, at irregular intervals. I headed down a corridor towards it to find the restaurant we'd visited. And at the piano, lost in thought, Tom!

He looked up. "Hello, Jeanie, it's good to see you. We need to talk. It's been so long."

I felt indignant. "Well who's fault's that, Tom? You and Nicholl … well it's not easy for me."

"Well, Nicholl and me, we just … clicked. It was fate I guess."

"That's what you said about us when we first met."

He began to play the note again, faster and harder.

"Stop it, Tom!"

The note turned into a beep, and I awoke once more. Goddammit, what was happening to me? The phone said 9.50. Right, out of bed *now*. No more snooze alarm!

I stood under the shower, feeling the hot water washing my sweaty body clean. I threw a dressing gown on and headed to the kitchen to make coffee. I saw a flashing light on the answerphone and pressed the 'play' button.

"Hello, Jeanie, it's me, Tom. Look, I need to speak with you. I want to help with the children's school fees and expenses, no strings attached. I'd like to meet. I can bring my lawyer if you want a chaperone. Do you remember, we once went out to a restaurant on an old liner moored at Saltfleetham? *The Silent Woman,* I think it was called. How about there? Let me know. Please."

I rushed to my phone. 10.15. I searched my messages. Nothing. No destination alerts! Smiling with relief, I dialled Tom's number.

November 9

"Be quite sure to follow all instructions," 'Missileer' Thomas Papineau reminded us, "to the letter."

Our white Dodge *Durango* turned off Interstate 80, just short of Sidney, Nebraska, heading north across the featureless Great Plains. There was just myself, journalist Katy Rutter, and my cameraman, Johnny 'Jonno' Moses. I longed to open the window and feel the dry, dusty, warm air on my face but I knew the guys preferred the air conditioning.

After a few miles Papineau turned off and headed along a track to some buildings, somewhat reminiscent of chicken barns. A brown sign stated 'U.S. Air Force, Global Strike Command, 92nd Missile Wing.' They weren't producing eggs here, they were prepared to blow up the world.

"Good afternoon!" A young, fresh faced man appeared. His name badge said Lieutenant Brad Rosner. Dressed in camouflage gear, he carried a clipboard. Papineau, Jonno and myself stood expectantly. Strangely, Rosner had oriental features, maybe Korean? He read us the usual riot act and we proceeded through a gate. "Follow me please."

We went into one of the buildings where a man and a woman, likewise dressed in camos, played table tennis. "Down time," explained Rosner.

Another officer came over with some camera gear for Jonno. We weren't allowed to use our own in case it interfered with their electrical systems. All four of us got into a cage lift, Rosner stabbed a red button and we started to descend.

"Good God!" I exclaimed, as I realised we were passing down the side of a huge missile, perhaps seventy feet high. The men laughed.

"We control ten of these Minuteman III missiles from here," said Rosner.

"Wow!" Jonno exclaimed.

It's OK, you can film," he said to Jonno, who held his camera uncertainly.

"How many of these are there?" I asked.

"Two on the base, but nearly five hundred spread around the country."

I didn't bother to ask if they were more powerful than the bomb that obliterated Hiroshima. I could guess the answer.

The lift stopped and we walked along a tunnel into a network of small control rooms, protected by an enormous steel door several feet thick. The equipment looked strangely old-fashioned.

"Hey, what's with the retro look?" asked Jonno.

Papineau smiled. "This facility was constructed in the sixties. They've kept the old panels. We kinda like it."

Papineau introduced us to the 'missileers' on duty, both in their early twenties, judging by their young faces; Lindsey Ferriell and Robert Halterman.

"Have a good time!" said Rosner, as he and Papineau turned to leave.

"Would you like some tea?" Ferriell asked.

We might have been in a kindergarten, rather than a nuclear command bunker.

After some small talk, Jonno set up the camera and I started the interview. "How do you feel working here?" I asked Ferriell. I noticed that even *sans* make up, she was quite pretty.

She smiled brightly, showing even, porcelain-white teeth. "Well, we've got a job to do, keeping our country safe, you just get used to it."

Halterman indicated a red LED display, probably state-of-the-art in the 1960s. "If the president decides on a launch, we'll get the code here. We can launch up to ten missiles in minutes."

'Great,' I thought. Jonno smiled at me and pulled a mock-worried face.

"How do you launch a missile?" I asked finally, and predictably, after recording several minutes of boring technical information.

"We turn these switches." Ferriell turned a knob that looked like an on-off switch from a wartime radio.

I gasped and my heart pounded. Halterman, a few feet away laughed and pointed to a similar one in front of him. "They have to be turned at the same time."

Just then a buzzer sounded.

I jumped. "What's that?"

Ferriell smiled. "Oh, we have to run a test routine. We do them throughout the day. You'll have to leave soon I'm afraid."

Suddenly a different buzzer sounded, higher pitched and louder, and the red LEDs lit up. Ferriell's smile evaporated and Halterman leapt up. "That's the president's code!" The LEDs displayed 'November 9.'

He feverishly grabbed a file from a shelf, opened it and ran his finger down a list. "*Jesus Christ*, that's the launch code. It's kosher!"

Ferriell's face was covered in sweat. She gestured towards us. "What about them?"

"There isn't time. Come on. On my mark." Halterman's voice was hoarse. "Three ... two ... one ...." There was a crushing silence. The missileers exchanged shell-shocked glances. Time seemed to stop. Then, "Launch!" They both turned their knobs simultaneously.

Ferriell sat back. She covered her face with her hands. "Oh God, oh God."

"What happens now?" I managed a whisper.

Halterman looked like a waxwork dummy starting to melt. He spoke in a dull monotone. "Orders are to wait."

Oh, Moo-ah Moo-ah!

"Well, people don't have to think for themselves nowadays, do they?"

"How d'you mean?"

"Well, in the 'old' days they didn't know the Earth was round or that it went around the Sun. Or that the circumference of a circle is pi times the diameter. People, ancient people, like the Pythagoreans, had to work it all out for themselves, actually reason stuff out! Now you just look it up online and think, 'oh, yeah.' You don't question it, you just accept it as the truth."

Sue laughed, blue eyes twinkling and the dimples in her smooth brown cheeks making her look adorable. "So, who are … *were* the Pythagoreans when they were at home?"

"They followed the beliefs of Pythagoras, that the universe was ordered around ratios of whole numbers, look never mind all that. I'm just saying that this so-called interstellar rock, Oh-Moo … whatever, it's got a bloody silly name, could be an alien artefact, a spaceship even."

"But it says on the news it's a rock. Similar to asteroids in the outer solar system." She stretched her long, tanned legs out along the sofa and reclined. "Anyway, it looks like a rock!"

"That's an artist's impression, you idiot!"

"Oh, are you sure?"

"Yes, of course I'm sure. No one's taken a photo of it. For God's sake!"

"Well it looked realistic."

"Yes, ever wondered why governments would commission fantastic artists to paint a couple of highly realistic rocks, when they know fuck all about what it *really* looks like!"

Sue put her hands over her eyes, as if wishing to shut out any doubt.

"Look it's travelling at nearly 30 kilometres a second, that's how they know it's not from our solar system, it's too fast. Then the brightness varies a lot, that's how they know it's spinning."

"Why would a spaceship spin?"

"I don't know, it might be damaged, derelict even. Or just some kind of unmanned probe."

She drew her knees up, showing a flash of pale lemon knickers. "What, you mean like a probe to Uranus?" She giggled.

I ignored her. "Anyway, how many asteroids are eight times as long as they are wide!"

"How should I know, I'm not interested in space stuff!"

I sighed. "Look, there's a guy on Twitter, reckons it's bright pink and likely titanium. That sound like a rock to you?"

She stood up, smoothing back her shoulder-length blonde hair. "Look, you ever thought, people are just making it out to be whatever they want it to be?"

"Huh, maybe. Who knows?" I clicked on Sky News on my laptop. "Bloody hell, hey, listen up! They've just detected another one, out beyond Neptune, same speed, same size, same rotation. You reckon that's just a coincidence? Multiple comets, asteroids or whatever, coming from another star system?"

"Well, we'll find out soon enough." She smoothed a hand over her breasts, opened the fridge and extracted a bottle of lemon-coloured nectar. She poured out a large glassful. "You want one?"

Out and out and out

Out of time, out of joint,
Out and about, what's the bloody point?
Out and out insanity,
Losing touch with reality.

Out of my mind, completely off my head,
Out and out stupidity, time to go to bed.
Out a space, out a luck,
Out a limits, who gives a tuck?

Out for the count, I don't mean Dracula,
Did you see Miss Jones, eating from a spatula?
Out of the EU, Rod Hull and Emu,
Brexit, Bricks it, Brocks it, Brew
a pot of tea, for thee and me,
Thine, fine, a cup for you.

All out superpower confrontation,
War, annihilate, tell it to the nation.
More money for bombs, you know it makes sense,
Bigger bombs, better bombs, we'll call it defence.
Out on the tiles, I can see for miles,
Out of touch? Moi? No, I likes it on the fence.

What could be better than a sexy cruise missile?
Plutonium's lovely, especially when it's fissile.
Satellite-guided bombs, multi re-entry warheads,
Nice little cluster bomblets,
Invented by the dead-heads.
Warhead, head of war,
Who knows what we're fighting for?

Have you ever met a bomb designer?
What a job, there's nothing finer!
Designer shirts, designer dresses,
Designer shoes, designer tresses.

But who designs the designers?
That's what we'd all like to know.
They sit in an office with a pen and a board,
and a book of explosives, written just so.

Materials properties, shatter coefficients,
Kill the most for a buck, you gotta be efficient!
But never mind the total, it's a bottomless pit,
Pay 'em a fortune, who gives a shit?

Out of their brains, off their pretty faces,
Listen closely now, we're out of car park spaces!
Out on the town, me and my clown,
Out of the picture, falling up, climbing down.
Out of order, out of shape,
Out of my league, I just gawp and gape.

Put me out to grass, I need to rest my arse,
Stammering, yammering, rumbling, tumbling,
Out in the fields, there forever bumbling.
Out of jail, out of the clink,
Get me more wine, I need another drink.

But 'out' is a useful word, out and out handy,
For a thousand idioms, just ask any dandy.
Bawl out, bail out, bang out, bat out,
Not forgetting ask out, if you're feeling randy.
A flexible friend, without any doubt,
So out, in, down, up, over and OUT!

On Strings

"Manager of data security and hacker extraordinaire! May I introduce the head of MI7, Baronetess Zilberstein?" The Speaker of the House of Commons gestured towards a short woman with the face of a man. Her hair was black and greasy, and reminded Grant Balfour of the 'pudding basin' haircuts he'd endured as a child. Her features were pudgy and grey, as if moulded from ancient plasticine. She dipped her head perfunctorily, but her thin, straight lips remained compressed.

Grant had been welcomed into the spacious chamber, carpeted in a deep ruby-red, by the Speaker. As a newly-elected Member of Parliament he was burning with pride and ambition. One step at a time, he'd told himself, but he was in an era and a place where he could make a real difference, both for his constituents and the wider world.

After a week of finding his feet in the myriad corridors and offices of the Houses of Parliament, he'd been summoned to a 'highly confidential' meeting. There were eight chairs, one presently unoccupied, at a brightly-polished, circular, mahogany table. Around it, sat the leaders of the five main political parties: The Conservative party, the Labour party, the Liberal Democrats, the Ulster Unionists, and the Irish Republican Party, *Sinn Féin*.

He gazed around at portraits of MPs from the combative past, hung on ancient oak-panelled walls. They glared back through their cracked varnish.

The Speaker continued, "Thank you for coming Mr. Balfour. Now, this meeting is to remain strictly confidential, and it is also independent of any party politics, you understand?"

Grant nodded, wondering what it was all about.

The Speaker gestured around the table. "I believe you know the rest of these gentlemen?"

Grant smiled. "Yes, I'm familiar with the Right Honourable gentlemen. I believe I've crossed swords with one or two already!"

A polite ripple of laughter went around the table.

A door opened and a man with silver-grey hair, neatly parted, wearing a blue pin-stripe suit, came in.

Grant almost fell off his chair with surprise. "But ... but you're ...."

The man stroked his thin grizzled beard and laughed. "Reports of my death were greatly exaggerated, to quote a famous homosexual." He took the remaining seat. "Now, Mr. Balfour, no doubt you're wondering what this is all about. Well, I'm not going to beat about the bush. You were elected to serve your constituents and our Queen, yes? A very noble desire. Unfortunately, it's not quite as simple as that."

"What?"

"You see, Mr Balfour, we are The Seven and we have certain other ... er, loyalties."

The others murmured in accord.

"We receive ... ah, certain directions ... from time to time, via the good Baronetess ...."

Her thin lips twitched beneath the greasy black basin.

"And it is our ..., er, duty, if you like ... to interpret and implement these directions."

Grant wondered what on Earth the old duffer was on about.

"Once we've decided on the implications of these ... er, directions, we pass them to the 'inner circle.' That comprises seventy MPs, they, in turn, communicate them to the Outer Circle – the remainder of our 650 MPs."

Suddenly, something clicked in Grant's mind. "You're saying some policies are decided ... um, externally of this house?"

The man slapped his hand on the table, making everyone jump. "Precisely!"

Grant felt indignant. He'd been elected to serve his constituents and his party, not some external ... external what? "Who, may I ask, is sending us these ... er, policy directives, then?"

The man smiled. "Ah, that I'm not at liberty to disclose. Let's just say, a foreign government, several thousand miles away, to whom we owe a debt of gratitude."

A wave of belligerence came over Grant. "And what if I don't agree to the demands of this, ... this 'foreign government'?

"Ah. Well, as Monsieur Rabelais once said, 'One falls to the ground in trying to sit on two stools.'"

"But what if I do what I was elected to do, vote with my conscience?"

The man put his hands over his eyes, as though he were protecting his soul. "Ah, in that case, er, something nasty will likely be found on your computer and you'll have the whip withdrawn."

"Thrown out of the party I've supported all my life?"

"Yes, if you want to put it like that, I'm afraid so. But if it's any consolation, everyone else is happy, well more or less, to toe the line."

Grant felt like he'd been punched in the gut. "So, I've got to kowtow to the Yanks or look for another job?"

There was a sudden silence in the room. Time was suspended, no one moved. Somewhere a fly buzzed at the edge of audibility. Then Zilberstein coughed. The man cleared his throat. "Who said anything about America?"

Out There

"America killed us Sam."

"Don't be ridiculous!"

"They've written us off. It's like we don't exist anymore."

I gazed out through the command room windows over the bow, at the uncountable millions of stars that surrounded us. "We'll be back. Our kids'll be all grown up!"

Randy laughed. "Little Anita was just five, bright as a sixpence. She'll be twenty-seven, maybe with her own kids!"

"Hard to imagine!"

"I want to go home, Sam." Randy's voice trembled.

"Come on, Randy, *you* signed up. No one forced you to. You'll be home before you know it!"

Exactly to what I was unsure. We were five years into a mission to Nephthys, a small rocky planet circling nearby Barnard's star. It would take us ten years, nearly all of that in hyper-sleep, Randy and me waking up once a year to check the systems. When we eventually arrived, the rest of the sleeping crew would awake and we'd descend to the planet to find a mining station prepared for us by androids, scheduled to land a year ahead of us. That was the plan anyway.

"See all these stars, Sam. There must be people, aliens, on the planets round 'em." Randy said the same, every time we 'awoke.'

"I guess so." Detectors on Earth had found Nephthys to be rich in rare earths, the metallic elements needed to make advanced handheld devices – videophones, holographic projectors and the like. The plan was to spend two years mining and refining the ores, then, with the holds full, back into hyper-sleep for the trip home. In our twenty-two-year absence, our families would be amply compensated.

These annual 'awakenings' felt weird. It took hours to reorientate oneself to the surroundings and to remember how to work the interfaces. But I enjoyed them. Just me and Randy, wandering alone in the colossal ship, constructed in Earth's orbit over a decade. Gazing out in wonder at the infinite universe.

"*Jesus*! Did you see that?" Randy shouted.

"What?"

"Something just went past! *Out there*!"

"What?"

"I dunno, some kind of light. It went across the windows, upwards." He made a gesture.

A couple of minutes went by, then, "There! D'you see it?"

Sure enough, something like a ball of light came from below us and shot in front and upwards. I felt excitement and fear in equal amounts.

Suddenly there was a beeping from a control panel on the far side of the room, about ten metres away. Red and yellow lights flashed rapidly. I raced over. "There's an incoming signal!" My training took over. *Calm down*! I addressed the computer. "OK, Max, switch the decoders on."

The computer responded. "Incoming signal is video. Recording. Should I display it, Sam?"

Randy had joined me and we both faced the large screen. "Go ahead Max."

We both gasped as an aerial shot of New York appeared, the viewpoint zooming around the Freedom Tower, sunlight reflecting brightly off its endless windows, before flying along the Brooklyn Bridge and up over one of its towers.

"*Wow*!" we both exclaimed in unison.

Now over St. Louis, it skimmed beneath the Gateway Arch before heading over sweeping plains with huge herds of cattle, then we were flying over snow-capped mountains, finally zooming into and along the Grand Canyon.

Suddenly it stopped near a group of hikers. A girl pointed towards us, her face a picture of curiosity, and their smiles vanished. She took a few paces towards us before the viewpoint took off again, soaring into the sky. Then it headed rapidly outwards and the canyon receded into the distance below, finally becoming a tiny speck. The blackness of space began to encroach on the brilliant blue northern hemisphere and the screen went blank.

We stood speechless, in awe of what we had just witnessed. Finally, I said, "Max, play it again."

There was a silence, then the computer spoke. "I'm sorry Sam, the video could not be saved."

We looked out of the window again for a while. Nothing moved. Finally, with the heaviest of hearts, I realised the show was over.

"Looks like someone's looking out for us," said Randy, eventually.

"Someone ... or some *thing*," I replied.

Payback Time

Melt down in thirty minutes' time, that's what his mother would do if she didn't get her 'anti-anxiety meds.' The traffic lights turned red. *Damn*! Joshua waited, his foot slipping forward on the clutch. To his right, he noticed a small pub with a thatched roof. Why had he never been in there? *The Coach and Tiger.* Hmm, unusual name!

Put it in neutral, get your foot comfortable, he thought. He applied the handbrake. Sooner than expected, the light turned green and the one solitary car in front, a dirty white Honda *Civic* with a nodding dog on the back shelf, sped off. Maybe he/she was a racing driver in their spare time? In Joshua's haste to get going he forgot to take the handbrake off and the engine stalled. The car behind hooted. *Fuck it!*

He looked in the mirror to see the driver, a bulky thirty-something male, looking belligerent. Joshua felt himself sweating. He tried the engine again. *Thank God!* The car started forward and he turned left, glad to see that the individual behind carried straight over the junction, doubtless cursing him as he did so.

That was the story of his life, he thought. So many false starts. Every time things were looking up – job, girlfriend, health, money – something would go wrong and it'd all come crashing down. Now, having moved to rural Shropshire, hoping for a new beginning, he'd become a servant to his nagging old mother.

He pulled out of town, accelerating, so that he sailed past the signs indicating the end of the speed restriction at sixty miles an hour. The stretch of road was clear so he kept his foot down until he was doing eighty, guiltily noticing a red sign on the left with the number of people killed on Shropshire's dangerous single carriage roads so far that year – 79. Well, if they *would* drive like maniacs. Then he supposed that a good number of those killed were *by* the maniacs. You could never account for that. You'd be driving along, minding your own business when a car coming the other way decides to overtake a tractor on a bend, and BANG, that was the end.

He signalled left, changed into second gear and took the turn, imagining his driving instructor, Natalie's, sexy voice. "Engine braking, nicely done." He smiled at the recollection.

Twenty minutes to go. He'd be back in under ten. No need for the old bag to blow a fuse! The road became rural, narrow and winding. Now he turned a bend to find a horse box stopped ahead. There was no visibility past it at all. *Unbelievable!*

He sat, fuming. Suddenly his mobile phone rang. He looked at the number. Mother! Let her leave a message!

It was her fault for mixing up the dates. "Those idiots at the doctors don't know what they're doing, losing my prescription. I posted it through the letter box on Sunday. Two working days, they say. It should have been ready by Tuesday!"

He'd pointed out it was two *clear* working days, therefore Wednesday, but had been given short shrift. Her medications had been out of stock at the doctor's dispensary, so he'd been dispatched post-haste to the branch in town to get them. She was bad enough *with* them, Heaven help him if she ran out!

Fifteen minutes to go. He got out and walked past the horse box to a white Subaru *Forester* SUV. A woman was seated in it, staring blankly through the windscreen. Joshua recognised her. Helen. Helen Robinson. He played pool with her husband, Trevor.

He rapped on the window and she sat up, as if waking from a trance. She wound the window down. A song was playing quietly on the radio – *Evergreen*. "Josh, I'm so sorry. I had one of my … er, turns. I'm not really fit to drive. Trev's away at a conference and I didn't know what to do." She sounded tearful.

"Look, show me how to drive this thing. I'll pull my car off the road, run you home and walk back, it's not far."

Helen's smile lit up her face. She put a hand on his arm. "Josh, that's *so* kind of you."

Joshua remembered a time, not too long ago, when he'd had no money for his asthma prescriptions. The days had gone past and the wheezing and coughing had grown worse. His mother had doubtless noticed but having no compassion for neither human nor animal alike, hadn't offered to help. Finally, as she was about to go on holiday, he'd 'given in,' and asked, almost pleaded with her to get his medicine for him.

Reluctantly, she'd agreed but had dillied and dallied until it was the doctors' lunchtime, then had deliberately taken as long as possible once they'd reopened, before finally going in the late afternoon, appearing to enjoy seeing him suffer in the meantime. 'Punishing' him for being short of funds, he'd surmised.

Well, 'payback time!' thought Joshua. '*Let* her melt down.' Hopefully she'd melt right through the floor and come out in China!

Riddle-me-ree

As a change from flash fiction stories, here are ten fairly mind-boggling riddles. The answers are given at the back of the book.

• I can only live where there is light but I will die if light shines on me. What am I?

• In 1990 a person is 15 years old. In 1995 that same person is ten years old. How can this be?

• Four men were fishing in a boat on a lake. The boat turned over and all four men sank to the bottom of the lake. And yet not one single man got wet. How could this be? *[and they weren't wearing wet suits!]*

• What disappears the moment you say its name?

• It is greater than God and more evil than the Devil. The poor have it, the rich need it, and if you eat it you will die. What is it?

• The more there is of me, the less you see. What am I?

• What comes once in a minute, twice in a moment, but never in a thousand years?

• You can see me in water, but I never get wet. What am I?

• What English word retains the same pronunciation when you take away four of its five letters?

• If Teresa's daughter is my daughter's mother, what am I to Teresa?

Phoning a Friend

Not wanting to dial, but wanting to dial, Jessica Sumner hesitated, her finger poised over her phone's key pad. She felt nervous. This was silly, she could simply say she'd dialled a wrong number. Her brain commanded her finger to press but her muscles refused to cooperate.

She'd upgraded her e-mail program and a window had popped up, asking permission to migrate her address book. She'd had the option to manually approve the entries. Having some time to kill, she'd checked through the list, one at a time, deleting contacts from her detested last job, waitressing at Burger Legend, and others she wanted to put out of her mind forever. How she'd hated that job, all those cowboys leering at her chest. It wasn't her fault she was so 'full figured'! She felt a pang of regret at the name Roland Korzybski though. She'd delete that one later she told herself.

Suddenly, seeing an old familiar name, she felt a lump in her throat and a burning sensation in her eyes. Eleanor Naddeo. Dear Ellie. Jessica felt a tear trickle down a cheek, almost relishing the chance to give in to overwhelming grief at the memory of her good friend.

Jessica had visited Eleanor almost every day towards the end, looking into the sunken yellow eyes in Ellie's gaunt face, feeling desperation whilst trying to exude optimism. "You'll be OK, Ellie, the doctors say the prognosis is good." The next thing had been Ellie's funeral, the coffin pulled on a carriage by two white horses, Jessica watching with tears streaming down her face. She choked back a sob at the memory. Come on, Jess, that was over two years ago. We have to move on! But still, she and Ellie had enjoyed so many good times growing up together.

Jessica cast her mind back to the last occasion they'd spent time together, before Ellie had got sick. They'd gone on a group trek to Morocco's Mount Toubkal, the highest peak in North Africa, amazed to find themselves the two youngest in the group of fifteen.

Jessica had caught campylobacter, a virulent form of food poisoning, and had collapsed, six days into the ten-day tour.

She'd been dreaming she was at home in bed, warm and cosy, but had returned to consciousness to find herself in a seated position, with the trek leader supporting her back, crying uncontrollably, a circle of concerned trekkers surrounding her. Then she'd had an acute attack of diarrhoea. Jessica allowed her mind to stray into a forbidden area. Two women had supported her, whilst Ellie had lowered Jessica's shorts and knickers, the rest of the group turning away discretely, although Jessica had been too far gone to care. She'd emptied her guts in an orange, stinking spray all over the rocky path.

Ellie had refused to go with the group, insisting on staying with Jessica and a guide. They'd taken mules back to the previous night's hovel, somewhere Jessica had never wanted to see ever again. Then she'd slept for 24 hours straight, Ellie bringing her water at intervals, and insisting she take some sips, "Come on, Jess, you have to replace fluid," before she would crash into oblivion again.

After two days, Abdul, the guide, had walked down the valley to a village with a phone, to call a taxi, returning at dusk. The following day the two girls had been driven back to Marrakech, a six-hour journey, punctuated only by a stop in a bustling market square to eat goat-meat kebabs. Their driver neither ate nor drank, it being Ramadan, but, sat, smiling and nodding encouragement as Jessica managed to chew and swallow a little strong, dark meat and sip Coca Cola. On reaching Marrakech, Ellie had insisted on sharing the £250 fare between them. *Enough*!

So now she had the inexplicable urge to dial Eleanor's old number one last time, just to see who was there. Crazy, she knew. *Do it!*

"Hello, Eleanor Naddeo."

It couldn't be, that was impossible!

"… Hello, is anybody there?"

"Y-yes, it's Jessica, Jessica Sumner." *Just hang up!*

"Hi, Jess, I haven't heard from you. It's been so long. Just so long. Are you still hanging with Roly?"

It must be a prank! "Who?"

"Roland Korzybski, your boyfriend, the biker."

The voice sounded *so* familiar. "No. No, I'm not. Ellie, is that really you?"

"Yes, of course it is, who did you think it was?" Eleanor laughed her unmistakable laugh, a kind of giggle that rose in pitch.

"Ellie, don't get me wrong, but you … you died. Two years ago. Liver cancer."

Eleanor laughed. "Yes, I remember being ill. I don't remember after that. But I'm OK now. I'm back at college, finishing my teacher training!"

I'll wake up in a minute, Jessica thought. She pinched her skin above her right wrist. "Ow!"

"Jess, are you OK?"

"Yes, yes, I'm fine. I just …. What college are you at?" Eleanor hesitated. "I … I forget the name right now. Sorry, I … I seem to forget stuff." She sounded upset.

"It's OK, Ellie, don't worry. It's just great to talk to you! How's your family?"

"Oh, mom's fine, dad's doing a lot of overtime, they're aiming to go on a world cruise next year!"

"Wow!"

"Chuck's got himself a new girlfriend, Sandy, a pom pom girl! He's finished college. He's working at MacDonald's whilst he finds himself a proper job."

"That's enterprising of him!"

"Yeah, and I get free Big Macs!" She laughed her unmistakable laugh again.

Jessica felt a stab of love and longing. "Ellie, can we meet? I want to see you."

Again, Eleanor's tinkling laugh. "Of course, why not? It's been so long!"

Just the thought of seeing Ellie again, illogical as it was, to throw her arms around her friend and hug her again, made her heart pound. "Wow, that'd be cool. Look, I'm free tomorrow afternoon …." Jessica realised the line had gone dead. Frantically, she pressed the redial button. Ellie's number popped up and she pressed the dial symbol. The number rang … and rang. *Come on Ellie!* Finally, someone picked up the phone. A man's voice answered. "Hello, Pizza Hut, how may I help?"

That was odd. "Er, could I speak to Ellie, … Eleanor Naddeo please?"

He sounded impatient. "Who?"

Jessica repeated her request.

"I'm sorry ma'am, there's no one here by that name."

Of course there is! "Eleanor … Ellie. She has long brown hair … in a pony tail."

"I'm sorry, ma'am, there's no one of that name here."

"I … er … can you …." The line went dead.

Jessica stood, an empty, hollow, sick feeling in her stomach. She pulled up the redial list on the phone. Yes, that was Ellie's number. Then … Of course! There must be a fault with the phone. That was it!

She knew Ellie's number backwards but even so, she went to the computer and her address book. She dialled Ellie's number manually, saying the digits out loud, her hand shaking as she typed the numbers in. Please let Ellie answer. *Please!* She pressed the call button. The number rang – once … twice … three times. *Come on!*

A familiar man's voice answered. "Hello, Pizza Hut, how may I help?

Pills for Thrills

"Profundity pills?"

"That's right, three for a tenner, I bought six!"

"Wow, well done!"

Libby smiled, "Yes, they'd just got a new batch in, they sell out fast, I was lucky to get so many!"

The government had just licensed a new recreational drug with one eye on the national debt. 'Profundity Pills – an exciting and *safe* way to relive your favourite books and films!' said the ads. The pills somehow disconnected parts of the brain for a couple of hours, so that you had virtually no memory of anything you'd ever read or watched. A bit like a couple of bottles of wine but without the hangover. Consequently, you could watch a film, like *Back to the Future,* with no idea of what was going to happen when Marty plugs in his guitar at the beginning, even if you'd seen it ten times before!

Libby went over to a case of DVDs, running her painted red nails over the spines before plucking one out. *Alien*!

"Wow!" I felt a genuine thrill and some trepidation at the idea of watching it again for the 'first time,' unaware of the grisly surprises to come. "Then we could watch *The Exorcist*" I said.

"Yuk!" she exclaimed, putting the two DVDs on a table.

It was the first time for Libby and me. She handed me two large green capsules. "This way we can watch both!"

I held the capsules in the palm of one hand and a glass of water in the other. "Here goes!" They went down quite easily, despite their size.

We sat on the sofa. After a few minutes Libby giggled. "I was just trying to remember the name of that book, the one about … Jesus … is it?"

"Oh, you mean the B …, the B …." I just couldn't remember the name!

I went over to the case of DVDs and scanned the titles. *Star Wars, Pirates of the Caribbean, Jaws.* Hmm, they seemed somehow familiar, but I had no recollection of every having seen them, or what they were about, apart from a vague supposition sparked by the titles. I looked around the room, everything seemed familiar, including Libby, I could even remember getting up in the morning, but I just couldn't remember watching any of those films. "I think we're ready!"

Libby picked up *Alien* and took it out of the case. "'In Space No-one Can Here You Scream!' This one sounds scary! What's this other one? *The Exorcist*, well we'll watch that after.

"Wow, that was amazing!" I said, nearly four hours later. "When that monster came out of …"

"Yes, and when that girl's head turned all the way round and she …"

"I'm not starting to remember properly yet, are you?"

"Not yet," said Libby. "Maybe we should watch another?" she giggled.

Just then the phone rang. It was my sister, Morag. "Hi, how's you and Libby?"

"We're fine, just tried those profundity pills, they were amazing!"

"Oh, yeah, I tried one yesterday. I watched *Groundhog Day*, I honestly couldn't remember it. Just so funny. Hey, did you see on the news about that idiot who jumped out of a window. Seems he never read the instructions and took two! Then he watched some horror films and couldn't stop hallucinating!"

I turned to Libby. "Hey, did you read the instructions?"

She shrugged. "I dunno. Why? What's the big deal?"

"You idiot! Seems like we could be in for some unpleasant dreams!"

"Oh my God." Her face was white. "Look!" She pointed at my stomach.

I looked down. Something was pushing against my shirt. From the inside.

Promise Her the Moon

"Be polite and listen carefully," said the old man to his four daughters, "and don't speak unless you're spoken to!"

Their names were Anshula, Bakula, Chandhini and Darshini. By the grace of God, they had been born exactly three years apart so that all four shared the same birthday – today, November 1st – unique in all the land.

Anshula was 16, Bakula 13, Chandhini 10, and little Darshini just seven. Now they waited, dressed in beautiful saris, Anshula in maroon, Bakula in ruby red, Chandhini in royal blue and finally, little Darshini in emerald green.

Their mother was considerably younger than her husband and now stood, nervously adjusting their saris and combing their long black hair. "He'll be here soon. Be sure to stand straight and smile!"

There was a knock on the door which made them all jump. The old man answered it to a messenger, who proclaimed, "The Great Prince will be here within the quarter hour, he approaches the edge of town."

"Thank you," said the old man, handing the messenger a coin. He turned to his daughters. "You may sit until his Royal Highness arrives."

The daughters sat down on two long sofas in the large, high-ceilinged chamber. The family were not rich but by virtue of the daughters' shared birthday, they had acquired a certain fame. People would visit them, regarding them as holy due to the coincidence, and were accustomed to leaving gifts of money, sides of meat, fine wines and the like.

After the longest fifteen minutes the family could remember, there came another knock at the door. A servant opened it to the Great Prince himself! His Royal Highness strode in, followed by an entourage of exotic characters. "Greetings to you all!" he pronounced in a deep, booming, royal voice.

The girls smiled nervously and curtseyed simultaneously, just as they had practised. The entourage spaced themselves around the large room whilst servants brought refreshments.

The Great Prince was tall, over six feet high, and magnificently dressed in a golden *achkan* with a crimson turban and *dupatta*. He was very handsome, with a tawny face, startling green eyes and thin lips that naturally gave the appearance of a smile. Finally, after some small talk with the parents, he clapped his hands for silence. The girls stood, trying to look calm, except little Darshini who wasn't nervous at all.

"Well my dears," he pronounced, "God has seen fit to give you all the same birthday and today Anshula, the eldest, is 16 years old. A Very Happy Birthday to you all!"

He kissed Anshula on both cheeks. Her brown face turned red and she felt faint. She determined not to wash for a week. He kissed the other girls likewise, having to bend low for little Darshini. "Now, I have very special gifts for you all!" he announced. This was followed by loud applause. When it had quieted down, he said, "To Anshula, I give the clouds!"

Anshula, looking perplexed, smiled and curtseyed. "You are most generous my Lord!"

"To Bakula, I give the moon!"

Bakula blinked her huge brown eyes and sweat lined her upper lip. "Thank you, Sir!"

His Highness moved along to Chandhini. "To you, Chandhini, I give the Sun!"

Chandhini curtseyed and smiled sheepishly. "Thank you Your Honour!"

Finally, he looked down on little Darshini, who looked up in anticipation, her blue eyes twinkling.

"Yes, and to little Darshini, an extra special present – all the stars in the sky!"

There was huge applause. The old man approached. "Thank you, your Highness, for your wonderful gifts!"

Suddenly a shrill voice piped up. "I don't understand. What use are the stars to me!"

The room fell silent, the old man gasped and a look of annoyance crossed the Great Prince's face.

He recovered his composure. "Well my dear little Darshini, Anshula may tax all who wish to fly their aeroplanes through her clouds, and she will be rich! And Bakula may tax all who gaze with wonder at her moon, she will be richer still!"

Little Darshini remained silent, scratching her head.

The Great Prince continued. "Chandhini may tax all those who wish to receive warmth and light from her sun, except me of course!" The entourage roared with laughter, followed by polite applause. "She will be the richest of all! And you, my dear little Darshini may tax all those lovers who hold hands and look longingly up at your stars!"

The little girl looked confused. "But what happens if they won't pay the tax?"

"Well then, it'll be 'off with their heads!'"

"What, you mean ..."

"Yes, the criminals will be executed," his Royal Highness exclaimed gleefully.

Little Darshini bit her lip and leant back to gaze up into the Great Prince's handsome face. "Please, Sir, I'd just like a little puppy."

The Great Prince regarded the little girl with surprise, narrowing his eyes. Just then the father came forward, bowing profusely. "I'm sorry your Highness, she is so young, she doesn't know what she is saying."

"Yes, I do!" exclaimed little Darshini vociferously.

The Great Prince was taken aback. He had been rather looking forward to some executions, there hadn't been any for quite a while. Then his frown turned to a smile and he clapped his hands. "Well, in that case, we shall leave the stars undisturbed in their Heaven for now, and you shall have your little puppy."

"Thank you, Sir," said little Darshini in a tremulous voice.

"I shall have one brought to you by this evening!"

The entourage clapped and cheered, and tears of joy welled in little Darshini's eyes.

"But you must promise to look after him properly and take him for walks every day!"

"I will, Sir!"

The Great Prince beamed. "Then all is well."

And so little Darshini became the proud owner of a little puppy. She made sure he was well fed and took him for a walk every day, just as she had promised, except when it was pouring with rain, when she thought neither the puppy nor His Royal Highness would mind. He grew up to be a strong, faithful dog, and, of course, she named him … Prince!

Red Nose Day

Ellen stood, gazing around the room in awe. Claire had said it was OK to look in here, but she felt somehow guilty, as if prying. Surrounding her, stood and sitting on the floor, and on shelves around the walls, were perhaps two hundred dolls.

She'd come to babysit her friend's five-year-old daughter, Bonny. Claire had told Ellen that she collected dolls, that she had 'a roomful' of them, but Ellen had never imagined Claire had been speaking literally. She'd put Bonny to bed after the little girl had fallen asleep watching a Disney DVD, made herself a sandwich, watched TV, and, growing bored, thought she'd look around the house. Look but don't touch. The babysitter's dictum.

In the front row was a female doll with a black tunic top and rose-coloured skirt. Wavy silver hair descended to her shoulders beneath a conical pale-yellow hat and bright blue eyes looked out from the lifelike face above pronounced pink cheeks. She bore a curiously neutral expression. You couldn't tell if she were happy, or cross even. Claire guessed the doll's costume was Swiss or German. The other dolls were of every size, shape and nationality. Chinese dolls with slanted eyes, Indian dolls in beautiful saris, babies in shawls, 'ladies' in emerald green finery, blonde hair piled high in immaculate curls.

Then there was a section of clown dolls, perhaps thirty in number, varying in height from just a foot or so, up to an almost life-size clown in a rocking chair. Its face was chalk-white, its eyes were black hollows and its grinning lips a garish red.

Ellen noticed that they universally sported red noses, the one unique identifying feature of a clown, she supposed. She heard the front door close and Claire call out, "Ellen, where are you?"

She checked her watch. Eleven o'clock. "Coming!" She closed the door quietly, hearing a creak from within. That was odd.

Downstairs, Claire was looking happy. "Hi, how was Bonny?"

"Oh, she was fine. We watched The Little Mermaid, and she fell asleep."

"She must've seen that one twenty times!" Claire went into the kitchen. Ellen followed. "What did you get up to?" Claire asked.

"Oh, after I'd put Bonny to bed, I watched TV then looked at your dolls. I didn't know you meant it when you said you had a roomful. They're amazing!"

Claire took some bread out of a container. "Yes, I collected them over the last thirty years. I'm making a sandwich. I'm starving, you want one?"

"No thanks, I already had one."

"What did you do with the carving knife?" Claire asked.
Ellen looked puzzled. The block that held the knives had an empty socket. "I'm sorry, I washed it. I thought I'd put it back."

"Don't worry." Claire opened a draw and picked out a serrated knife. "This'll do." She cut two slices and opened the fridge, taking out a pack of Lurpak Light and some slices of ham. "Which dolls did you like best?"

Ellen laughed. "Well, I'll tell you which one I *didn't* like. That big clown doll in the rocking chair!"

Claire turned, looking pale. "What d'you mean? I don't have a big clown doll. I sit in that rocker myself!"

"What?"

"Listen!"

Heavy footsteps were coming down the stairs.

Red Snow

It is snowing at the checkpoint and John and Abbie are outside, gazing over the border to the Taebaek mountains, and freedom.

"You come, please," says the guard, his green tunic emblazoned with enigmatic decorations and his oversized green cap looking surprisingly uncomic.

I look through the window to see Abbie throw a snowball at her dad. They are both laughing. "But we're going soon, the bus'll be here."

"You come."

North Korean guards aren't people you ignore. He leads me into a small, austere office. Pictures of Kim Il-sung, Kim Jong-il, and Kim Jong-un hang on the wall above a desk. Their official cleaning cloth lies folded neatly on top of a filing cabinet nearby. I remember hearing about a woman who lost her cloth and used a different type. A random inspection resulted in three harsh months in a Gulag. Could that be true, I wonder?

The man at the desk looks up. His tunic has twice as many emblems and decorations as the guard. A colonel, apparently. The guard was young, not unfriendly. This man's face is older, gaunt. It looks like he doesn't smile often, if at all. "Mrs. Hernandez. There's an irregularity with your visa."

"What, no, we've been through this. It's all been sorted!"

The man pushes his chair back and sits with his hands clasped together and his chin resting on them. "Mrs. Hernandez. There's something we need you to do. Then … no problem with the visa."

It is snowing and we're getting on the plane. The white flakes are settling on Abbie's golden hair as we cross the gangway. A young, pretty, Korean woman with a smart blue jacket and matching cap, wearing a very short skirt, smiles a greeting. I stare at her in a daze. I feel I'm about to crumble. *Stay strong, just till the plane's in the air.* Then I can go to the toilet and dissolve.

I'd been taken to a room. Three women were sitting on a bench. Their faces were frightened but resigned, their eyes huge with pleading.

"You pick one," said the colonel.

"Why me?"

He shrugged. "Orders."

I made the impossible choice, the oldest one, but still only middle-aged. I caught her eyes for a split second but it was enough. We went outside to a snow-covered yard, the flakes coming down harder now. My hands were shaking. The colonel handed me a heavy pistol with a squat silencer. He showed me the safety catch, put the gun against his head in demonstration, and motioned the woman to kneel.

It is snowing at Las Angeles airport. Is it snowing everywhere in the world, I wonder? Everyone is there to greet us. John's mum and dad, Abbie's friends, my sister Madeleine – 'Mads,' and a newspaper reporter from our home town.

I smile, wave, and reply to questions on autopilot. In my mind there's one image. Beautiful huge white snowflakes swirling and settling on the ground by the woman's head – instantly turning red.

Reflections of a Traitor

Like something out of a James Bond film, I was to observe and photograph a Russian agent being handed secrets. The setting, Painter's Fairground, set up for the week on a field just out of town.

It was getting dark and I wandered between the brightly lit and gaudily painted stalls, laden with brilliantly coloured boxes containing tacky plastic toys. I inhaled the smell of electricity, petrol engines and candy floss, whilst my ears were assailed by the noise and excitement of the rides. The bumper cars careening across their conductive floor, sparks flying from the connecting rods as they moved across the ceiling. Crazily driven by laughing teenagers, girls made up to look ten years older, twenty-five instead of fifteen, accompanied by lanky youths in coloured tops and tight jeans.

I passed the Ghost Train, hearing the vehicle thundering through the wooden shack, children screaming in *faux* fright, and always, the relentless chugging of generators everywhere. I tried in vain to imagine someone designing a Ghost Train and the 'spooky house' it ran through. And factories manufacturing them in some godforsaken place.

"Hey, Pal, wanna try your luck?" A barker with a time-worn face and pork-pie hat addressed me from a shooting gallery where little ducks ran on rails.

"Sure." I put two pound coins into his brown leather hand and took a rifle. It was equipped with ten .22 calibre metal pellets and unnecessarily heavy. He showed me how to load the rifle, then walked to the other end of the stall, leaving me to it, to talk to what looked to be a grandfather with his grandson, a gangly youth with thick-lensed glasses and acne.

My first shot told me that the sight was slightly out of alignment, presumably to handicap the shooter and save on prizes. Allowing for the discrepancy, there was a satisfying 'ting' as a slow-moving fat duck went down. Then another. I aimed at the row behind, where the ducks were smaller and moved faster, giving correspondingly higher points for a hit. My first shot missed but 'ting,' 'ting,' 'ting,' three in a row! I noticed the stall-holder looking at me curiously and the youth gaping with admiration. Deciding it would be prudent not to show my hand too obviously, I aimed at the back row, where the ducks were smaller and faster still, and deliberately missed three, finding my aim for the last shot. 'Ting.' One went down to my satisfaction.

"Well done, buddy," the barker forced a grin. "Looks like you've done it before!"

I made a non-committal sound as he gestured to a shelf of prizes appropriate to my score. I selected a large soft toy – a basset hound – and handed it to a small girl nearby. She smiled shyly and ran off to her mother, pointing me out to her.

Time to move on. I walked through the noisy throng to the merry-go-round, blasting out up-tempo fairground music from what appeared to be an authentic organ engine. Rows of brightly bedecked horses rotated, moving up and down, mostly without riders, but some with smaller children. Then, to my astonishment, mounted on a gold horse with a red saddle, my 'target' came into view. Known simply as Oleg, he was sixty-two and a professor of linguistics. He wore a black suit, his hair matched his suit and was Brylcreemed and parted on the right, his nose was long and beaky, and his lips were thin. He looked straight through me as he passed, smiling and giving the appearance of enjoying the ride. What on Earth was he playing at, drawing attention to himself like that?

I feigned interest in a darts stall whilst waiting for him to come around again.

There was a little girl in a green dress with blonde hair I remembered, then two boys, brothers I presumed, both with curly ginger hair, then … nothing. Oleg's horse was now unoccupied! I ran around the carousel in case I was mistaken but, no, he was nowhere to be seen. How was that possible?

The information we'd got was that the switch was to be at quarter past eight. It wasn't even eight yet. Had he met his contact earlier than planned? I started to feel worried. If I blew this assignment it would count against me and there was another agent, the arrogant Toby Mellors, younger and ex-Oxford

185

University, vying for my role and the substantial salary it carried.

There were many people milling around still, parents and grandparents with their young and not-so-young offspring, and groups of teenagers, fooling around as teenagers are wont to do, good-naturedly swearing at each other.

I passed a mirror maze and there in the kaleidoscope of hundreds of reflections, right at the back, or what looked like the back, I thought I saw a black suit and parted, greased-down black hair.

I paid my entry money to a woman with an aged gypsy-like face and incongruous bright blonde hair and went in, feeling satisfaction at the reflection of my athletic appearance and what I hoped to be nondescript look. Music was blasting out from a crowded, nearby *Waltzer* ride – *Green Onions,* that perennial fairground favourite.

The maze confused by having plain glass panels as well as mirrors, but by finding and sticking to a likely pattern of turns – left, left, right – I made my way towards the back, catching sight of what I perceived to be Oleg's reflection from time to time. There was someone else too, moving around, as if playing cat and mouse with either Oleg or myself or both. I reached into my jacket pocket and reassuringly caressed a small revolver, equipped with a silencer.

The mirrors here reflected solely myself – fat, thin, even inverted. Suddenly I found myself in a small open space with two men, surrounded by a crowd in the mirrors about us, and I looked from Oleg to the other man and back with total astonishment. Oleg handed me a notebook and smiled. "Low tech," he said, with a trace of Russian accent.

I glanced inside it. Written in English, it said 'British Spies – Moscow, Leningrad, Saint Petersburg and environs.' The next two pages had been torn out. The rest of the book seemed to contain a kind of journal but using some sort of code I didn't recognize. Oleg opened his jacket to show the missing pages in a pocket and laughed, handing the book back to the other man.

I took out my revolver. "You know I could kill you both, right here?" I said.

The familiar face spoke. "I don't think so, old man, you see, I fitted your gun with blanks this afternoon. Mine on the other hand, are the real McCoy." He pulled out a squat black revolver, quickly screwing a silencer on and hardly flinching as I pulled the trigger of mine, producing a 'phut,' barely noticeable above the general fairground hubbub. He laughed and pointed the gun at my forehead. "Time to start a new life, old man, looks like I'll be moving up in the organization after all!"

Return of the Gnome

9.00

So, it's nine in the morning and I'm on my first call, a pickup from The Admiral Derek in Castlehorn, driving to Lincoln. I pull up outside. No sign of anyone. I get out of the taxi and enter the hallowed doors of the hotel. Claude, the doorman greets me. "Good morning, John, here for a pickup?"

"Yes, a Mr. Evans-Smith."

Claude rolls his eyes. "I'll just call him." The long gold-braided red coat and smart cap disappear down a corridor.

Shortly, a young man appears. He wears a black suit, white shirt and red tie. His hair is light brown and is swept back and brylcreemed. He sports a thin pencil moustache. "Oh, I say, you must be the taxi fellah!"

Taken aback, I nod. "Yes, that's right. Thalham cabs. Should we go?"

He smiles an odd smile. "Oh, it's not for me. I want you to take something to Lincoln museum. They're expecting it, don't you know."

"Oh, they didn't tell me. It'll still be full price, £45, including my return journey."

"By Jove, that's a bit steep! Still, needs must."

10.00

So here I am, driving into Lincoln, a garden gnome sporting a blue tunic and tall conical red hat sitting on the passenger seat beside me. Mr. Evans-Smith had been very particular about that. "Don't put him in the boot. I'm paying a passenger fare and he must be treated as such. He's to sit in the front passenger seat at all times!"

I pull up, self-consciously, at a pedestrian crossing in the old town. Two teenaged girls cross. Suddenly one spies the gnome. She points it out to her friend.

"Oi, haven't you got no gnome to go to?" her friend shouts and they both roar with laughter.

As I drive off the first one jiggles her large breasts together and pouts her red-lipsticked lips at me. Silly tart! And she only looks about fifteen!

Suddenly I see a man waving frantically at me, stepping into the road ahead. He is middle-aged and well dressed in a smart grey suit. For once there is no car behind, so I pull up and wind the window down.

He gives me an odd look when he sees the gnome but carries on. "Can you take me to Riverside Road, it's, um, urgent. I called a taxi and it hasn't turned up!"

Well, I manage to keep a straight face. "Riverside Road?" I say, all innocent-like. "Sure, hop in. I'll just put my little friend on the back seat!"

I'm not actually licenced to pick anyone up out of my area but what the hell? It's clear he's not short of a few bob. I'm assuming he's off to 'Elsie's,' the town's best known 'house of ill repute.'

I pick up the gnome. He has a grey beard and a curiously pale face. I notice a small chip in his hat. His little black eyes gaze vacantly at me as I dump him unceremoniously on the back seat.

11.00

I'm sitting by the river at The Old Barge, drinking a pint of shandy and wondering what the hell to do? I still can't believe it. I dropped my gent at Elsie's, it was indeed where he was headed – and where he was no doubt relishing the pleasures of the flesh at this very moment – and pocketed a tenner for a ten-minute drive, including a handsome tip. Easy money!

Then I thought I should put my little passenger back in his rightful place. Who knows, maybe a member of the museum staff might observe me arriving and report back to Mr. Evans-Smith, who might phone my boss. You never know.

Well, blow me, the back seat was empty! I searched frantically but *nada*, the gnome had disappeared, gone, vanished – seemingly into thin air!

15.00

Well, I'm back on the rank at Castlehorn, feeling happier. I couldn't understand what had happened to the gnome. It seemed impossible that my passenger could have somehow taken it off the back seat without me noticing. Anyway, I did the only thing I could think of. Drove out to the nearest garden centre and bought another gnome! As similar to the missing one as I could find.

I thought I'd be rumbled at the museum but a young man with a spotty face and huge thick-lensed glasses took it without showing any interest. Fortunately!

Apparently, it was just to brighten up a display, celebrating the discovery of a hoard of gold coins, unearthed during a catastrophic flood fifty years ago this month. There were several gnomes there, in varying colours and stances, standing around on a model riverbank in a huge glass case, with the coins displayed on a blue velvet panel behind them.

I couldn't understand the logic of me bringing one twenty-five miles but I had been well paid for it, so why worry?

23.00

I'm watching the telly with a glass of cold *Pilsner Urquell* to hand. Fortunately, there'd been no repercussions over the 'replacement gnome,' from either the museum or Mr. Evans-Smith, so far anyway, touch wood. I'd been kept busy with fares all afternoon so I'm tired and ready for my bed. I'm hoping my dreams will be 'gnome-free'!

08.45

Well, I'm on the point of leaving for work when there's a knock at the door. A bit early for the postman in these parts, I think, but open the door to see – no one! Kids messing about probably. Then I look down and jump. *There* is a little blue-vested, red-hatted figure.

I pick it up and gasp with astonishment. I recognise the chip in the hat. But above his now-ruddy cheeks, the black eyes twinkle mischievously.

Well, there's only one thing to do. I march into the back garden and give him pride of place at the little pond there. I'd never realised how much it needed a garden gnome!

Salmon and Soul

Tunsgate Green stood, thinking of Ruth, back in the cottage, typing away at her wretched manuscript. Some romantic nonsense, mainly to make up for the total lack of it in their lives, he imagined. Once she'd been young, vivacious, sexy even. He snorted. Hard to imagine that now! Their love life currently resembled this salt marsh – dead flat.

He gazed over the dry beige marshland to the distant level horizon, the faintest deep blue ribbon set against the pale blue sky indicating the start of the North Sea, next stop the fjords and islands of western Norway, 400 miles away.

They'd come to Stiffkey, on the Norfolk coast, to try to rekindle something of their relationship, but with Ruth immersed in her fictional romantic world, and him stalking the lonely marshes and empty beaches, they rarely seemed to meet when one or the other wasn't tired. She could be irritatingly churlish too, which didn't help, and he probably wasn't much better, he admitted.

He missed Shiva, his black Labrador and companion of the last twelve years. She'd developed stomach cancer and had to be put to sleep six weeks earlier. Ruth had made sympathetic noises, but she didn't really care. He'd been devastated. He realized he still was, as tears came to his eyes at the thought.

A gentle cool breeze ruffled the stubby coarse grass. It was warm and he felt sweaty, even though he'd not walked fast. Out there he knew appearances could be deceptive. Salt water lurked under the soil, always eager for a victim, perhaps an overzealous dog, or even a careless walker. At night, spirits of footpads and pirates were said to roam the endless flat landscape, damned to do so by virtue of their heinous deeds in life.

He walked back alongside a creek of bright blue water. The soil was exposed here, clay-brown, but dry from the heat of summer. There was no sign of modern life, no fences, telegraph poles, nothing. Just this ancient path, scuffed by centuries of wayfarers.

Coming into the village he encountered the Stiffkey Stores. A pale-red pitched roof surmounted walls made from small stones, some grey, some black, cemented together somehow. A faded blue awning, stained green with moss, overhung a dark curtainless window. In front of the store stood a trailer full of pots of colourful flowers. Someone had recently given it a lick of fresh grey paint.

He pushed the door open and a bell rang. To the left was an old brown wooden counter with an ancient till at the near end. Shelves on the far wall contained tins of soup, loaves of white bread, bags of sugar and the like. Against the wall to the right was a stand containing potatoes with soil on them, large, almost-fluorescent orange carrots, huge cauliflowers, and other vegetables and fruit.

"Hello." A young woman behind the counter, dressed in an enormous thick bottle-green turtle neck pullover, smiled brightly. She had shoulder-length blonde hair, and an attractive, tanned face, unadorned by makeup. On the counter, in front of her, lay a salmon. Its scales held shades of purple and red. Freshly caught, he surmised.

"Hello," he said, surprised. He'd met old Mr. Blush on his one previous visit to buy some stamps. "Did you catch that yourself?" he found himself asking.

"No, I created it!" She laughed a warm laugh, showing perfect white teeth. "What's your name?"

"Oh, it's, ... don't laugh. Tunsgate! Apparently, I was conceived there. My mother never knew my father's name. What's yours?"

"She smiled, it's Nancy, but you know me as Calluna ... in the other place."

He began to wonder if she was all right in the head. She seemed somehow familiar though and exuded an aura of friendship. "What do you mean, you created this salmon!"

She stood up and smoothed the green wool down over her breasts. She laughed her warm laugh again. "There are four of us, you – Arthemis, that's what you're called, me, Nathum and Senji. Our guide and teacher is Shato. He sometimes comes to us as an Irish leprechaun, other times as a beautiful young woman! Your ego-mind doesn't remember, but inside, deep inside, your superconscious mind, the mind of your soul, remembers very well!"

Something in what she was saying rang a distant, faint bell. "I … er, I don't know. It's interesting what you're saying but …."

She came out from behind the counter and he noticed she had one pale blue eye, and one jade green eye. He felt a jolt of recognition. His imagination though, surely?

"We were on what we call Earth Two, a 'practice world.' Now we are at level three we can practise, with Shato's help, channeling energy to make things. At first small pebbles and rocks, then plants, then … fish!" She laughed. "It took a long time. Many, many, *many* lifetimes!"

She approached and put her arms around him. Tunsgate closed his eyes, hugging her back. Yes, he knew her. Deep inside. He could feel the love of a soul mate emanating from her. Then she broke away. "I have to close the shop now." She wrapped the salmon in greaseproof paper and put it in a brown paper bag. "Here, a present from Calluna!"

Ruth was in the small kitchen, pouring boiling water into a large blue china teapot. "What did you do?" she asked.

He enjoyed the familiar, fragrant smell. "Oh, just walked along the coastal path. I miss Shiva."

"I know, darling, she was a lovely dog." She came over and, to his astonishment, hugged him, kissing him on the cheek. He couldn't remember the last time she'd done that.

He continued, "I called into the store. There was an amazing young woman there. Said she knew me from a previous life!" He felt embarrassed.

Ruth laughed. "I wonder who that was, there's only old Mr. and Mrs. Blush run the store."

"She was about twenty-five, blonde hair, attractive. She gave me this salmon!"

"Oh, that'd be from the salmon farm just down the coast. They've got a son. He works there. There's no daughter though. Well …."

"Well what?"

Ruth poured strong brown tea into two blue enamelled mugs and splashed in milk from a carton. "Well there *was* a daughter. Old Mrs. Blush told me the girl used to ride a horse along the coast. One day, about ten years ago, she went out and neither she nor the horse ever came back."

"That's terrible!"

"Yes, some said the horse was a water kelpie and had taken her back to the sea. More likely they went onto the marsh and just got swallowed up, poor girl. Her name was Nancy."

He started. "Nancy. That was the name of the girl in the shop!"

Ruth looked up. Her lips were glossy and he noticed she'd applied some powder to her normally pale cheeks. "Old Mrs. Blush told me Nancy had an unusual characteristic … she had one blue eye …"

"… and one green," he said.

Ruth looked into her mug. "Truth can be stranger than fiction … sometimes."

"I suppose so."

She smiled. "Look, let's drink our tea, then …." She nodded towards the bedroom door.

Saint Peter

"Take your shoes off please, Peter, dear. We don't want to tramp sand over Mrs. Johnson's carpet, do we?"

Peter smiled and eased off his stained white trainers with the toes of his opposite feet, kicking them into a corner.

Mrs. Johnson bent down to retrieve them, recoiling slightly and holding them at arm's length as she gingerly placed them onto a polished mahogany shoe rack. She stood up, brushing down her beige Aran-wool cardigan over her large, lumpy breasts. She spoke in a deep, throaty voice. "Do come through to the lounge. I've heard so much about you, Peter."

"Oh, yeah, right, thanks."

"My husband's still at the church. He'll be along presently. When he's finished the service."

We proceeded along a deep-carpeted corridor. Photographs of smiling family members hung on the walls and a tall grandfather clock ticked ponderously, attempting to keep the silence at bay.

Peter sat on a red-leather sofa with his back to a bay window, overlooking a neat garden which receded into the distance. He wore blue jeans; a black leather jacket and his long hair was washed and in a neat pony tail. "This room's very nice Mrs. Johnson."

"Oh, thank you, yes, there are many family heirlooms, as you can see. She gestured around at glass cabinets. All under lock and key!" She blushed furiously. "Oh, er, I mean …."

"Of course, Mrs. Johnson." Peter gave a charming smile. "You can't be too careful around here."

I'd met Peter at the drug rehabilitation clinic where I work. People imagined living by the coast in a quiet seaside town to be idyllic, but the reality was rather different. Little work, a lot of young and not-so-young people with nothing to do, save drink, take drugs, and steal things to buy them.

They'd found Peter at the bottom of a fifteen-foot dyke one night, out of his head on alcohol and heroin. Quite by chance, a dog walker wandering late at night had heard muffled shouts and investigated. Someone had been lowered on a rope and hauled Peter out, dazed and unaware of what was happening, cursing and shouting abuse at his rescuer. The nights were cold and he'd only been wearing jeans and a T-shirt. He could easily have died from hypothermia.

So, he'd come to us for methadone treatment and gradually turned his life around. He'd cut down on alcohol, quit living on the beach in a ramshackle caravan and been given a council mobile-home. He'd even got a job at the small resort down the coast, taking fares for the rides at the fairground there. Chatting to customers gave meaning to his life, he would say, and "I don't want no stuffy office job!"

Now the vicar had asked Peter to consider giving a talk to young people about the dangers of drugs. It had to be said that they didn't seem like addicts in the making, but around here, you just couldn't tell. Peter, himself, had once been an angelic choirboy by all accounts.

"Would you like some tea, Peter, dear?" asked Mrs. Johnson.

"Yeah, thanks, that'd be nice. D'you want a hand?" He made to get up.

"No, no, that's fine. Just stay here with Mildred, I won't be two ticks." She disappeared down the corridor.

After she'd gone Peter got up and walked over to a glass case housing porcelain figurines, peering into it through small leaded panes. I knew at least two of them were from the reign of George the Third and the collection had been willed down to Sue in the testaments of her forebears.

He turned towards me. "So, any idea how many kids I'll be talking to?"

"Oh, I think it's mainly the older children from local churches, maybe fifty to a hundred. Are you nervous?" I laughed.

His face took on a serious demeanour. "No. I just want to get the message across. I don't want to see any of 'em wasting twenty years of their lives on junk, like I did."

I glowed with pride. My faith in him had proved justified.

"Could I use the loo, Mildred?"

"Yes, of course, go down the corridor, it's the door next to the clock."

He left and I followed shortly, joining Mrs. Johnson – Sue – in the kitchen. She was bustling around, preparing ham and tomato sandwiches, and putting dainty fairy cakes on a cake stand. A large brown earthenware teapot stood on a wooden tray, exuding warmth and the fragrant smell of tea. We chatted about the forthcoming jumble sale. Just then Sue's husband, the vicar, appeared at the kitchen door. "Hello, darling." He kissed Sue's cheek. "Hello, Mildred, lovely to see you. Is ... he here?"

"Yes, he's waiting in the lounge. He seems a nice young man," said Sue.

He sounded worried. "Look, has some fellow just been here, trying to sell something?"

"What? What on Earth makes you say that?"

"Well, I almost bumped into a man carrying a suitcase just now, it looked like he'd come out of our drive, I wasn't sure. He went the other way, towards the main road."

"What did he look like?" she asked.

"Oh, about thirty-five, jeans, black leather jacket, I think he had a what d'you call them ... a pony tail."

My heart sank to my knees. I felt a pain in my gut, I couldn't breathe. Like the time my ten-year-old brother had punched me in the solar plexus at the age of eight 'for practice.' I'd gone down like a ninepin, wheezing and gasping in agony for breath. Mind you, dad had strapped his backside until it was red and raw. He could scarcely sit down for a week. Happy days!

"There was a suitcase in the lounge, woollens for the jumble sale," exclaimed Sue.

We raced down the corridor to the lounge. The cabinet that had held the porcelain figurines was empty. The wooden doors hung open, splintered where they'd been jimmied.

I knew those pieces were of great sentimental value as well as being worth thousands. With tears of shame flooding my eyes, I realised that Peter had taken us all for a ride. He wouldn't be taking any more fares at the fairground, that was for sure.

Salvador

Waves lap at his toes. Gentle, quiet, rippling waves. Benny Saris stares out over the undulating blueness. *Here goes.* He begins to wade out. The water is freezing and goosebumps cover his body like a rash. Muscles cramp agonisingly in his groin. He looks back at the desolate beach and the empty guesthouses on the front. It's no good, suicide is the only option.

He'd awoken one week earlier after a heavy night, drinking almost two bottles of wine and ordering books on Amazon until the early hours. He'd looked at his phone. Almost midday. His head felt groggy, blurred. Funny, there was neither phone nor Wi-Fi signal. He got up and went into his small, shabby kitchen, drew the curtain and looked down on the street far below. The road was empty, just parked cars. No one in sight. He cast his mind back. In the five years he'd lived in the dingy flat, he couldn't remember that. There was always traffic, passersby on their anonymous business, people waiting at the bus stop. He filled the kettle and flicked the switch. *Damn!* The power was off. He stood at the window. Silence. Absolute silence.

Benny went around his cramped flat, flicking switches. Nothing worked. *Bloody Hell, this is weird!* He pulled on a sweater and jeans. Going out onto the landing, he jabbed the lift button. Nothing. He began to worry. He rang old man Stalewski's doorbell, then knocked loudly on the door. No response. Perhaps the old bastard had died? He jogged down the stairs, thinking to call at his friend Sonia Schliefer's, but something kept him going, flight after flight, until he arrived in the lobby. He went out into the street and it hit him like a brick to the head. *Where is everyone?*

The street had an aura of malaise, an indefinable look of neglect. Paving stones that had seen a million footsteps, abandoned. He crossed over to *Sanjays*. The door wasn't locked. Yesterday's newspapers stood in a stand. The usual racks of chocolate bars stood on the counter. He helped himself to a couple, then walked to a door – 'Staff Only.' Pushing it open, he found himself in a short corridor. Light came in through a dirty skylight. On one side was a stock room, piled haphazardly to the ceiling with newspapers and magazines, cans of soup, beans, pot noodles and suchlike. On the other side lay a tiny kitchen and toilet. The toilet bowl was dirty and stained green. In the kitchen stood a cup with brown liquid in it. He smelt it. Instant coffee. It was stone cold. *What the Hell's happened to everyone?*

Benny felt a shiver run down his spine. Perhaps it was some kind of drill? One he just hadn't heard about. *Yes, of course!* He struggled to convince himself.

He spotted a radio behind the counter, battery powered, thank God! He pressed a sweat-stained knob and the radio burst into life, a loud, monotonous hiss. He turned the tuning knob and then changed the bands. The hiss came and went at different pitches, but no music, no pseudo-cheery DJ, nothing.

Now, with the freezing sea up to his neck he knows there's no turning back. A small wave hits him in the face, soaking his hair and making him retch with the salt. He remembers walking the streets of the seaside town, shouting for help, companionship, he didn't know what. Then going into houses, at first entertained by the wonderful entrapments of other people's lives. Knowing he could have anything, take any painting, ornament, crockery, jewellery … if he wanted.

Maybe he'd died, gone to Hell, but didn't realise?

He feels his numbed feet leave the seabed and swallows another mouthful of salty water. He retches again and nearly throws up. Suddenly he hears a sound he recognises, a sound from a thousand years ago. He suspects he's delirious.

But no, it's definitely there. With his heart pounding he turns and swims a few strokes until his feet are back on the seabed once more. He looks around and sees a black object approaching. *My God!* It can't be! The object comes closer – it's a dog, a black Labrador! The creature paddles towards him, whining and barking between pants. He swims towards it. Close now, he sees the dog's eyes, wide, brown, the whites a little bloodshot. Then its paws are on his chest and, bobbing in the sea, the dog tries to lick his face. It's going crazy now, barking excitedly.

"Steady on boy, you're OK!" The frantic touch of the animal's paws makes him think. There's a caravan park a few miles down the coast. Caravans have batteries and gas canisters, don't they? Refrigeration and power! He realises he is, after all, not alone. He has a responsibility to care for this animal now. Maybe there are other people too? They swim to the shore together.

Back on the beach, both wet through and shivering, he notices the dog has a collar. "Here boy!" He examines a metal disc. *Salvador*. How ironic! His eyes fill with tears.

Shameless

Cooee! Over here! I'm waiting and ready for you! Look! Don't you admire my hourglass figure? True, not as slim as some, but then again, I'm not so young any more. But I think I'm wearing pretty well, wouldn't you say?

Don't you admire the gold bands I wear on my neck? My rich mahogany body, the intricate rosette I wear at my waist?

Now, I'll be the first to admit I've not always been faithful. You watched me go off to the Czech Republic with another, and you didn't even try to stop me. And worse, it was with a woman! An oriental wench, twenty years older than me! I blush when I remember that there's even a video of us together. For that I beg your forgiveness.

So, reach out for me. I'm longing for the caress of your fingers, the excitement of your skilful touch, waiting to abandon myself to you, I don't care! It may sound shameless but I want to surrender to you!

Don't listen to *her*, look at *me*! See, I wear bands on *my* neck too, but of better quality, and above them, a piece of precious ivory. And, 'tis true we are of similar age, but see how much younger *I* look, my face smooth and unblemished. I know you adore my curvaceous body, and I thrill to the touch of your hands upon my waist.

And *I* have breeding. I was born in far off Japan before I came to London, when young. My father was a skilled craftsman. Look at her! She can't even tell you where *she* was born, and *her* father was just a humble factory worker!

I've always remained faithful to you, never run off with any 'floozie,' like her. And I hear she even let herself be caressed in public, whilst being filmed, no less! Honestly, she has no shame!

So, come, my dear, grace me with your gentle touch and I will sing so sweetly for you!

He entered the music room, looking round at the instruments hanging on the walls and stood on stands. For some reason, the first two he ever acquired caught his attention. Yes, there was his *Saxon*, bought from a mail-order catalogue for £30, what 43 years ago? Orange-faced, and a body of dull brown mahogany. Of anonymous 'foreign' manufacture. Nevertheless, its tone had improved with age. He'd had the frets filed too and changed the tuners himself. He'd even had a *golpeador* fitted for flamenco.

Then there was his *Takumi*. Bought from Ivor Mairants Music Centre in Soho, perhaps three years later than the Saxon? £150. Ivor himself had demonstrated it, playing *Variations on a Theme by Mozart* by Fernando Sor. His thumbnail had been broken, so the bass was soft.

He remembered taking it to a luthier in Muswell Hill to have the 'action' lowered, the man working on it with a cigarette in his mouth. A long cylinder of ash defied gravity, hanging directly over the instrument as the man slackened the strings. He'd stood, expecting it to fall, then been told to return in a couple of hours, before discovering the fate of the ash.

Then he thought of his partner twenty years ago. How she'd gone on a guitar orchestra tour to the Czech Republic and taken his *Saxon*, her own instrument needing repair. Later, she'd paid for extensive rework on the *Takumi* – the top sanded down and French polished; silver dots laid along the edge of the neck, the saddle lowered and the 'tie block' changed to incorporate bridge pins, in order to get the strings as low as possible. Quite recently he'd had the French polishing redone.

Then his eye caught the exciting contours of his Jackson *Randy Rhoads RR-5,* an electric model with an asymmetric V shape. It had a longer, thinner 'fin' on the top, to rest the arm on, and perfect balance with a strap. It was finished in cream with a black pinstripe, with gold hardware, and a gold 'V' shaped tailpiece, where the strings went through the body. A pricey and 'flashy' instrument. Yes, he would practice on that one today. Sorry girls!

Shine On

"Arabic numerals, that's their proper name."

Emily sat at the heavy wooden table in front of the fire, school book open, pencil poised. "Why?"

"Oh, I suppose they were invented in the Middle East, or North Africa. Countries that have Arabs in them!"

Emily wore her blue school blouse still. It matched her eyes, the colour of robins' eggs. Her hair was shoulder length, blonde as straw. "What was before that?"

"Well, we had Roman numerals, you know, like on the grandfather clock on the landing. Come on, finish your homework."

Fiona Mathews went to the door, watching as her daughter filled in a school mathematics quiz. She was a bright one, like her dad, she thought. She felt a lump in her throat. *Don't go there.*

The farmhouse kitchen was large, high ceilinged, and the walls were whitewashed. The floor was grey stone flags covered with a worn red rug. There was a large Aga kitchen range, in a faded, scratched and dented royal blue, which, when both ovens were occasionally in use together, made the room almost unbearably hot, despite its size.

Along two walls were work surfaces in natural wood, ancient and scored, and below them, cupboards painted an olive-green. Not a colour to Fiona's taste. She intended to repaint them cream. One day … when she had time. She sighed. Better check the readings. "Back in a while sweetheart. Be good."

Emily didn't look up. Fiona went out into the yard, closing the heavy wooden door behind her. Outside it was cold, starting to get dark. Crossing the yard, she could smell the pungent odour of cows in the cowshed. She recoiled at a chilly wind on her face. She passed her dull maroon Vauxhall Victor estate, then walked along a path to a small building. She opened the door and snapped on the lights, marvelling at the new-fangled fluorescent tubes that lit up the laboratory with garish white. Only a generation ago, the only illumination in the farmhouse had been the flickering orange-white flames of wax candles, and the quiet hiss of the occasional gas lamp.

Presently she clicked a radio on to dull the solitude. It was a song she liked. *Eleanor Rigby* by the Beatles, that week's number one.

"Hey man, how much further?" A young man huddled in a great-coat, unshaven, long black hair flopping over a Romanesque face, lay across the rear seat of a battered Bedford van. The headlights traced the track between high dry-stone walls, suddenly illuminating a sign, 'Swarfdale farm 3 miles.'

The driver, a tall, thin man in his twenties, laughed. He had the long, misshapen face of a gravedigger and black hair combed across his forehead. "Three miles. Hey, break out the whisky, Sid, … or were you thinking of acid?"

The man in the passenger seat turned around to face the back seat. He was good-looking, his face thin-lipped, and framed by curly brown hair to his collar. "Hey, Sid, leave off the fucking acid!"

"I never brought no fucking acid!"

"Like we believe you," laughed the driver.

The headlights lit up the old grey stone of a farmhouse. "Hey, we're here." The driver stopped the engine and looked behind Sid to the back of the van, piled high with guitar cases, keyboards, amplifiers, drums, and box after box of equipment and cables. "Let's unload in the morning. I'm knackered. It'll be OK out here."

Fiona opened the laboratory door to leave and flicked the lights off. Her job was to monitor radiation levels in the milk of farms within a fifty-mile radius. She felt satisfaction. All tests had been carried out successfully and isotope levels were normal.

Across the valley she saw distant headlights and heard the sound of a sliding van door crashing open, and men laughing. That was odd, she thought. The farm was unoccupied at present. She stood and watched. The headlights went out, then three dark shapes crossed the farmyard. Shortly afterwards, lights came on within the building. Hmm. They must be visitors staying at the farm. She'd heard the owners were letting the farm out whilst they were out of the country. She shivered. Up above, deep purple clouds scudded erratically across a moonlit sky. It was September, but here in the Derbyshire Dales, the seasons changed quickly. Better check Emily had finished her homework, then she could serve out their evening meal. She looked out again over the valley to the distant farmhouse lights and wondered.

"One, two, FREE, FOUR!" There was a crash of cymbals, a jab of organ and a thundering bass riff. The drums settled into a repetitive rhythm, interspersed with figures played on the drum rims, giving a clicking, clacking sound, whilst the bass pounded out a different metre, producing a beguiling, hypnotic polyrhythm.

The man at the organ bent forward, long brown hair covering his lean, handsome face, as his fingers noodled over the twin keyboards, producing tantalising fragments of otherworldly melody, interspersed with jarring chords.

On the floor sat Sid, holding a black electric guitar covered with small round mirrors, a design of his own creation. In his left hand he held a cigarette lighter which, from time to time, he slid up and down the strings close to the bridge, whilst pounding them with a plectrum, producing a high-pitched swooping, wailing sound.

After several minutes, the bassist, the tall man with the long gravedigger's face, signalled with his head. There was a drum fill, a riff was repeated in unison four times, then the music ended abruptly. Sid jumped up. "That was fucking great!"

"It was OK," said the drummer, a man with a moustache and long dark hair. He'd arrived that morning to join his bandmates. "Those 'mandies' are scrambling your brain. Let's do it again. With the tape rolling this time."

Fiona looked up from her test tubes. What on earth was that noise? She went to the door of the laboratory and looked out across the valley. A blue van stood there, in the distance, along with a Mini Cooper, parked outside Swarfdale farm. She hadn't noticed the car last night, she realised. She guessed they must be musicians, but that noise sounded like the soundtrack to a nightmare.

She looked at her watch and noticed it was time to pick Emily up from school. She'd been listening longer than she'd realised.

When her Vauxhall Victor estate pulled back into the farmyard, she noticed a young man at the back door. She got out of the car. "Hi, can I help?"

"Yes, I'm from over the valley. I'm here with some friends. Musicians. We're staying for a week. Can I come in?"

She noticed the face beneath the long curly black hair was very handsome. And his eyes were extremely dark, the pupils wide open. Like black holes in the sky, she thought. She felt her body reacting to his presence. It had been so long since …. "Yes, come in, please do."

They all went into the kitchen and she put the kettle on. "I'm Fiona. This is Emily."

Emily stared, then found her voice, "Hello."

"My name's Sid. I just came to say, I hope we're not disturbing you. We're working on some tracks for an album." He laughed. "I don't think it'll make us a fortune."

"Oh, no, no. It's not very loud over here and it sounds … er, very interesting." Fiona realised she was blushing furiously.

He seemed not to notice. "What's that you've got there?" he asked Emily. She held a small cage where a white mouse ran in a wheel.

"He's my pet mouse. I let him out sometimes, but you have to be careful he doesn't run and hide."

"What's his name?"

"Oh, I call him Gerald, after my friend's brother."

"This is nice!" He took down an empty china vase from the mantlepiece, noticing Fiona's concerned face. "Don't worry, I won't break it!" He reached out for a pad of paper and a couple of Emily's crayons.

Fiona watched with astonishment as his fingers deftly sketched the vase, his wide black eyes darting between the sketch pad and the vessel, whilst he chewed his lip. "There, for

207

you!" He gave the sketch to Emily and replaced the vase on the mantlepiece with exaggerated care.

Fiona laughed and poured out thick fragrant tea from a huge brown pot with cracked glaze. "Help yourself to milk and sugar." Then, "Emily, take your mouse into the lounge, you can let him out in the corner." She turned to Sid. "You should see Emily play with Gerald. She's so funny. She lets him run up her arms and legs!"

Sid sipped his tea. "Look, I have to go soon. We've two more songs to work on. Perhaps …?"

Fiona's jade green eyes met his black holes. "You could come tomorrow. Tell me about your music. Say one o'clock."

"One o'clock it shall be." Sid stood, bowed, gave a charming smile, winked, and was gone.

Silence is an Empty Space

She was brought up among people who couldn't understand her. Why, at the age of three, she would demand crayons to draw stick men – almost an obsession. Gradually they took on eyes, noses, mouths – now neat but at the same time scary. Then facial expressions, ears, hair, feet and hands, and clothes.

Then aged four, Elizabeth would shut herself away, writing words, gradually stringing them into sentences, accompanied by little pictures in green, red and yellow crayon. 'The cat sat on the mat,' 'The bat sat on the cat.'

"Lizzy, why don't you want to go and play with your friends. Little Josephine next door, she likes you. I'll take you to the park together."

"It's OK, mum," she'd say, now five, going to her room and writing and drawing on her notepad. 'The black-as-soot vampire bat dive-bombed the funny tabby cat.'

But the kids at school didn't want a 'clever clogs' in their class and she knew her mother and father had to struggle to feed her and her two siblings. Writing, painting and drawing came low on their menu of survival. And so, Elizabeth learned to dumb-down her precociousness, to be more like the other kids. She'd read instead, soaking up the art of Shakespeare along with the imagination of Ray Bradbury and the horror of H P Lovecraft, and take her little Jack Russell, Winnie, for walks.

Now it was 2018 and she was sixty years old. She traced the lines on her cheeks and jaws in the mirror, wondering where the time had gone? Wondering what had happened to that little girl with the world at her feet?

She felt her eyes moisten as she remembered the death of her mother. Something imprinted on her mind forever. It was the day before her fourteenth birthday when she'd watched her mother's back going out of the door. Her mother wore a red coat with a fur trim and a matching red hat. "I'll just be ten minutes love, be good!"

It had been December 1972 – she remembered Carly Simon's *You're So Vain* was playing on the radio – and her mother was wearing black leather boots; there'd been snow on the ground. She was just going for some cigarettes but she never came back. A van had skidded on ice and careered onto the pavement, crushing her against a post box. Elizabeth wiped her eyes, putting out of her mind the awful week of visiting her mother in hospital, whilst she fought, in vain, for her life.

Dad had taken it badly. He would come home from work and drink himself into oblivion. She'd had to look after her two younger siblings – her sister, Sally, four years younger than her, and a brother, David, six years younger.

An aunt had made an occasional appearance but they'd had to survive on their own, so she'd taken a job at sixteen. Working on the checkout at Woolworths. But she'd done well there. Promoted to supervisor a year later, then to branch manager a couple of years after that.

Then had come Kenneth. She sighed. He'd seemed so wonderful. She knew she was no glamour queen and she'd been flattered with his attentions.

"Ken, darling, guess what?"

"What, sweetheart, did you hear from your dad?"

"No, better than that. I'm pregnant!"

And so little Abraham had been born. Only to be diagnosed with severe autism a few years later when it was found he could barely read or write. Then Arthur. He too had been autistic, though not so severe. But she'd loved them both and done all she could to help them grow up and develop. When Abe was ten had come the second great shock of her life. Ken had suffered a heart attack in the street and dropped down dead at the age of thirty-six.

She pulled down on her left cheek, just below the eyelid. Licking a finger, she rotated a contact lens, trying to improve the focus. Her hair was blonde with just a touch of grey in the odd place, still natural. She presumed it wouldn't be long before she'd need chemical help. It was just these damned 'marionette lines' on her chin. She'd only recently learned the term but now, whenever she looked in the mirror, she thought of an ageing Lady Penelope from the puppet show Thunderbirds she'd loved as a child.

She looked once more at the envelope she'd rested on the toilet cistern and shivered. It was stamped 'Mortimer Frampton.'

Sarah smiled. "Lizzy, you should get out more!"

"I'm OK, I've got my quilting to work on."

"Jan and I are signed up for a creative writing course at the Walled Garden. What about you? You could come too."

"Oh, I don't know. I … I used to write, when I was a little kid, then … then life got in the way." She gave a hollow laugh. No point in telling Sarah her life story. "I'll think about it."

"Lizzy, you always say that!"

But she'd done more than think about it. Writing had become a part of her life now, a world she could retreat to, away from the mundane, grim reality. A year down the line she'd submitted a children's story to half a dozen publishers, thanks to her tutor's encouragement, but not really expected a reply.

That was eight months ago. She'd given up hope, but now, today, this. And Mortimer Frampton, the most prestigious of the lot! She took their reply and held it up to the light, as if hoping to see the response through the thick cream envelope.

She rubbed the smooth paper against her cheek, then took it into her bedroom and switched on the shredder. It would break her heart to read a rejection letter and anyway, she didn't need fame and fortune. She'd grown used to the solitude and the silence and, after all, there was her quilt to work on.

Souls and Arrows

Old Man

He looked across the village green to a small huddle of folks, dressed in T-shirts and shorts, mostly. They surrounded a boy, tall and skinny, his long brown hair flopping over his face. The boy, holding a long bow, reminded him of a lamppost gone wrong. Seemingly without effort, the boy drew the bow and loosed an arrow, standing motionless as it thudded into the centre of the distant target, joining two others there. A ripple of applause went around the small crowd watching. Yes, he'd do. He'd do very nicely!

Boy

He'd noticed the old man standing at the periphery of the crowd. It was hard not to. Although the sky was filled with cumulonimbus clouds, towering up to distant anvil-shaped plateaus, the air was full of the warmth of summer. He, himself, wore a red T-shirt, green shorts and sandals. The old man, on the other hand, wore a black trench coat and top hat. Maybe it was some kind of costume. Yes, of course, that was it!

He handed the bow and arrow to the next competitor, wishing him luck, as the old man approached.

"You shot them arrows real good!" The old man spoke with an American accent.

He noticed the old man's thin lips and green eyes, the pupils just black slits. Like a snake, he thought. "Thanks."

Old Man

"What's your name, son?"

"It's Sam, er, Sam Torresi."

"How d'you learn to shoot so well?"

"My grandad owns an archery shop, he teaches me ...." He hesitated, unsure whether to confide in a stranger. He pushed his unruly mop of hair back from his sweaty forehead. "I'm at theatre school in town now though … so I'm out of practice."

"Theatre school. Hmm. Well I figure I can help you out there, son."

"How?" The boy looked wary but interested. Good!

"Well, so happens I can make you an offer that'll get you what you want."

"I'd like to be famous. In the movies!"

"Exactly! And I can get you just that!" His thin lips formed a smile, showing yellowed, smoker's teeth.

Boy

He regarded the old man's face. The cheeks were hollow, the skin tawny, but curiously unlined, as if he'd had an endless series of facelifts. "Yeah, as if! Look are you selling something?"

"I guess I'm sellin' … dreams." The old man reached into his coat and pulled out a photograph and a wrinkled, folded-up letter. "You ever hear of Elvis Presley?"

He reached out to take the documents. Momentarily he touched the old man's hand. It was like ice. He read the inscription below the smiling handsome face. 'To Tom, thanks for making my dreams come true, affectionately Elvis.' The letter had the same handwriting and talked about shows and recording dates.

"How do I know this is real? And who are you?"

Old Man

"They call me The Colonel. I knew Elvis's momma and poppa, Gladys and Vern. I managed him for over twenty years!"

The boy regarded him with curiosity. "But then you'd be real old, I mean *real* old!"

He laughed. "When you have money, you can have … things that ordinary folk don't know about."

The boy blinked, silent now. Almost hooked!

213

"Look, let's cut to the chase. I'll make you famous. In return, I'll give you a deal. You shoot one of your arrows, only one mind. If it hits the bullseye then there's no charge."

Boy

He knew he couldn't miss but played along. "What if it doesn't?"

The old man removed his top hat and held it against his chest, revealing long wispy grey hair. Suddenly he looked very old. "You meet me here, in this exact spot, in eighty years' time, eight o'clock on Christmas Eve. Then you pay the price I ask."

He imagined the green transformed, white with a blanket of snow. Heated tents adorned the field and coloured lights hung from poles. In the centre was a huge Christmas tree, covered in sparkling white lights and glittering baubles. Crowds of warmly dressed folk laughed and smiled, drinking hot beverages and mulled wine. And the old man stood there, in his black trench coat and top hat. As black as death. He shuddered. "OK."

The old man followed him to the now-empty target range and watched him retrieve the bow and an arrow from a tent. No one paid attention to them.

"Remember, Christmas Eve, eighty years from now. Right here. Eight o'clock in the evening. Only if you miss, mind!"

He nodded and stood straight, at the shooting mark, the arrow in place. The old man smiled. He hesitated, then grinned back. What the old man said didn't make sense, but he nevertheless couldn't help but believe him.

He drew the bow and, feeling a strange mixture of nervousness and confidence, sighted the arrow just as his grandfather had taught him. He took a deep breath. Just then, a huge black bird swooped down in front of him, flapping its wings and disappearing off over the field, making him flinch as he released the arrow. With a sinking feeling in his guts he saw he'd missed the bullseye. "That wasn't fair. I'm taking it again!" He looked around but the old man was nowhere to be seen.

He returned the bow and arrow to the tent. Huh, never mind, the whole thing was nonsense!

On coming out, a man was waiting. He looked vaguely familiar. His face was flat, not handsome. "Hi, I've been hearing good things about you!" The man proffered a card.

He felt surprise, but, yes, he was probably top of the class in most acting disciplines. His singing and dancing were coming along too. "Yeah, sure." He took a proffered card from the man's hand and examined it. "Quentin Tarantino, hey, I've heard of you!"

"We're auditioning for a live action version of Young Robin Hood. It'll be a warts an' all account!" Tarantino smiled and winked. "You've every chance of being chosen."

Statue at Liberty

"America comes first though, right?" said the president. Aides Don Daley and Victor 'Day-Glo' Rigby exchanged nervous glances. The president stood, facing a statue. A voice came into their minds, deep, educated. 'No, *we* come first, *then* America.'

The president stuttered. "Oh, yes … of course … I meant, er …."

Slits in the green eyes widened imperceptibly. 'You will first do *our* bidding, *then* the bidding of your people. You will cut spending on your Environmental Protection Agency climate change program. Drastically!'

The president had sat in the oval office, finally, and incredibly, alone. The inauguration procedure, with its endless speeches and razzamatazz, was over. Photographs of every permutation of his family had been taken. Finally, Day-Glo had ushered everyone out. "Come on folks, I think Mr. President needs some time to himself!" Before leaving, he'd turned. "Mr. President, there's an urgent letter for you from Mr. Obama in your desk."

In the unaccustomed silence, the president wiped his face with a handkerchief and looked in a cabinet. Thank God! Several bottles and glasses stood inside. He poured himself a generous measure of whisky and added several cubes of ice from a refrigerated compartment. He took a gulp and felt his brain reel from the alcohol. Better have a look at this goddamn letter!

'Greetings Mr. President, firstly there's something you must know. Take the lift at 9 p.m. tonight. Press six and nine simultaneously for five seconds ….' The president's jaw dropped. The letter continued with the usual congratulatory material. It signed off, 'Good luck, you will need it! Barack.'

He'd taken the lift as instructed to find himself descending below the lowest level for what seemed an age. Finally, the door opened onto a corridor where Daley and Day-Glo were waiting.

"What's going on? What's this about?"

"You'll see sir. Don't worry."

They proceeded into a large chamber, illuminated by numerous candles around the walls. In the middle of the room was a statue of a seated Egyptian figure. It had the head of a jackal. Daley and Day-Glo stood on either side of him. The president felt annoyed. What the hell was going on? Suddenly a voice came into his mind, making him jump.

'Greetings. You have been elected president, and like every president before you we extend our congratulations.'

The statue's eyelids slid upwards, revealing green, snake-like eyes. The president started, then felt Daley's reassuring hand on his shoulder. "Who are you? What's this about?"

'We came to this planet many millennia ago to aid your development. It was *we* who constructed the pyramids. Because of our ... appearance ... we are currently hidden, but we continue to direct your affairs. In return you co-operate with us.'

"Aid our development? What about all the millions of people killed in wars!"

'The fate of individuals is not our concern. War leads to innovation, innovation requires power, power produces heat, and heat ... warms the planet.'

"What? What's that to you!"

'Our ... people ... abhor the cold. When the mean planetary temperature has increased another five degrees, then they will come *en masse*, and we can reveal ourselves.'

The president's mind boggled. So, the rumours were true. Lizards, or something similar, really *had* been pulling the strings! Goddammit. As if he hadn't got enough on his plate already! "Look, we appreciate your help, sorry, I don't know your name, but there's a lot of people not happy with global warming!" What the hell could these creatures do about it anyway, if they were hidden away in statues and the like?

"My name is Anubis!"

Daley and Day-Glo looked alarmed. Day-Glo spoke hurriedly, "Mr. President, er, it's best you agree sir!"

The president felt emboldened. No, *he* was in charge goddamn it! "So, it's, er, nice to meet you, Mr, er, Anubis, but I can't agree to this."

The aides gasped.

Slowly, ponderously, the figure rose, rocking its canine head from side to side. Now standing eight feet tall, it stretched its arms out and opened its hands to reveal a slender thumb, two fingers and three long, sharp claws.

The president gulped. "Of course, on second thoughts, er, *you* know best. Sure, I'll cut the program. No problem!"

Sycamore the Wise

The sun was setting over the field and Sycamore made his way to a small spinney in one corner, stopping on occasion to perk his long, furry ears up, and to feel the warm summer air playing on his long whiskers, whilst he sniffed the evening breeze. *All clear!* He entered the trees and heard the quiet guttural calls of his mother. He found her in a depression in a bed of moss with his two brothers and sister in attendance.

"Sycamore, what took you so long?"

He'd fallen asleep after feasting on a pile of carrots he'd chanced upon. "Sorry, mother, I thought I smelled a fox, and lay low for a while."

"Hmm. Well, anyway, you may now all suckle from me." She stretched out on the moss, exposing her belly and four enlarged nipples, which the leverets – young hares – quickly latched onto.

Sycamore was in heaven as he drank the warm, sweet milk, feeling his mother's warmth and his siblings' closeness.

When they had finished, their mother lapped up any urine they had expelled, so as to cover their tracks. Then her voice became serious. "Now the moon has gone through one cycle, it is time to make your own way in life. I will no longer be here to suckle you, and you must continue to wean on the fruits of the woods and farmers' fields."

"But will we still see you, mother?" asked Blackberry, Sycamore's brother, with a tear in his eye.

"Yes, son, I will still frequent the same woods and fields, but it will only be a few moon-cycles before you will father leverets of your own. And just a few more before Bluebell, your sister, gives birth to her first litter."

"How exactly does that happen?" asked Sycamore, bemused.

"You will find out son, never fear!"

An older hare lolloped onto the moss. His coat had many curls and grizzled areas.

Mother cleared her throat. "Now, I want to introduce someone to you. This is Uncle Ditch."

"Hello young 'uns, well, you have all grown so much this past moon-cycle that you are now free to go further afield. I will stay close but never wander more than two fields from me. If you get lost, then I will come to this spot at sunfall. Meet me here."

The young hares nodded, feeling a mixture of excitement and apprehension.

"Now, you know about foxes, owls and eagles, and man, with his fire-sticks, traps and poisons. But I need to warn you of one further thing."

"What's that?" chirped up Hedgerow, the other brother.

"Patience, Hedgerow!" laughed Uncle Ditch. "Well, you've seen a slow-machine, something that moves around the fields on its own with a man in it, turning the earth with a lot of noise?"

"Yes," they all answered.

"Well, beyond these fields lies a track, made by man from something black and hard. From time to time a machine will come along, much faster than the slow-machine, and at night, with two huge glaring golden eyes, bigger even than the eyes of the biggest owl in the forest! And how they shine!"

Sycamore felt a shiver pass through his fur. "Will they attack us?"

"No, but if you see one, you must run. Run as fast as you can, faster than the wind, faster than the clouds that scud across the sky on a stormy night! And pray to the Great Hare for deliverance!"

Just then a young buck hare appeared.

"Greetings Juniper," said Uncle Ditch.

Juniper bowed. "Uncle Ditch, I have terrible news. Chestnut, he … he's gone to the Great Meadow in the Sky." He began to cry.

Sycamore felt his eyes watering, even though he had never met Chestnut.

"What happened?" asked Uncle Ditch.

"He was on the black track when a fast-machine came along with its golden eyes blazing. He ran and he ran and he ran, but it caught him. He was mortally wounded. There was nothing I could do to save him."

"His soul will go the Great Meadow, and his flesh will feed the crows," said Uncle Ditch sadly.

Sycamore piped up, "If we hares cannot outrun these fast-machines, then why do we even try? Why don't we run away and hide until they've passed? ... Ow!" he exclaimed, as his mother whacked him around the head.

"How dare you question Uncle Ditch and the wisdom of our kind!" she scolded. "You will do as you are told!"

Sycamore felt all eyes on him. He felt indignant but acquiesced. "Yes, mother, sorry."

But as the meeting wound to a close, he told himself that *he* would never try to outrun something that could go faster than him and would never get tired. Where was the sense in that?

By running and hiding until the fast-machines had passed, Sycamore lived to a ripe old age. But eventually the time came, as it does for us all, for his soul to leave the old, faithful body that had fathered many, many leverets, and to pass on to the Great Meadow in the Sky. There, he was overjoyed to become reacquainted with his dear mother again, and with so many other relatives and friends who had also passed into spirit.

Now they are free to run and feast on lush grass and crops, safe from the threat of predators and fast-machines, and under the loving care of The Great Hare.

So, if you are driving at night and a hare runs in the headlights in front of you, then please be kind and drive slowly until it has run off the road. Not every hare has heard – or chosen to pay heed to – the teaching of Sycamore the Wise and his descendants.

Tangled Lives

I felt embarrassed. "Eavesdropper, *moi*?"

The girl looked at me accusatorily, but with humour behind her pale grey eyes. She wasn't pretty, not even attractive really, but she had 'something.' Her skin was quite dark, healthy looking, and she wore silver-rimmed glasses. Maybe it was her generous shape. Perhaps it conformed to a subconscious template we males lust after?

"Well, what were you up to then?" She glanced back at her friend, a fat girl with bright blonde hair, presently shovelling spaghetti Bolognese into her face, then looked me square in the eyes, raising her eyebrows.

"OK, perhaps I was … a bit. I'm a writer; it's a way of getting realistic dialogue … and ideas for stories."

"What did you hear then?"

I laughed. "Not much really, just that you both sound desperate for a man!"

"Cheeky sod!" She blushed. "Perhaps I am. Have you written many books then?"

"I'm working on a novel."

"Oh." She sounded disappointed. She looked around, as if she were thinking to re-join her friend.

"Wait. I've written some stories. Look! I hurriedly took out my phone and found my book on Amazon. Look, that's me, David Bird. *Stories from the Undergrowth.*" There was a little picture of me.

She looked from me to the picture, and to me again. "Wow. So, you're a famous author!"

"Sort of!" I thought it prudent not to tell her it was self-published and that sales were currently in single figures.

Her eyes lit up. "Look, it sounds exciting. Maybe I could help?"

"Ah, I dunno."

"Look, I'll go around the bar, see if I can hear anything interesting. I'll pretend to look at my phone, OK?"

I decided to humour her, I could always make my escape. "All right, thanks. What's your name by the way?"

She smiled. "Leanne, I wondered if you'd ask!"

"Pleased to meet you, Leanne." I shook her hot, clammy hand.

There was a restaurant area, about half full, and a large bar, separated into three levels, presently quite crowded, where you could also eat food. I'd discovered this was a good place for eavesdropping, and two stories in my book owed their genesis to it.

In a far corner I could see a middle-aged couple who looked like they were arguing. She was large with long platinum hair, small oval black-rimmed glasses, and a lined, saggy face. He had a short grey moustache and beard, and a skull that would have made a billiard ball envious. I wended my way towards them, aiming for a nearby cigarette machine, simulating a conversation with a talkative partner on my phone, giving time to eavesdrop on a tête-à-tête worthy of a modern-day Rabelais.

"All I'm saying, Jack, is to put your foot down a bit. She's living in our house and while she's still at home, she should abide by our rules."

"I know, darling, but she's twenty-four, she's got a life of her own now. It's not easy communicating with her, you know."

"Maybe, but she comes back at all hours, drunk usually, crashing and banging about. And then there's her ... well, I hesitate to call them boyfriends."

"Well, we were young and randy once!"

"Well, maybe *you* were. I preferred to keep my knickers *on* – unless I was having a piss or a shit."

"Yes, I noticed!"

"Never mind that, something must be done, Jack, d'you hear me?"

Suddenly, out of the corner of my eye, I saw Leanne beckoning from across the crowded room. She looked worried. I went over to her. "Did you get anything?"

"Yeah, some men playing pool, 'round the corner. They were talking about beating someone to a pulp."

"Oh, my god, did they say why?"

"Yes, apparently some guy is shagging one of their wives."

223

"Did they say who?"

"Yes, one David Bird esquire!" She glared at me.

I felt my stomach go queasy. "Look, I think I'd better go. It was great meeting you."

She looked concerned. "I think you should. Will I see you again?"

Just then, Jack came over. "Leanne!"

"Oh, hello Dad, fancy meeting you here!"

That seemed as good a time as any to take my leave.

The Artifact

'Out in space no-one can hear you scream.' Well, Alice could hear screams all right. Her three-year-old twins, Adam and Toni, fighting.

Adam wailed as Toni held an angry-looking, bright-blue shark just out of his reach. Being taller, she would lift it higher, just beyond his grasp, as he jumped up for it.

"Toni, you know how much he likes that toy. Give it back right now or you don't go to see daddy's shuttle come in."

Toni threw the toy at Adam's chest, knocking him over. Adam began to cry.

"Pack it in you two, I haven't got time for this." Toni could be so cruel to Adam. She couldn't understand where Toni got it from. Both she and Tom, her husband, had been placid, sociable children.

A screen beeped, high on the playroom wall and a message scrolled, 'shuttle ETA 45 minutes.' The display showed a sweeping view over a segment of the planet Mars, where a rash of mountains rose above the dull orange surface. They looked so small, she thought, but, in reality, she knew many of them to be over two miles high.

Elsewhere, the volcano, Olympus Mons, lurched 14 miles skywards, looking for all the world like a gigantic, squat boil.

The tenuous atmosphere of the planet formed a haze on the curved horizon, and beyond it, the sun blazed in the inky blackness.

A communicator sounded. Alice pressed a button and Tom's face appeared.

"Hi, Ally, we're on our way. They've found something they want taking back home, we're bringing it up."

That was unusual. "What is it?"

"Well, it's some kind of artefact. It's kinda weird ...." The signal broke up. "... shaped like a ...." Then it cut off completely.

Alice sat with the children, gazing at the silver sails of the space station, and the shuttle dock below, set against the infinite blackness of space. Alice thought over the revelations of the last six months whilst Adam and Toni played hand-held games. At first the digs had revealed stone tools, twenty metres below the frozen red desert, to great excitement. Then in another excavation site, metal objects, long strips of some strange alloy were found, deeply buried.

At first, they'd been told to keep it all under wraps, not to let the Earth public know. "The plebs won't know how to handle this," the director had told them.

But it was too big, too important, and soon, too many whistleblowers had ignored the mandate. Back on Earth, rumours of 'outlandish conspiracy theories' became science facts.

Now Tom, Alice, and two planetary scientists, David and Heinz, stood in a lab. The twins were next door watching videos of Earth. Lights blazed on an object lying on a table. It was ivory-coloured, about eight feet in length, a foot wide, and just over an inch thick. The width tapered towards the rounded ends, where it also curved up slightly. There was a small hole where a sample had been taken.

"What's the lab say?" asked Tom.

David ran a hand over his bald head. "It seems to be some kind of plastic, can you believe?"

Tom and Alice exchanged glances. "What the hell is it?" Tom asked.

"Christ knows," responded Heinz, a young man with ginger hair and beard.

Adam appeared in the doorway, jumping up and down excitedly. "Mummy, daddy, I know what it is!"

Alice smiled. "Don't be silly, darling!"

"I do, I do, come and look!" He ran back into the rec room.

"Go and see what he wants," sighed Tom, raising his eyebrows.

In the rec room a video played. Alice gasped. "Tom, David, Heinz, you might want to see this!" she called out.

The others trouped in. They all gazed at a gigantic wave where an athletic young man balanced half way down its huge green face. David smiled. "Yes, I'll admit there's a similarity. Welcome to surf city – on Mars!"

They all laughed, then a communicator beeped. "It's the lab," said David, as he walked over to pick up a handset.

The others stood watching the surfer riding the wave, in awe. How beautiful the sea back on Earth looked. Alice felt a pang of nostalgia.

They were startled by the sound of a handset hitting the floor. David stood, ashen-faced.

"Hey, what's up?" asked Heinz.

David's tone was wooden. "… They dated that artefact. I just got the result."

"Well, how old?"

"It's incredible. It's … it's sixty-six million years old!"

"What, you mean …?"

"Yes, whatever killed the dinosaurs wiped these … people out too."

"And that … er, thing next door?"

David shrugged his shoulders. "I guess it is what it looks like. The oceans must have been evaporated by the heat of the impact."

Alice looked up at the screen again, where the video of the surfer still played. She tried to imagine an orange sky, a huge red wave, and balancing on the ivory surfboard, a tall, slim ochre-coloured humanoid, young and adroit, thinking thoughts that we could never begin to imagine.

She wondered what Earth would be like in sixty-six million years' time.

"Mum, can we go now? I'm bored." Toni's shrill voice brought her back down to Mars.

The Final Crossing

Other times Justin Schneider would have stayed in his warm, lighted cabin, or mingled in the bar, but he'd needed some *real* air. He wanted to breath the sea breeze and feel alive. Out on the stern it was cold, wet and misty, and his companion's words were suddenly drowned out by the gargantuan blare of a foghorn. The ferry bucked in the heavy sea and he held onto the handrail tightly, gazing down nervously at the green-black waves crashing below.

Justin had recognised his companion from the television. Mike Murphy, some kind of political figure, seen occasionally on tedious news clips about Ireland. A tall man with receding hair and a lean face, wearing a heavy charcoal overcoat, he'd been gazing fixedly out to sea, as if seeking answers to unsurmountable problems.

In life, though, he seemed a different man, animated and imaginative. "Would you look at the waves now," Murphy was saying. "The power of a wave, it's something. 36 kilowatts of power potential per meter of wave crest!"

"But how would you harness the power of these waves, for example?" Justin asked, gesticulating downwards.

"Well, that's for the Good Lord to tell us, and for the boffins to pay good heed to!" Murphy laughed. "But look how they've extracted gas and oil from the sea bed!" He winced as a spray of salty water splashed over them both. "And what, pray, brings you to this cold, damp spot, when you could be warm inside, watching the football on the big screen?"

"I don't like football," said Justin, "and … and there's something else …."

Murphy's eyes gazed sympathetically at him, like a faithful dog's. "Yes?"

He found himself opening up. "Well, it's my dad, he always wanted to be buried at sea." The ferry bucked again and Justin steadied himself. It was growing dark and starting to rain. "I have his ashes. Inside." He gestured towards the lighted cabins.

"Now's as good a time as any," said Murphy.

"Well, I was hoping for some sunshine."

Murphy pulled his overcoat tight against the wind. He had a persuasive, easy-going manner. "There's no time like the present. Just wait for a lull in the wind." He smiled.

Justin hesitated. Perhaps Murphy was right. He reasoned he could scatter the ashes in the presence of, well, a kind of celebrity. That would make a more memorable sending off. Perhaps Murphy would even say a prayer?

He went down the deck, balancing carefully against the rocking of the ferry. Inside he caught sight of a television screen, stopping him dead in his tracks. A group of football fans sat watching a news bulletin featuring a shockingly familiar face. He opened the door and listened, stunned. "… and it's been announced that councillor Michael Murphy is being sought for questioning into the murder of a catholic, Father Patrick O'Connor in 1975 …."

The football match resumed to a cheer and the swill of beer. He retraced his steps to the deck. At least he owed it to Murphy to let him know, Justin thought. As he battled through the rain and the gloom towards the stern, he saw something dark on the deck. A heavy black overcoat, lying on the wet planks, empty sleeves blowing in the wind like a priest's supplicating arms, but its occupant … gone.

The Ideomotor Effect

While I wait for news, and now my hands have stopped shaking, I want to record the incident that happened tonight.

My parents had gone into London to see an opera and still aren't back at nearly half past midnight. They said I could have a couple of schoolfriends around as long as we promised to be 'sensible.' Fat chance! So, Shelley and Julie had called round, together, about seven o'clock. They'd brought some DVDs and Julie had snuck a couple of bottles of beer from her brother's stash. Shelley had brought a large carrier bag. Like all teenage girls, we swapped news and giggled about the boys we fancied, then we put on a DVD, *The Omen.*

Well, it was pretty scary, and nasty too, the way people got killed, being sliced in two by a faulty lift and crushed between train carriages, for example. Afterwards, Shelley said, "God, that was horrible. Look, I brought something we can play, I'll go and get it." She headed for the kitchen.

Julie laughed. "Paul used to look like Damien when he was young. He used to get mad when we called him Damien!" Paul was Julie's brother.

Shelley returned with a rectangular box. She opened it and took out a board with the letters of the alphabet and the numbers one to ten printed on it, along with the words 'yes,' 'no,' and 'good bye.' The board was decorated with star symbols and a sun and a moon, both characterized with evil-looking faces. At the top of the board was a skull and, on either side of it, bat-like wings.

"Oh, my God!" I exclaimed, "A Ouija board, this is scary! ... I know, I'll light some candles!"

Shelley laughed, "My gran used it to contact spirits!"

Soon we sat at one end of the dining table, two candles burning in holders in the centre of the table and the room lights turned off. Our half-drunk bottles of beer stood on coasters, we didn't want to stain the table, being thoughtful girls at heart. I took a swig of mine, I wasn't sure of the taste, but it made me feel good.

Shelley explained how it worked. "All put a finger on this. It's called a *planche*tte."

It was a heart-shaped piece of wood with a pointed end that ran on small castors. It moved around slightly under our finger pressure. "I'll start." In a serious voice, she continued, "Is there anybody there?" Nothing happened. Julie giggled. Shelley asked again and the planchette remained where it was. "This is silly," I said, as Shelley asked a third time. Suddenly the planchette made a rapid movement directly to the word 'Yes.' My heart was pounding. It must have been Shelley or Julie moving it, surely? I was certain it wasn't me. My finger was only pressing lightly. Shelley continued, "Who's there?" The planchette spelt out 'A F-R-I-E-N-D.'

We asked silly questions, the sort of things teenage girls ask. When will I get a boyfriend? Will I go out with Russell? Will mum and dad buy me a horse? The planchette would spell out the answer we wanted to hear, or else a jumble of letters that didn't make much sense. After half an hour I was getting bored. "Let's watch another DVD."

Julie laughed. "I brought *The Exorcist*. That's a good one!"

"Hang on, said Shelley, I want to ask it something. She hesitated, then, "When will I die?"

Julie and I looked at each other, disconcerted.

The planchette moved to the row of numbers. Again, my finger wasn't pressing hard. I looked at Shelley and Julie. Their faces were serious and their fingers didn't *look* to be moving the planchette. But surely, they must have been?

We held our breath as, slowly, the planchette picked out 2-0-8-7. "Phew, that's a relief," laughed Shelley, "wonder what it'll be like then?"

Then my turn. The planchette spelled out 2-0-9-2. "Wow, I'll be ...." My brain struggled. I was never one for sums. "uh, ninety-three!" We all laughed.

"Let me try," said Julie. This time the planchette moved away from the numbers and spelt out three letters, H-O-Y. "Hoy, what's that supposed to mean, this is silly. C'mon let's watch that DVD."

We pushed the pointer to 'good bye' and Shelley put the board and planchette away in their box and took it into the kitchen. We extinguished the candles. I think we were all a bit spooked by that so we were geared up to be frightened by *The Exorcist!*

"Is there any more beer?" asked Julie.

"Here, you can finish mine." I handed her my bottle which was still about a quarter full. I'd decided I wasn't terribly keen on the taste of beer.

So, we sat, watching as a girl, about our age, became more and more 'disturbed' and ghastly things began to happen, the special effects team of the day going overboard with the gore. Suddenly the doorbell rang and we jumped out of our skins.

"It'll only be Paul," laughed Julie, going to answer. "They said they'd call round."

Her brother, Paul, and his girlfriend, Maria, came into the room. Paul was a few years older than Julie, tall, dark and handsome, as they say. Maria, his girlfriend, was a few years older than Paul, had olive skin and long dark hair. I felt self-conscious, and envious of her looks.

We paused the DVD and Paul poured us all out some wine he'd brought. "Don't tell your parents!" It was chilled and quite sweet. I liked it! I'd make sure the glasses were thoroughly washed and put away before mum and dad got back!

They asked what we'd been doing. When we said we'd been playing with a Ouija board, Maria looked shocked. "*Dios mio, eso es peligroso* – dangerous!"

Paul laughed, "Come on, it's harmless fun, don't be dramatic!"

"No, Paul, you can contact *espíritus malignos* – evil spirits."

"It's all done by subconscious movements, the 'ideomotor effect.' I've read about it, it's all rubbish. Scientists have tested it out."

Just then there came a soft tapping from the kitchen.

What's that? Maria exclaimed.

Tap-tap-tap

We looked at one another.

It came again, tap-tap-tap-tap.

"I'll go and see," said Shelley.

We told Paul and Maria about the dates we would die and about the nonsense word. Paul laughed, "one of you was moving it subconsciously!" Maria turned pale. "H-O-Y, *hoy,* in Spanish, that means *today!"*

A scream came from the kitchen and Shelley came running in. Her eyes were wide and her face white. "The planchette was tapping against the board – in the box!"

We looked at each other in disbelief. Suddenly all the lights went out. Julie screamed. "Oh, my God, I'm getting out of here!" She pushed past us in the dark and ran to the door, then out and down the hall. Some light entered the room as we heard the front door open, then there was a cry and silence.

The lights came back on. Paul went to see what had happened and came back grim-faced. "Julie's fallen, she's unconscious. She must have tripped on the step. She's cracked her head open."

We called an ambulance. Paul and Maria went with Julie. I'm waiting for them to call from the hospital. Until then, I can't possibly sleep, just write this and hope that she'll be OK. I know one thing, I'm done with Ouija boards – for good.

The Magic Onion

Heidi came in with a string bag of onions and dumped them on the kitchen table. I looked up from my computer screen. "What's with all the onions?"

"The guy on the market was giving them away!"

"What? Couldn't he sell them?"

"They were packing up. There weren't any customers really and it was starting to rain. It was cold too. I think he just wanted to get rid of them."

"Oh. Would you like some tea?"

She took off her navy-blue fleece, tossing her long brown curls back, and hung it up. She smiled. "Yeah, thanks, that'd be nice."

I got up and filled the kettle. I ignited the gas ring, watching the blue flame hiss and burn for a moment, enjoying its warmth, then put the kettle on.

Heidi came over and put an arm round my shoulder, kissing my cheek. "What are you doing?"

"Oh, just writing e-mails. Boring stuff."

"I remember grandma used to have a lovely recipe for eggs. She'd cut a big onion ring and fry it on one side. Then she'd turn it over and crack an egg into it. She'd add some water and cover it for a few minutes. We'd have them on toast. I learnt how to do it myself and I'd eat three at a time!"

"Greedy guts! You'll have to make me some." The kettle was whistling. I put teabags into a large brown pot and poured boiling water onto them, inhaling the familiar, comforting odour. "My dad used to clean spoons with them!"

"What?"

"Yeah, he'd get an onion, slice it, then crush the slices. He'd put them in a pot with a little water and leave it for a while. Then he'd dab a cloth in the mixture and rub it on the spoons until they were clean and shiny. I used to clean my penknife blades with it. I had one of those Victorinox things."

"What, were you in the Scouts or something?"

I laughed "Yeah, I was always prepared!"

We both sat at the kitchen table. I closed my computer lid. Heidi took some scissors and cut the string bag. She selected an onion, shut her eyes and held it to her nose, inhaling deeply. "I think people are like onions."

She could be deep could Heidi. "How d'you mean?"

"Well, on the outside they can be a bit rotten but inside they're OK."

"True."

"Then, there are translucent layers, but you can only see through a couple. You don't know what's *really* inside. You think they're kind to animals, peel a layer off and it turns out they put a hamster in a microwave. That kind of thing."

"That's horrible!"

"People've done it. Then sometimes they're hard on the outside but soft, rotten in places, on the inside."

I poured the tea into two large blue enamel mugs. "Mum was like that." I took a bottle of milk from the fridge and poured some into our cups. Neither of us took sugar.

She continued, "Sometimes there's like another layer of skin inside, like an onion inside an onion." She sipped some tea and smiled. "That's like a schizo I suppose!"

I cupped my mug in my hands, enjoying the warmth and looking into Heidi's green eyes. "I'll tell you something. Just you and me, right?"

"Yeah, sure."

"Well you remember my dad's funeral?"

"Yeah, of course. You were well upset. Don't blame you though."

I took an onion, rolling it slowly between my hands. "Not exactly, I had one of these – cut into pieces and wrapped in foil. In a jacket pocket."

She sat up. "What d'you mean?"

"Well every now and then I'd go somewhere private, get a piece out and put it up to my eyes."

Heidi looked shocked.

"Dad was like an onion all right. Nice on the outside. Different layers for different folk. Bitter at the core."

The Medium is the Message

"Hello Sherina, yes, I've received your payment, how can I help?"

"Well, the world's divided into two kinds of people. Those who hear voices in their heads and those who don't. Some get paid for it and some get locked away!"

"Ha ha, yes, I get paid for it, dear!"

"Oh, getting on for thirty years!"

"Well, we have 'guides' – people in spirit. They co-ordinate who comes through."

"Yes, they do a great job, it can get pretty busy! OK, I'm hearing the name Dianne, it's a female energy, I'm feeling a lot of love, is it your mother, dear?"

"All right, I'm feeling a sharp pain in my chest. Did she have heart problems before she passed, perhaps a heart attack? Ah, I feel she passed quickly."

"Oh, I'm sorry, dear, but she's with me now, she says she's fine now, and she sends her love … Sherina, are you OK, love?"

"Ah, yes, she's just come to say hello, to let you know she's fine!"

"Well, she's showing me a garden with two swings, and two dogs, one's a rough collie, black and white, the other's a big brown thing, I'm not great on dogs!"

"Oh, yes, it is! He's got a long muzzle and a big black nose."

"Yes, my love, she's bringing that through as a memory link, then. From when you were little, then … You've got photographs on the mantlepiece of her, she's showing me?"

"Yes, have you noticed them being moved?"

"She's been there and moved them, my love. To let you know she's still around."

"Yes, she's often with you. Did you know?"

"Well, now you know, perhaps you'll be more aware of her?"

"Ha ha. On, no, spirit won't intrude if it's private. Like if you're in the loo!"

"But she's saying she's not keen on, Ian, is it? Yes, is he a boyfriend, dear? She'd question his motives."

"That's right. And sometimes he brings a friend, she's saying."

"Yes, well we won't go there, dear!"

"No, it's not for me to judge dear, I'm just the messenger. But, maybe listen to what mum has to say, eh?"

"Yes, and can I give you Andrea?"

"OK, well, she's telling me that Andrea's not to be trusted, do you understand, please?"

"No, don't sign anything! That's what she's telling me, anyway."

"Well, it's up to you. I'm just the messenger. Perhaps speak to a financial adviser, love?"

"Ha, well you can choose your friends, but not your family, in-laws included!"

"OK, now, I understand you've been having bad headaches?"

"And it's something you've suffered from for quite a while?"

"Well, she's saying to try shamanic healing, she thinks it'll help."

"Just look online. Where are you, my love?"

"Oh, there'll be a few around there. As I say, just check online, OK?"

"And can I give you October for a big anniversary or birthday?"

"Oh, yes, birthdays and anniversaries are still important to those in spirit, dear. They can go anywhere, at any time, and join in the fun!"

"Ha, yes, she's showing me a big cake, it's got a *lot* of candles on it!"

"All right my love, and mum's giving you a bag of sherbet lemons! I was never too keen on those, they used to scrape the roof of my mouth!"

"Ha, that's why she's giving you them then!"

"All right, my love, I'll leave you with her love and say God bless."

"You're very welcome, my love. And remember what she said about Ian and his … his, er, friends, eh?"

"All right, my love, Goodbye. Thank you."

The Ministry of Truth, Revisited

Some had warned me it'd be like this, but I hadn't believed them. Now I looked at my entry in Wikipedia once more, still feeling sick to my stomach.

Corwin Blackthorne (b.1957) a self-proclaimed 'spiritual' healer, established a 'sanctuary' in St. Olaves, Wiltshire in 2003, when the number of patients visiting his home became too great. He claims to have healed thousands from arthritis, depression, asthma, and even cancer. However, studies by the British Medical Journal showed no evidence to support this claim and were unable to verify a single cure. Subsequently, some ex-patients have accused Blackthorne of fraud ....

My wife, Jean, appeared and put an arm around me. "Darling, don't torture yourself, think of all the people you've helped. They know you're a good man. Look at Sue Jones, last week. She's been walking around town without her sticks, singing your praises."

I kissed her cheek, still smarting from the inaccuracy of the article. "I know. But anyone who *doesn't* know me will believe this, this shit!"

I'd got a friend who knew about these things to correct the Wikipedia entry on me. To say that the BMA study was on terminal cancer patients only, where, truth to tell, most were beyond any kind of healing beyond a complete miracle. Also, only *one* person had accused me of fraud, the ludicrous Jaspar Simons, a local squire who was busy suing all and sundry for alleged misdemeanours relating to the renovation of his stately home. But now, 'someone' had gone in and altered the article back to the previous version.

It had been back in 1987, when I'd attended a spiritualist church with the encouragement of friends, that a medium had told me I had healing powers. As a child, I remembered seeing my grandparents around the house, although they'd both died years before, but had been told by my parents 'not to be silly,' and that it was 'just a vivid imagination.' Suddenly I hadn't been so sure. Then, following a brief training, had come years of experience, and great success.

Now, we lived in a large house with an old orangery, whose glass facades, high ceiling and large stone pots, planted with fruit trees, were conducive to encouraging healing energies, which I sensed and could be directed into the subject. All paid for by donations from patients, I only charged a subsistence fee.

Two weeks after seeing my entry redacted back to the original pack of lies, Jean came to me. "Darling, there's someone to see you. Someone official I think."

"Who?"

"He didn't say."

"OK, show him in." I decided I'd give him five minutes.

A distinguished-looking man, dressed in a smart grey suit came in. He looked to be in his early sixties. "Mr. Blackthorne?"

"Yes."

"My name is James Spader. I'm from the Government's Department of Perception Management, the 'Ministry of Truth,' as some call it!" He laughed and offered his hand.

I shook it. Dry and warm. "Take a seat. Please." I gestured to a sumptuous green-cushioned cane chair. "What can I help you with?"

Spader adjusted silver-rimmed glasses on his aquiline nose. "Look, Mr. Blackthorne, I'm not going to beat about the bush. We want you to let your Wikipedia entry stand."

"What!"

"Look, we'll make it worth your while."

"Why?"

Spader took out a cloth and wiped his lenses. "Think of the damage it could do to the pharmaceutical industry, to the doctors' lifestyle. We can't have people believing they only have to pay a few quid and they'll be cured!"

"But that IS the case," I replied, feeling incensed.

"Yes, of course it is. I know that and you know that. But the … plebs, don't. And we want to keep it like that."

I was lost for words.

"That's the way it is and, I'm afraid, er, that's the way it's got to stay." His thin lips compressed into a smile.

"Are there other departments, er, like yours?" I asked, curious now.

"Well it's all hush-hush of course, but, between you and me, yes. Ghosts, UFOs, crop circles, aliens, fake child abductions, spirit communication, etc., they all have to be ... debunked, I suppose you'd say. On Facebook, Twitter, Wikipedia, forums, in the papers, on TV. You name it. We've hundreds working on all the monitoring and 'correction' required."

"But why? Why not let the people know the truth? At the end of the day, you guys are elected by us!"

"True, but well, orders from on high, that's all I can say. You carry on with your ... good work, we won't stop that, just don't interfere with any media ... 'interpretations,' there's a good chap."

I sighed. What was the point of banging my head against a brick wall? "OK, how much is it worth then?"

Spader smiled a wry smile. "Well, maybe you'd prefer a bigger property? We could facilitate that. This house is nice, but a man of your stature ... well, perhaps you'd like a more impressive healing space?"

"Well, actually, there is somewhere, somewhere nearby actually. Owned by a chap called Jaspar Simons ...."

The Mound Folk

With a heavy heart, I've decided to set down here an event from my distant youth, one that's been troubling me for many a year. I'm now five years short of my century, not long for this Earthly plane and I need to get it off my chest.

Well, it would have been back in about 1933, those inter-war years I so fondly remember, when hope burned in all our breasts, and optimism exuded from every pore. We'd gone on a school trip to South Wales and were staying in a youth hostel, a converted lifeboat house. I remember the normally wooden or steel launching ramp had been concreted over for some reason.

Anyway, youth hostels were known to be austere in those days, not tarted up to fourth-rate hotels like they are now. This one was more austere than most. Bare stick-like furniture, cold, damp and no hot water or electricity. So, in the evenings we'd congregate in a corner of the refectory where logs blazed in an open fire and there was table football and darts.

Well, I loved table football, the excitement of pushing and pulling the rods to position the players, the powerful flick of the wrist to send the ball flying and the split-second reactions needed to block a ball from your goal. All to the excited shouts and laughter of a bunch of schoolboys.

So, there we were, on our first evening, about to start our evening meal. Curiously, I can remember it even now. Parsnip soup and bread, followed by beef stew with dumplings, potatoes and carrots, that we'd spent an hour peeling beforehand. First, though, the hostel manager, 'Skipper,' asked us to bow our heads as he said grace.

In the silence I could hear waves crashing on the rocks outside, and the quiet hiss of gas lamps. When Skipper had finished, he cleared his throat. "… and, listen carefully, no one is to leave the hostel in the hours of darkness."

"I hope that doesn't include me," laughed our teacher Mr. Hughes, "I thought I'd take a walk down the coast to the village pub, … just for linguistic studies, you understand."

We all laughed.

"I'm sorry, Mr. Hughes, that *does* include you, sir, it can be dangerous out there, er, … the wind and the waves …."

"He doesn't want us to bump into any Mound Folk, that's what it's about!" Joseph, my class mate, whispered from his bunk in the dormitory. From the snoring and heavy breathing surrounding us, it sounded like we were the only two still awake.

"What are you on about?"

"They're elves, tall and thin. They live on the moors hereabouts, under those mounds you see sometimes."

"How do you know?"

"Sally, the lady who brings milk in the mornings told me. At night their menfolk make jewellery, pots and pans, and fashion swords. The women bake and brew and herd their cattle. And they love to dance! Sally says they play the fiddle like you've never heard. Even the trees and stones have to dance! If you hear it though, you can't stop dancing, unless someone cuts the fiddler's strings. And if it gets light before you stop dancing, well, you turn to stone!"

"Do you believe that?"

"Well, I'm going to find out!"

"No, Joseph, don't, you might … get lost … or something."

Not one for following rules, he'd pulled on some clothes and crept out of the hostel via a back-door Sally had shown him, locked at night, but the key left in the lock.

And that was the last time I ever saw him.

In the cold light of day, I awoke. I could hear waves thundering on the shingle outside but there was dead silence in the dormitory. Then I looked over at Joseph's bunk and was horrified to find it empty.

I couldn't sleep after that and I found Mr. Hughes, bedraggled and unshaven in his bed, and told him Joseph wasn't there. There followed a day of frantic searching, us boys at first, then the local bobbies, then even the army were brought in.

There was no sign of Joseph. Eventually it was assumed that he must have fallen into the sea and drowned. A tragic accident.

A memorial service would be held and a tree planted in his name.

But on our last day there, we'd had some free time and I walked up onto the moor and to one of the mounds Joseph had referred to. *There* was a stone obelisk, nearly five feet high. It looked quite new, the sides showing no sign of wind erosion.

I circled the stone, pulling my collar up against a high wind, and wondering. Then, as I turned to walk back to the hostel for lunch and the bus home, I heard a high-pitched wail. It could have been the merciless wind whipping the bare turf, or perhaps a gull high above, being thrown across the sky, or maybe even the sound of a small boy crying out desperately from his stone prison – for help that could never come.

The Neighbour

March was a bad month for romance, she decided. No decent looking guy had looked her way, in the right way, for several weeks. She looked at herself in the mirror. Long brown hair, good skin. Not much wrong there. Maybe it was her breath? She cupped her hand over her mouth and nose, inhaling the odour of garlic – but who didn't like garlic?

The phone rang. She answered. "Hello, Sonia McEwen."

A breathy male voice rasped. "Hi Sonia, you don't know me. I live on the floor below, I see you going to work, we haven't spoken."

"Then why are you phoning me? Hey, how d'you get this number?"

"… I guess I thought you looked lonely. Maybe we could meet?"

He sounded about thirty, ten years younger than her. "I don't think so."

"Well, whaddya like doing?"

She hesitated. "Well, I go to church."

"So, you like God?"

"I s'pose so!"

"Me too, look I'm coming up right now, I'll bring my bible." The phone went dead.

Dreading the knock at the door she stood and waited.

Dread turned to resignation then to disappointment.

After twenty minutes she gave up. March was *not* the month for romance."

The Optimist Creed

Christian D. Larson (1866 – 1955). First published in 1912.

I Promise Myself …

• To be so strong that nothing can disturb my peace of mind.

• To talk health, happiness, and prosperity to every person I meet.

• To make all my friends feel that there is something in them.

• To look at the sunny side of everything and make my optimism come true.

• To think only of the best, to work only for the best, and to expect only the best.

• To be just as enthusiastic about the success of others as I am about my own.

• To forget the mistakes of the past and press on to the greater achievements of the future.

• To wear a cheerful countenance at all times and give every living creature I meet a smile.

• To give so much time to the improvement of myself that I have no time to criticize others.

• To be too large for worry, too noble for anger, too strong for fear, and too happy to permit the presence of trouble.

• To think well of myself and to proclaim this fact to the world, not in loud words, but in great deeds.

• To live in the faith that the whole world is on my side, so long as I am true to the best that is in me.

The Psychic on the Hill

"What does he do all day, d'you think?" Alison said, standing at our bedroom window, looking out across the valley and up at the dilapidated farmhouse on the hill on the far side.

I swivelled my chair around at my writing desk. "Didn't you hear? Jenny says he's a clairvoyant, does readings over the phone for people."

Alison looked in the mirror, restlessly brushing her long chestnut-brown hair. "What? How does that work, then?"

"I don't know how he does it, but they do tarot readings and stuff over the phone, don't they?"

"Hmm. That's interesting. What, you mean people pay for it, without him seeing them?"

"That's what Jenny says. She cleans for him on Fridays, didn't you know? Says he seems a nice bloke, keeps himself to himself. 'Very spiritual,' that's what she says.
D'you think he'd give me a message from mum?"

I sighed. "I don't know. Maybe. Why don't you give him a call?"

In slow motion, her long, slim fingers replaced her hairbrush on the dressing table. "OK, perhaps I will."

So that's how it had started. Seems Roger, as he was called, didn't want to do face-to-face stuff, would only work over the phone. That seemed odd to me. But I'd asked around and he was by no means alone. The internet was full of people claiming to contact the dead over the phone for you, and it wasn't cheap either.

But now Alison would phone him at least once a week, for advice from her mother, grandmother and other deceased relatives and friends.

She seemed to be shelling out money left, right and centre on her credit cards but I had to admit she seemed much happier nowadays, so in that respect it was worth every penny. She hadn't been the easiest woman to live with this past year, since her mother passed away.

"It's all a big fraud," laughed Jonathan, one of my drinking buddies at the pub, as he returned to our table with a tray of pints of beer. He clumsily handed them round, spilling beer to form a growing puddle.

"When you die, you die, that's the end!" said Frank, my next-door-but-one neighbour. He took a large gulp of beer, leaving a moustache of froth on his upper lip. He wiped it off with the back of his hand, then wiped his hand on his trousers.

"What about God, Jesus, er, all that Bible stuff?" said Richard, an accountant and captain of the pool team.

"Invented by man," said Frank, letting out a large cheese-and-onion belch that I could smell from the other side of the table. "Look, it's like ancient man couldn't explain stuff – thunder, lightning, eclipses, that kinda thing, so they had to invent a supernatural reason."

Paul, a postman and general know-it-all, chimed in. "Every country's got a religion and all those religions say you live on. In Heaven or whatever. Stands to reason they can't all be wrong!"

Frank laughed. "Every country's got tales of 'little people' – goblins, elves, dragons, mermaids – you name it. 'Stands to reason they can't all be wrong,'" he said in an affected voice, mimicking Paul.

"Who can't be wrong?" asked Edna, the landlady, reaching across to pick up some empty glasses and exposing two huge pink orbs struggling to remain in her low-cut T-shirt.

"Oh, never mind," said Frank. He guffawed. "You don't get many of those to the pound," nodding his head in the direction of Edna's breasts.

"Oh, I do like a man with originality," laughed Edna, good-humouredly.

When she'd gone, Paul said, "Well, there's one way to find out whether Roger's genuine or not isn't there?"

"What's that?" I asked. "Phone him for a reading, you mean?"

"No, I mean, one of us can go up and see him in person!"

I rang the bell apprehensively, glancing around at the stained, curtained windows, then down at the lush green fields in the valley. Well I could understand why Roger wouldn't want people coming around to such a dump!

There was no sound from within. I felt the urge to flee but I'd drawn the short straw. I couldn't show my face again without getting some kind of result. I rang again. Nothing. All was silent, save for a chill breeze rattling around in the ramshackle wooden porch. I rang a third time then took several paces back and looked at the curtained windows. Nothing moved.

I walked around the extensive buildings, tracing my fingers over the ivy-covered brickwork, noticing the occasional conspicuously-clean window, the handiwork of Jenny, no doubt. I came to a rough driveway, all broken tarmac and potholes. But no sign of a car. There was a lean-to garage with filthy cream panelling but it was locked and there were no windows. A little further on was a green wooden door. It looked serviceable. I went to knock but instead, on impulse, turned the handle and it opened! Inside there was a curious smell, perhaps resembling the odour of an Egyptian tomb opened for the first time in a thousand years. "Hello," I called. "Hello!" The only response came from a grandfather clock, ticking at the foot of a staircase in a wood-panelled hallway. All quiet, no one at home.

I headed up the stairs, noticing the remnants of a paisley pattern on the ancient worn carpet, itself of an indeterminate pinky-grey colour. I peered into the bedrooms. There were six, five of them shrouded with white cloths. The sixth was obviously the one Roger used, and quite neat and clean too, surprisingly. Obviously, the money spent on Jenny's elbow grease was paying off. Then through a side door in the bedroom I spotted some office equipment. I stood and listened. All was deathly quiet. I walked through to find a small switchboard with a computer connected to it, sitting on the green leather of a large mahogany desk. By a phone was a pack of cards, face down. A single card, likewise face down, sat alone, right in the centre of the desk. Beyond was a bay window, gazing out over the valley, and our house clearly visible in the mid-distance. I noticed Allie's knickers and bras visible on a washing line at the back.

The phone rang, making me jump. An answerphone kicked in and I heard a woman speaking with a Welsh accent, asking if Roger would be available at ten o'clock the following night to give a reading? Suddenly, the connected computer sprang into life and I stood there with my jaw heading progressively towards the floor. A map of Britain appeared, then it zoomed in on a county, then a town, then a street, and finally a house. A column on the right gave data about the house price, its occupants, their ages, occupations, income, and photographs of them too. There were Facebook and DVLA sub-screens giving information about Facebook friends, groups and interests, and the date of manufacture of their car, the tax status and renewal date and the date the next MOT was due. And that was for starters! I didn't know what program he was running but I guessed it didn't come cheap or whether it was even legal for the public to see. I half-expected it to say what they'd eaten for breakfast that morning!

The call ended and the screen went blank. Wow, well would I have a story to tell my friends!

I picked up the cards and flicked through them. It was a tarot deck, I recognised the suits – cups, rods, swords and pentacles – and some of the trumps – The Devil, The Hanged Man, and Death. I wondered why he bothered? I tapped them back into a neat deck and put them to one side. And what of the single card? I flipped it over. Hah! What else could it have been but the only unnumbered card – a man resplendent in a black tunic with a bold floral design, carrying a stave with a tied kerchief at one end, accompanied by a small white dog, and about to step off a cliff whilst gazing skywards in innocence – The Fool.

"Insurance."

My heart missed a beat and I whirled around, startled.
Roger gave a disarming smile and sat down in an armchair. "Take a seat." He gestured towards a burgundy leather sofa. "I was in MI6. Old habits die hard. I don't need any of it, really, but ... sometimes the er, connection is weak and a few salient facts can help reassure the client."

"It's hardly ethical though, is it?"

"Ethical, what's that? One person's view versus another's. Look, there's cold reading, hot reading and mediumship ... I use 'em all to give accurate readings. Whether the info comes from spirit or MI6, what does it matter? Anyway, MI6's data stops with the living! Look, I'll do a reading for you, right now. He got up and sat at the desk shuffling the tarot pack. Just you, me, the cards and any spirit friends who care to pop in. If you've got time of course?"

Well, I'd learned something very interesting from Roger. The DVLA information was in the public domain. Just punch in a registration number on their website and get a big list of data about any car! I pushed my way through the crowded bar and the curtain of beer-aroma towards my buddies.

"Here he comes, the man with all the answers!" laughed Frank.

I sat down and reached out for a pint of beer waiting for me.

"What did you get?" asked Paul. "Did you see Roger?"

"Yes, I saw Roger. Well, my mum visits me and makes the lights flicker, my grandfather thinks Allie and I should be starting a family and my granny says I should ask my sister-in-law for her ring back, she wants Allie to have it."

"Hardly proof of life after death! Didn't you get any hard evidence?" asked Frank.

"Yes, your MOT was due a fortnight ago and your car tax is six weeks overdue!"

He almost choked on his beer.

The Shell People

Action is required. The Shell People are multiplying! Infiltrating to higher and higher positions in organisations – political, social, and industrial. I turn to my controller, Digby. He is tall, gaunt, wearing a heavy brown woollen overcoat and matching Homburg hat, as is his wont.

"What's the plan?" I ask.

Digby smiles and I'm reminded of his uneven, yellow, smoker's teeth. "The Magician's on his way, and we've two drones patched into the security screens." He indicates a row of monitors, currently scanning the football crowd. The Director's decided we need them alive, find out what makes them tick, dissect them while they're still breathing if we have to." He gestures to my 'rig' – in an aluminium flight case propped in a corner. "This time you'll have M99 cartridges. Etorphine."

I shrug. I just do what I'm paid to do. Even so, I know the heat is on. The rumours are spreading. The papers are stamping them down, 'wild conspiracy theories, vile trolls,' all the rest of it, but how much longer can they keep the lid on?

Yvonne, my wife, knows I'm with security, but she doesn't ask too many questions, just smiles and raises her pretty eyebrows. "I wish I knew what you're up to, John, you don't have to tell me everything you know."

The door crashes open. Wild grey hair and a grey beard surround a lined, leathery face. "Hello, Digby, sorry I'm late, bloody car battery was flat." Piercing grey eyes look me up and down. It's the Magician. "I see a lot of yellow and red in your aura, John, you have a nice energy today." He smiles a smile that knocks decades off.

The volume is building outside, Dire Straits' *Walk of Life* is playing over the PA. I take my rig outside and up a fire escape, the noise of the crowd hitting me like a slap to the face.

Earlier, I tell Yvonne, "Look I'm not supposed to speak to anyone about this. If you tell anyone, anyone at all, and it reaches the Director, well, they'll be fishing me out of the canal. Understand?"

She nods earnestly.

"Well, there are these … 'people,' we call them the Shell People, cos that's all they are really, a shell, they're not … human."

"What!"

"Just listen. We don't know where they're from, whether they're aliens or from another dimension or whatever, but they're masters of identity theft. And they're telepathic. They're infiltrating organisations and putting antisocial ideas into people's heads. Some may even have been elected to parliament."

"That's incredible!"

"Well, we're not sure what they're up to, but their aim seems to be to cause instability, to make people unhappy with their lot, in short, to foment unrest."

Yvonne sits open-mouthed.

"And our job is to stop them."

"How?"

"Well, one thing we've learned, they don't have an aura, you know, that psychic coloured thing around us. So, we've got this guy, The Magician, he's got incredible psychic abilities, he looks for people with no aura. Crowds are good for that."

"Then what?"

I mime, pointing a pretend-rifle at Yvonne and pull the imaginary trigger.

There's a roar from the crowd and the thud of the ball being kicked. Up here, it's windy, but I've got a sheltered spot. I'm lying down on a thermal rug and I've pads on my elbows to protect them. After what seems an age, I scan the crowd through the telescopic sight, feeling bored. I observe a good-looking girl in red. She leans forwards, and I adjust the rifle to look down her dress, pleasantly surprised to see she's not wearing a bra. As her heavy, bare breasts swing forward, a burst of radio in my ear brings me back to earth.

"John, The Magicians spotted one. He's 99% certain. Up in the second box from the right at the far end. Young woman with a white fur jacket and hat."

Well, she's easy to spot. Attractive, looks well-to-do, but seemingly ordinary otherwise. I'm worried about the other 1%. "Is he sure?"

There's a short delay, then. "Sure enough. Go for it, John. We've got our St. John's guys ready."

Yes, I bet they had. Ready to rush in and 'rescue' a lady who had mysteriously 'fainted.'

I get her neck in my sight. There's a fellow gesticulating next to her. I recognise him as a club official although I forget his name. Owns racehorses if I remember correctly. I tense, finger on the trigger, waiting for the moment.

The moment comes very soon. There's a deafening roar as a goal is scored. On autopilot, I pull the trigger. Watching through the telescopic sight I see the dart hit her cheek, I've misjudged the wind. Her pretty smiling face collapses inwards like a punctured football and for a split-second I see bulbous red eyes, and the glistening, waving legs and antennae of something that resembles a five-foot-high earwig. Then the human form returns and she's fainting into the arms of the concerned official. I see our guys entering the box in their St. John's Ambulance getup.

What I saw makes me feel sick to my stomach, but she's in the hands of the dissection boys now. Job done.

The Visitation

"Head for the hills, 'cos I'm looking for thrills ...," sang Hamish, his Scottish burr prolonging 'thrills.'

"I could use some of those," laughed Julia, a short, stocky woman in her sixties.

I hoped she didn't have me in mind.

The sun was sinking, lengthening the shadows of *saguaro* cacti, towering here and there along our way. Ahead, in the distance, across miles of flat, arid, semi-desert scrubland, lay a low range of hills, our destination.

Normally we'd have had a bumpy journey in an SUV but the prof's plan had us dropped off on this side of the centre, giving us a chance to 'acclimatise' before our two-week residence, by plodding through the hot desert for hours. Every few minutes he'd take out a notebook and write mysterious observations, sometimes pulling out a tape measure and gauging the length of a cactus arm or the height of an inconspicuous, shrivelled brown plant.

It was still warm, the motionless dry air oppressive, and I was hot and sweaty. Damn Hamish! I shifted my backpack into a more comfortable position – this gear weighed a ton – and assessed the party. There was Professor Hamish McPherson, our erstwhile leader, then Julia Surey, a paramedic – no stranger to carrying defibrillators up flights of stairs, judging by her biceps. Then Valencia Lopez, a slight, brown, forty-something scientist from Paraguay, John 'Garry' Garau and myself, Sam Piccarreta, both in our thirties and qualified animal psychologists.

"I saw something move!" exclaimed Valencia, pointing across the endless flat dry scrub that stretched to the distant horizon.

"Could be a coyote," said Hamish.

She took out some binoculars, scanning the desert. "It looked bigger, more upright."

After a minute Hamish spoke. "Come on, we should get to the centre before dark." As always, he spoke quietly, insistently. A kind, easy-going man who preferred to lead by example, he nevertheless had an unstoppable drive when it came to getting what he, or the team, wanted or needed.

I looked at Val, wondering. I'd never heard her mention a husband, or a partner of any kind come to think of it. She wasn't bad looking. I watched the sway of her narrow hips as we started again, imagining running my hands over her naked thighs. Come on Sam, snap out of it! The desert was getting to me and I'd only been here five minutes!

It was almost dusk when we reached the high wire fence surrounding the centre, a network of squat concrete buildings, set against a deepening turquoise sky. Soon stars would begin to peek through the dwindling light, preparing for their lonely, cold sojourn. A large sign stated Big Cat Conservation Trust. Hamish rang a bell, a gate opened and a man appeared.

Hamish greeted him without introduction. "How are the animals tonight?"

"They seem restless, very restless. It's strange. I've never seen them quite like this."

"Huh, that's odd."

We peered down into a sunken enclosure where a pair of Lynx lived. They were both patrolling the walls, agitatedly, but in opposite directions, rubbing their faces together briefly on each pass.

There were forty big cats here – lynx, cougars, bobcats, ocelots and jaguars, mainly in high-walled outside pens, furnished with platforms and shelters. Some had lived here since the centre was built seven years ago, but mainly they were released back into the wild after a year or two.

An enormous crack of thunder startled me awake in my small room. That was unusual. Then another, almost overhead, making my heart pound. Outside, the cats were yowling. Then a sound we didn't often hear – heavy pouring rain crashing down on the roof and outside, turning the dust into mud. I could smell the scent of it through the air conditioning, and knew it'd wash the world outside clean. The plants would be grateful I thought. No, that's silly, plants can't think. Not as we know it, anyway. I drifted back to sleep to the rhythm of the rain.

The next thing I knew was a frantic pounding on my door. My clock said 06.42. *What the hell?*

"Sam, Sam, something awful's happened!" It was Valencia. Her face was streaked with tears and she could hardly speak. The others were gathered on the veranda. The sun was up and the heat of the day was already building.

She led me down some steps and hit a number pad. The door into the jaguar enclosure opened. There they were, or what was left of them. Maia and Gaia. Their eyes were missing and their bodies had been stripped of flesh in places. Neatly incised down to the bone. "They've had their blood taken."

"What!" I could see the remaining flesh was whitish. "Are there any others?"

"They're all like this, except for the ocelots"

They were kept indoors at present. "Oh my God!"

Back on the veranda, the professor spoke. "I've radioed it in. The police will come out later this morning."

"I don't understand." Valencia was crying. "Who would do this?"

"Whoever, or ... whatever, did this, they weren't from ... around here," said Hamish.

"What'll happen?" I asked.

Hamish smiled wryly, "They'll say it's natural causes ... or cults."

I gazed out across the desert and gasped at a purple bloom. As if the life taken from the cats had been transferred into the normally drab and desolate vegetation, a sea of flowers was springing into existence.

The Tale of Tobias Squire

"Princes … and paupers, all are buried here, sir." The old man spat into the grave he was digging in the rich brown earth.

I'd chanced upon an ancient church, deep in the Norfolk countryside. A long walk down a meandering single-track lane that looked like it would fizzle out in the middle of nowhere. Instead, there was a sizeable farm, this church, ensconced in shadow amongst mature trees, and two cottages, predictably named 'Church Cottages nos. 1 and 2,' as indicated by an incongruously modern sign.

"Princes? Are you sure?"

"As sure as my name's Tobias Squire!" He climbed out of the hole, coughing with the exertion. His face was wizened and he wore a heavy black overcoat, despite the warm spring day. "Do you doubt me sir?" he asked, his head askance and thin lips compressed in silent mirth. He reached into a coat pocket and pulled out a tin, containing tobacco and cigarette papers.

"No, no, of course not, it's just … out here, I mean, um …."

The old man sat down on a weathered wooden bench and rolled a cigarette. "Out here, sir, well, it ain't like the cities." He laughed a phlegm-laden laugh. "There's things go on out here you city folks'd have nary an idea of."

Feeling somewhat indignant, I challenged him. "Prince who, then?"

The old man looked up at the sky and spoke softly, "Prince Korrigan."

"Prince Korrigan?" I said, wondering if the old fellow was crazy. "What kind of name is that?"

"Well, that's what I calls him, anyhows." He gestured towards a distant corner of the graveyard, beyond enormous square yew trees. Take a look over yonder, sir."

I strolled over, walking between rows of ancient, haphazardly-toppled and indecipherable gravestones, to a white stone tomb. It outshone its neighbours like a supernova outshines the brightest star in the sky. A colossal rectangular box of pure white marble with sporadic carved seals – a lion wearing a crown, and a unicorn. And one simple date – 1877. No name, no motto, nothing.

I had to admit that it *could* conceivably be the tomb of a prince by virtue of its opulence and returned to find the old man puffing on his roll-up and staring up at the cerulean sky.

"So, who's buried there then? It doesn't say."

He jolted out of his reverie, looking at me as if I were a complete stranger. Then his antiquated mind categorized me and responded. "He never had a name, he died the day after he was born … or that's what they thought!"

"What on Earth d'you mean?"

"He was *taken*, taken by the fairies! They left a piece of wood in his place. An *enchanted* piece of wood, mind. To all appearances, the double of the newborn!"

"You daft old bugger!" I exclaimed, deciding I'd had enough of the silly old fool.

"People believe what it is they believe, sir," he said, and turned his face away.

"Well, I wish you a good day." Leaving the graveyard, I began to retrace my steps along the lane, presently hearing the sound of his spade upon the earth once more. So, I wondered, if this supposed prince was substituted at birth, what happened to him after he grew up, and was he perhaps alive, even now, sustained by fairie magic, and working on their agenda, maybe even in public?

As I sauntered along, feeling the warm sun on my face and listening to the birds singing, a thought came to mind. 'There are more things in heaven and earth, Horatio, than are dreamt of in *your* philosophy.'

Three Lives

"I'm a servant, milord, a maid to Sir Oswald's household."

"And are you happy there?" I asked.

"No, milord, cursed be the day I came into this house!"

"What do you see around you?"

"Stone flags, milord, and a great fire. There's a kettle o'water a'heatin' for the washing."

"Is it the scullery?"

"Yes, milord, there be a great kitchen for the cooking."

"Is there anyone else there?"

(subject laughs) "Yes, milord, there's Jack, the vartlet. He sits by the fire, his face red as any fox!"

"Do you like Jack?"

"Yes, milord, he's a knave, jolly as a pie!"

"That's good. And what about Sir Oswald."

(subject seems nervous) "He … he, by my troth, he doth take advantage. When my lady is away, I must needs go to his chamber of a night. He maketh me unclothe myself – naked as a needle, and … and …."

"Can't you refuse?"

(subject appears tearful) "What wilt thou say, milord, I must needs, or I'll be flashing my queint as a trull down in the town, a penny a time!"

"Isn't there anyone you can talk to?"

(subject starts to cry) "No, milord, there's none as wish to upset his Lordship!"

I place a hand on the subject's forehead. "On the count of three you feel completely calm and come forward in time to your next life, at roughly the same age."

(subject nods)

"One Two *Three*!"

(subject looks around, smiling)

"Where are you?"

"In the children's room, sir. I see boxes of their toys."

"And what year is it?"

(long pause) "Good Queen Victoria reigns, … er, I'm not sure, sir."

"What is your position?"

"Oh, I'm a nanny to two dear children, sir."

"Where do you live?"

"Oh, I live with the family, sir, the James's. It's somewhere in London, near to the river."

"What age are you?"

"Eight and twenty, sir."

"And do you like your work?"

"Mostly. The children, Jacob and Jemima, are lovely, and the master is a gent!"

"What about the mistress?"

(long pause) "Hard as nails she is, sir, always finding fault with me, especially when the master's not around. Once I'd taken the children out, down to the pond to sail their toy yachts, and Jacob fell over and cut his knee bad. Well it weren't my fault, sir, but the mistress, she went mad. The master being away, she took me into her study and gave me ten strokes of her cane on my behind." (subject begins to cry) "I couldn't sit properly for four days, sir!"

"OK. I'm going to count down from ten, and on the count of one, you will be back in the present moment, feeling calm and happy, with full memory of this session. Do you understand?"
"Yes, sir."

"Ten, nine, eight ... two, ONE!"

(subject sits up)

"That was heavy!"

"You see now. Your problem of over-dominance, especially of, er, subordinates, is linked, intrinsically, to these last two lives."

(subject nods)

"In both cases, you were subject to sexual and physical abuse, on a regular basis."

"Yes, it wasn't much fun!"

"I'm going to give you some hypnotic suggestions, based on this session. They'll help you see people for who they are, warts and all, as *people*, not objects or possessions to be pushed around."

David smiles, relieved. "Thank you."

Time of Death

"Become aware of your surroundings and return to the room," said Valentina.

I felt lethargic, unwilling to come out of the meditation, even though it hadn't been very successful.

"Joanna, return to the room and open your eyes."

I did so reluctantly. She smiled at me. "Well, what did you see?"

I'd been doing a 'future life progression' meditation with a friend of my sister's, a supposed clairvoyant. "That's just it, nothing!"

"Nothing!"

"Well, when you said to imagine the clock one hour ahead, two hours ahead etc., and to look around each time, it was fine until nine o'clock. I could imagine touching the furniture, looking out of the window, going outside, walking round the garden, but after that ... just blackness."

Valentina's face was pale. She looked worried. She took my hand. Hers felt cold and clammy. She closed her eyes. I could see them flickering under the eyelids, as though she were dreaming. Shortly they snapped open.

"What is it?" I asked.

"Nothing," she said, "I just asked my spirit guide what it meant. He said not to worry." She got up, avoiding my eyes. "I have to go now Joanna, take care." She smiled a sad smile and left the room. I felt shaky. What did it all mean?

"Hello Jack, Joanna's not well. She says she's terribly sorry to let you down and she'll call you tomorrow ... oh, stomach pains, food poisoning she thinks ... yes, I will, thank you ... yes, goodbye." I turned to my sister, sitting on the sofa, rocking backwards and forwards, as if possessed. "Joanna, you've got to get this crazy idea out of your head!" She'd called round in a state after doing a meditation with Valentina, a friend of mine, saying she was going to die by nine o'clock. For Heaven's sake!

"Look, Valentina was hiding something, she couldn't explain why I couldn't see anything after nine."

"Listen Jo, it was nothing! Another day you'd be able to do it!"

"Well, I'm not going out with Jack. The car might crash or I get could get killed by a mugger."

"Look, stay here till I get back, then you'll be safe! I'm going to choral society, so I'll be back late. Just take it easy. Why not have a bath and relax?"

Joanna stopped rocking and gave a weak smile. "OK."

It was gone eleven when I got back. The rehearsal had taken my mind off Joanna's silly idea until Pete, a friend who'd given me a lift, dropped me off outside my house. I looked at the darkened windows and remembered. My heart thudded. "Pete, sorry love, could you wait a minute, I've just got to check my sister's OK."

"Sure, what's the problem?"

"Oh, nothing, see you in a minute."

I unlocked the front door. Inside, except for the ponderous tick of the grandfather clock in the hallway, the house was dark and silent. Had Jo gone home? I went down the corridor to the bathroom. A light shone from under the door. I knocked. "Jo … Jo. Are you there?" All was quiet.

I hesitated, then opened the door and froze with shock. In the bath, naked, lifeless, was my sister. Her head, eyes open, was under water, surrounded by a halo of floating brown hair. I could scarcely breath. I put a shaking hand in the tepid water and closed her eyes.

The clock that had stood by the taps was gone. I noticed it in the water, down by her knees. I fished it out and looked in horror. The hands showed exactly nine p.m.

Time Out of Joint

It is raining, it's nine o'clock in the morning, and I've taken all the vases off the shelves and the pictures off the walls like that nice Mr. Hughes at UTC asked me to.

I do like the rain, I like to stand in it and close my eyes, feel it on my face and on my bare hands and arms.

I'd been doing that at eight thirty whilst my tea was brewing, when I'd heard the phone ring.

"Good morning, is that Mr. Gordon Smith?"

"Yes, who's calling?"

"It's Roger Hughes, I'm calling from Universal Time Control."

"Who?"

"Well, it's all rather hush-hush, but people think time's a simple matter, running in one direction at an even pace."

"Er, well, doesn't it?"

"Actually, no! It's more a case of millions of 'time bubbles,' 'temporal capsules,' as we, er, boffins call them. Sometimes they can go out of sync."

I really wanted to go and stand in the rain again.

"So, your 'bubble' is running about eight minutes fast. You think it's eight thirty but it's actually eight twenty-two!"

"Oh, well, how would I know?"

"Well, you'd only notice it if you physically crossed into a normal bubble, then suddenly, you'd find your watch would be eight minutes faster than everyone else's."

"How big are these bubbles then?"

"Ah, well, that depends. Some are tiny, some are enormous, and they fluctuate in size too! Anyway, we can reset you at nine fifteen, the *real* nine fifteen! There might be a bit of vibration so to be on the safe side, just make sure pictures, vases etc. are secure, there's a good fellow."

It is raining again and the sun's playing hide and seek. There's a beautiful rainbow and I'm sitting under a patio umbrella, thinking about time. Just to check, not that I disbelieved Mr. Hughes you understand, but just, you know, to be sure, I'd put the television on. If that was being broadcast from a different 'bubble' then surely it couldn't pass into mine twenty minutes early?

Well, the local station announced nine o'clock when my watch said nine, then I looked at the BBC and that said the same. Well, just as I was thinking the whole thing was an elaborate practical joke, I realised that it *would* be nine o'clock elsewhere from my perspective. It was only from Mr. Hughes' point of view – wherever on Earth or off it that was – that you'd know I was out of sync. So, until I was 'reset,' I was effectively eight minutes in the future.

It is raining and I'm dancing in it!

Well, bang on quarter past nine the whole house had quivered, very briefly, like a stiff jelly given a quick flick. I'd looked at my watch and, blow me, it had jumped back eight minutes. This time stuff was bloomin' confusing!

So, everything, was back to normal. With just one exception. Immediately after I'd been 'reset,' I'd made a quick phone call to my sister in Sydney with some info gleaned from the internet in the meanwhile. She'd just had time to put everything she could muster on a horse that couldn't lose. Running in the 8.15 evening race at Canterbury Park, its name, believe it or not, was Timedancer!

Timothy the Armchair

"Oh, look, darling, we simply *must* get rid of this *ghastly* furniture!"

Reginald Wright rolled his eyes. "What's wrong with it?"

"Well, it doesn't match for starters! And this green – *thing* – is ancient! Look, let's order a new suite from McIntyre's. They can do us a custom job. Top-of-the-range leather and how about a deep ruby-red? It'd suit this room to a tee!"

Reginald held his tongue. Melissa was always right. Why argue? Her mother had died and left them a respectable sum. Now Melissa had her eyes on this old pile, Dalefern Manor, along with it's almost-equally-old furniture. He replaced the dusty white sheets over the suite. "Fancy a snifter at the Coach and Horses?"

"That'd be nice, Reggie my darling, but look, let me call round at McIntyre's first."

Reginald sighed. "Whatever you say, dear."

Timothy was an armchair, nothing more, nothing less. For fifty years he'd stood in this living room, with its high Georgian ceiling, chandelier and huge fireplace with towering bookcases on either side. There were three bay windows. One gazed out onto a driveway, with an ancient stone church beyond, another onto a neat front lawn and trees, and the third onto a croquet lawn. He'd heard that beyond the croquet lawn were more lawns, leading to a large circular pond, covered with wide green lily pads and inhabited by secretive carp and tench. Something he yearned to see, but knew he never would.

Once he'd had a sister – another armchair – and a brother, a beautiful sofa, both clothed in deep-green studded leather, as was he, although his was now rubbed and worn. He remembered only vaguely a workshop, the zinging of circular saws, the hammering of leather mallets and the overwhelming, sweet smell of sawdust. All to the shouting and laughter of the fellows there. His creators. God – collectively, he supposed.

Then came a brief period standing in a showroom with his siblings, proudly commanding a larger area than any of the other suites, much to their chagrin.

Then had come his first owners. Sandra and Kenneth. They'd poked and prodded him, dumped their fat backsides down on his tender leather. Bounced up and down, disturbing the inertia of his springs. Ummed and aahed, haggling over the price, as if he and his siblings weren't worth every penny! Then finally they'd been carefully wrapped, put in a large lorry and brought to this house.

So many memories over the years! Generations of excitable children jumping on him. Rambunctious visitors laughing and shouting at noisy Christmas get-togethers. Shouting and yelling of a different kind during spring-quivering family rows. And all those bottoms! Sometimes clothed in harsh tweed, other times soft, warm and naked. And he blushed to think how some had abused him. Wine – and worse – spilt over his beautiful leather on more than one occasion too!

Then one sad, sad day his brother and sister were taken away and replaced with a three-seater, *cloth-covered* sofa and armchair, the latter with a control to lift the mistress, Hannah, out and support her arthritic legs. At first, they had remained aloof and, in truth, he'd regarded them with disdain, but as the weeks, months and years rolled past they'd become friends.

But now Hannah and Derek were gone, to the great workshop in the sky, he presumed, and he and his friends, Olly the sofa, and Mavis the reclining chair, had been draped in white sheets and left to ruminate.

Timothy awoke with a start. There was a deep rumbling sound of an engine, a slamming of vehicle doors and men's voices. Sounds he recognised only too well – a removal lorry!

"Olly, d'you think they're taking us away?" said Mavis, in a tremulous voice.

"Oh, dear Mavis, I think perhaps so. You heard what that awful woman said about getting furniture from McIntyre's. Timothy, what can we do?"

Timothy didn't know what to say. It seemed there wasn't an awful lot they *could* do.

"This sofa and that chair, the reclining one, they're to go. And this green leather thing. Just a minute. Darling … *Darling*!"

"You called, dear?"

"Yes, d'you you really want to keep this awful old thing? You could have a lovely new one from McIntyre's!"

Timothy felt the shock of Reginald's bulky frame crashing onto his springs, bouncing up and down, stretching and exercising them. But exercise they were still most capable of doing, even after all these years!

He'd been carried upstairs, somewhere he'd never been before, down a corridor and into a study. The walls were lined with shelves and there were boxes and boxes of books everywhere, waiting to be unpacked.

A piano stood in a corner with a beautiful carved stool covered in pink leather. Reginald stood up, patted Timothy fondly and left the room, smiling to himself.

The piano stool addressed Timothy. "Well, hello, big boy! My name's Susie, are you going to be in this room with me?"

Timothy blushed. "Well, yes, er, I think so. My name's Timothy."

Susie giggled. "He's a bit of a porker, that one – Reginald – isn't he? By the way, do you mind if I call you Tim?"

"Oh, er, all right."

"Oh, how lovely! You and I will be great friends! I can tell you stories of pianists who've sat on me and you can tell me of your adventures downstairs!"

Timothy looked out of the window and his springs almost burst with happiness. For there in the distance was the one thing he'd yearned to see all his life; the round pond, with its lily pads and its silver water, rippling and sparkling in the early morning sunshine.

Tiny Yellow Kites

The roaring sun
Bakes shimmering sand.
A beetle emerges from nowhere,
Senses the heat
And vanishes.

Under the small wooden bridge,
Beneath wide green lily pads,
In cathedral-still depths,
slide golden carp.

Two butterflies flying high above trees,
Like tiny yellow kites.
Drifting far apart,
Coming together miraculously
To kiss again.

Touché

Stanislav Kowalski replaced the cigarette between his lips, inhaling the smoke deeply. He held it in his lungs as long as he could, until dizzy from the nicotine, then exhaled slowly with pursed lips, forming smoke rings in the warm still air of the May evening. He didn't know why he smoked, he just did. People said he should give up, but then what would he do when waiting on the used car lot, as he did now?

He looked down the road towards the edge of the woods, where an old water tower lurked high up in the trees. As always, when the light was fading, he fancied it to resemble an alien creature, like the fearsome tripods in *War of the Worlds*, except this had four legs. Or the horrible tank-like creatures in Wyndham's *The Kraken Wakes,* with their octopus-like inhabitants, which would emerge to capture people with their sticky tendrils. Then back inside the 'tanks' with multiple victims neatly rolled up in the tentacles for God knows what horrific fate. He shuddered as he remembered reading how two of the 'octopuses' latched onto the same woman, tearing her in half.

He was awoken from his nightmare reverie by the hoot of a vehicle's horn. He hadn't even noticed the small silver car pull up. He went over and a woman wound down the window.

"Do you have any trucks or vans?" she asked, without greeting. She was plain, about forty, with thick-lensed glasses and brown hair fastened in a pony tail. She wore no makeup.

"Well, yes, we do. We've a couple in right now, a Ford Transit, and a Toyota Hilux, that's a pickup truck."

She got out of the car and sized him up. About thirty, unshaven, needing a haircut, and she recoiled from the stench of cigarette smoke. His face was quite handsome though, she noticed. "OK, let's have a look."

He dropped his cigarette, stubbing it out with his foot, then led her through rows of cars, carefully spaced to give the illusion of more stock than they actually had, to the two vehicles in question. "What did you want it for?" he asked, then noticed her surprised glare. "If you don't mind me asking?"

"Well, actually, it's for moving hives, bee hives."

"Oh, do you need to move many?"

She looked him up and down. "Twelve." She gazed around the car lot, then gestured across the road, to the view over the vale. A panorama of neat green and brown fields with Haw Hill, in the foreground. "They say that hill's a natural formation. Looks artificial to me. Like a burial mound."

"They found some gold coins there, about ten years ago, just below the summit."

To his surprise, she smiled, suddenly looking ten years younger.

"What's your name?" she asked.

"It's Stanislav. Er, people call me Stan."

"Look, you probably don't know, but hives are pretty heavy, I think the truck would be better."

"Well, how often do you move them?" Ignoring his partner's advice, he added, "I mean, it seems very expensive to buy a truck, when you could just rent one."

Her eyes blinked rapidly several times behind the thick lenses. "Oh, not often, but I move them for other people too. Sometimes it's to pollinate a special crop, other times it's just to sell them. You have to move them three miles or more, or the little buggers'll fly back to where their nest was. Like homing pigeons!" She laughed, a high-pitched, rippling sound. "That can cause problems!'"

He found himself smiling. "Back in Poland my uncle runs a bee-keeping museum. You know, hives, clothing, smokers, frames – that sort of thing. To be honest I was never really interested."

She patted the side of the truck. "What can you do on the price?"

"Let's go to the office, we can talk terms there," said Stanislav. "What's your name by the way?"

"It's … Miss Dawson." She started to follow him. "Bees are a lot more interesting than humans *I* always think."

"They're just insects that sting."

She looked around at the vehicles. "Judging by your prices, you've got something in common then!"

271

What's in Store?

Waves in Plasmas. I flicked through pages of mind-boggling equations in the heavy hardback book. *The Susceptibility and Dielectric Tensors.* How the hell could I have understood this stuff? Thirty years later it might as well have been in Chinese! At the sound of muffled hammering I threw the book back into a box of old textbooks and went out of my storage unit into the corridor. Four units away a bright light showed under a door. *What the hell are they doing in there!*

I'd arrived at the *IndieStorage* warehouse at 7 p.m. on a Tuesday, as per my usual routine, after teaching the guitar for four hours. There, I'd spend until 8.15 p.m. sorting through boxes of books and papers and then walk into the town centre to the *Cock*, an ancient pub, distinguished by its whitewashed walls, criss-crossed with black oak beams, that stood at a crossroads. There I'd meet Jim, my old friend and drinking partner for the last fifteen years.

It was March; cold and dark on the isolated industrial estate. Heavy low cloud blotted out the moon and it felt like it might snow. A couple of lamp posts cast a cold light into the murk. I'd approached a large steel shutter and tapped my code into a panel. With a loud clanking the shutter began to roll up. I smiled at the thought of the first time I'd come here, I'd expected a small door, not a huge shutter for lorries to unload at, and my heart had pounded as the unexpected noise shattered the silence. I'd felt embarrassed and afraid someone would suddenly appear, demanding to know what I was doing.

Now I knew the ropes there was no problem. I stepped inside the building and, leaving the shutter up, went through to a gate. I entered my code again and it opened, giving me access to four floors of storage units, mostly five feet by ten, over one hundred units per level.

I always found the place eerie, lights only came on when you passed sensors, there was no discernible heating, and there were cameras everywhere. Some of the units had huge pictures of exotic doors stuck to their mundane thin steel ones, giving the appearance of the entrance to a castle, or a bank vault. I wondered if you had to pay extra for those?

I liked to wander around the empty, echoing corridors, wondering if some bored security guard was following my movements on a screen in a distant control room. Once I'd espied a unit slightly ajar. I'd opened the door, to find it was empty, and been startled by an ear-splitting siren. I'd looked pleadingly at a nearby camera and seconds later the din had been shut off, whether by an operator or automatically, I didn't know. After that I'd never touched any door other than my own!

In all the times I'd gone there I'd only ever met one other soul, so I was taken aback to hear raised voices when I exited the lift and headed through the maze of corridors towards my unit. As I approached, I saw a black man, perhaps sixty years old, with a grey crew cut and a matching rash of stubble, clad in a thick maroon sweater and jeans, arguing with a woman. She wore a long, beige gabardine mackintosh, was perhaps fifty, and taller than him. Straggly blonde hair fell over a makeup-caked face. She wore garish red lipstick and her eyelids were heavily made up with blue powder.

The man was gesticulating with a hacksaw, and they were speaking a strange language I didn't recognise at all. I thought about turning around and going back, but they caught sight of me and fell silent. As I self-consciously walked past, the woman smiled and said 'good evening' with a peculiar foreign accent. I noticed she had lipstick on her teeth, which were nicotine-yellow. Her voice was husky and I saw her chest appeared to be completely flat. The man merely stared, open-mouthed, at me, as if I had two heads.

They seemed perturbed that my unit was so close to theirs, but I had work to do. Sorting through eighty boxes that had previously languished in my parents' garage for years, before they'd moved to another part of the country.

There was no light in the units themselves, only in the corridors, and they would turn off after five minutes, leaving just isolated dim security lights. To overcome that I would normally work in the entrance to my unit, with empty boxes for

273

sorting books spread out into the corridor, where my presence would constantly trigger a sensor

So, I'd been going through boxes of old university text books and other scientific ones I'd collected, sorting them into alphabetical order of author. Maybe I could sell some on Amazon? Or maybe science had advanced so much that they were now redundant?

From time to time I became aware of the odd couple talking animatedly in their strange language, sometimes raising their voices, and dragging things around. I wondered if they had furniture stored in there and mulled over taking a walk down the corridor to the toilet to take a peek.

As I began to fill some boxes in the corridor, I noticed that they'd closed their door. They must have had some kind of battery-powered lantern though, as bright light shone from beneath it. Then there came the sound of sawing and a strange intermittent thumping sound, disturbing my concentration. *Damn them!*

Presently I heard their door open and sounds of dragging and clanking. I retreated into my unit and peered out to see the woman pulling a trolley. The man followed, dragging a huge wooden box. With some effort, the woman picked up the other end and they manhandled it onto the trolley. She noticed me looking at them but gave no sign. In silence they padlocked the door and wheeled the trolley down the corridor. Soon I heard the distant sound of the lift.

Thankfully able to concentrate again I managed to sort through a further six boxes of books, before stacking everything back inside the unit and padlocking it. 8.15 p.m. on the dot. Excellent!

As I walked down the corridor towards the lift, I noticed something on the yellow floor tiles outside their door. Taking some tissue from my pocket I wiped it, then looked at the stain with surprise. *Hmm.* Well, I'd have something to talk to Jim about. I knew fresh blood when I saw it!

When Something Stinks

"This is WKKZ, bringing you the brightest music and the brightest discussion!" announced the smooth voice of DJ Kenny Bright, "and just before the news at 1 a.m. we have Donny on the line, I believe. Donny, hello, can you hear me?"

"Hi, Kenny, yes, I can, how are you doing?"

"I'm great, Donny, how are you?"

"I'm good, thank you, Kenny."

"OK. I believe you wanted to talk about cover-ups. Is that right?"

"Yes, Kenny, that's right. You know, I don't believe we're told the truth about anything anymore."

"Well, I know there's been a lot of talk about 'fake news'."

"Well, there's fake and there's fake, isn't there?"

"How d'you mean?"

"Well, for example, they tell us that plane, MH370 just disappeared off the radar. Damned pilot just flew off and murdered two hundred and fifty people!"

"Well, no one knows what happened."

"That's just it, Kenny, of course someone knows, probably quite a lot of people know, as a matter of fact. But the media here just follow the party line. Suicide-murder pilot and all the rest of it. Anything else is just a 'conspiracy theory'!"

Bright coughed a phlegm-laden cough. "Excuse me." He continued, "Surely they're just reporting the information put out by the Malaysian authorities?"

"Well, you know that base we have, Diego Garcia, in the middle of nowhere?"

"Yeah, sure."

"Did you know they closed it for twenty-four hours the night MH370 disappeared? Seems under the cover of darkness a very large unidentified plane landed."

"So what?"

"So what, man! Put two and two together."

"Well, I'm not going to put two and two together to make five!"

"Listen, man, someone on that base blew the whistle. Told people that hundreds of passengers were taken off a 'mystery plane' that landed in the middle of the night, divided into groups and flown off to different interrogation centres."

"*Someone on that base,*" Bright's tone turned sarcastic. "Like who?"

"Well, he gave that information incognito, obviously. But he gave evidence that showed he knew the intimate workings of the base."

"And you've seen this evidence?"

"Listen, Kenny, man, you know I haven't. I'm taking the word of certain investigators – Barney Murillo, Ruben Pemberton, Rhys Gray, you know those guys?"

"I've heard of them. Conspiracy theorists is about right. Although some might have stronger words to say about them!"

"Look, man, Barney Murillo was the guy who first blew the whistle on that English paedo DJ, Jimmy Saville. Everyone knew he was at it, no one spoke up. Barney wrote about it time and again on his blog, got called every name under the sun for it. Turned out, after Saville died, the British police announced he was one of the worst paedophiles ever!"

"Well, Britain … England has paedophiles coming out of the woodwork, that's what they're like over there."

"Yeah, man, right. *The point* is that Murillo had a 'conspiracy theory' that turned out to be correct! Based on investigation and facts!"

"OK, OK, but, look, there's a list of conspiracy theories out there as long as my arm!"

"So, let's talk about another. 9/11."

"Sorry, Donny, I'm not going to go there, I don't want to upset our listeners."

"I'm not going to go there, Kenny. I just wanna talk about the Solomon Brothers building, that huge office block that came down the same day."

"Yes, it was set on fire by falling debris from the towers and collapsed due to burning office furniture. It was proven."

"Yeah, it was in the report, sure. The *government* report. Problem was, a load of people heard demolition charges going off, just before it collapsed."

"Rubbish!"

"It's on camera, as is the building going down."

"Maybe it was fireworks?"

"Fireworks, my ass, that building went down in free fall! Only way it could have done that was by demolition."

"Says who?"

"Demolition experts. Want me to name 'em?"

"Well, actually, no, Donny, we have to break now for the news. Well, thank you for your interesting ... ideas. But the rest of us have to live in the *real* world. Nice talking to you."

A jingle for a foot deodorant commercial cut in. 'When something stinks ....'

Where's Superman When He's Needed?

Monday

Took the coach to Skegness with mother. I loathe the place, all crowded streets, tacky 'souvenir' shops and the ubiquitous smell of frying, but she wanted a day out. The tide was in, so the beach wasn't wide. We sat on the sand in an area of large black boulders. I think they're to stop erosion. She read her latest book-circle title, *Superman – A Retrospective*. I listened to Tommy Bolin's *Teaser*, the brilliant legacy of another heroin 'victim.' What a waste.

There was some sort of mist that made our eyes sting. We came back early. Others on the coach complaining about it. One lady's eyes were red and streaming, other people were coughing.

Tuesday

My eyes felt sore today. Mother complained too. Read on the internet that hundreds affected. People told to keep away from Skegness and other places along the coast. Authorities haven't a clue what's going on. A chemical 'spill' at sea the most likely culprit, apparently.

Wednesday

Well, the 'mist problem' seems to have got worse. It's now affecting the whole coastal area, people being told to stay indoors whilst the authorities find out what's going on. My eyes are OK now but mother coughing a lot. I told her to see the doc, but she says she 'doesn't want to be a nuisance'! She seems confused, talking about Christopher Reeve as if he's a close personal friend! Dementia is cruel.

Thursday

This thing is serious! Sky's even changed the headline from 'Mystery Mist' to 'Killer Fog,' on account of the number of car crashes there've been. It's affecting the whole East Midlands coast and has come up to fifty miles inland. Authorities say they 'are working on identifying the problem.' Tossers!

Friday

Well, the fog's reached us here in Welby. You can't see anything out of the windows and it's impossible to drive. You can't have the headlights on – too much reflection – and you have to keep the windows closed. Mother's saying that Superman will sort it out. She's gone completely doolally, poor old soul!

Saturday

Donna called round on horseback – with gas masks! Seems she'd bought a 'his 'n' hers' set of WW2 gas masks at auction a few years ago and found they're still OK. Amazing!

She'd brought Jamjar on a tether. I hadn't ridden for years but he's a gentle soul. The horses' eyes don't seem affected but they're a bit spooked by this bloody fog. We rode into town to try to get some bread and milk. It was so weird riding down the high street. You couldn't see the shops until a few feet away and it was deathly quiet. All closed, but the Co-op windows had been broken. All the fresh stuff had been looted but we found some dried milk and Ryvita.

I managed to bring back a boxload of CDs, well if I hadn't taken them, someone else would've. A mixed bag, including some ancient stuff. Been listening to the Beach Boys' *Surfin' U.S.A.* Still sounds so good, but don't think there'll be much surfing going on around here for a while.

Sunday

PM on the telly saying there's no need for panic. Silly cow, she should come out here! The source of the fog's still unknown, but they're now saying it might be some kind of chemical warfare. Great! It could be the Russians, the Chinese, or even North Korea, not that it makes much difference. It's reached the East End now though, so everyone is finally taking it seriously. Mother's still asking if Superman is coming to the rescue. If only!

279

Your Head in Our Hands

"Remove any doubts from your mind, Mrs. Hawking. Our facilities here at Newton Cryonics are state-of-the-art. True, there may have been one or two, er, hiccups at the beginning, *elsewhere*, but you can have total faith in *us*, our cryogenic process has proved its reliability."

"Alfred's finding it hard to breath now. He's not got long …."

"Ah, good, now Miss Kelly outside will go through the protocol and form-filling with you. There's just one thing. Did he want the full body or just the head?"

"Oh, what would you recommend?"

"Well, for most it comes down to price. Keeping the whole body at minus two hundred degrees is considerably more expensive over the long term than just the head."

Mrs. Alexa Hawking looked out of the window at the huge concrete hemisphere ensconced among neat lawns and flowerbeds that stretched out ahead. She fingered her white hair nervously. "Oh, just his head …. How long …?"

Dr. Zanoun gave a wry smile. "I can't give you any definite figures, Mrs. Hawking. It could a hundred years, it could be five hundred …." He made a gesture as if juggling invisible balls. "But rest assured, your husband's head will be safe in our hands."

'Hello, message for Dr. Jared Wise, Dr. Abraham Klein wishes to see you urgently.' A soft, artificial-intelligent voice came into Jared's mind. He tore his gaze away from an enormous round window, through which he'd been watching multi-coloured sky-pods dart between towering pyramidal blocks a thousand stories high.

Jared walked down a gleaming white corridor whose windows gave over the city below, into Klein's enormous circular office, also in brilliant white. Huge oval windows behind Klein's desk and in the ceiling far above showed puffy white clouds in a bright blue sky. Dr. Klein looked worried, Jared thought, very worried.

"Take a seat, Dr. Wise." Klein gestured to a sumptuous white chair and retreated behind his desk, also white. He sat down and rested his chin on the inverted V of his fingertips. "There's a problem."

"Yes? With the heads?"

"Yes, with the heads."

Jared knew that today was the second day of reanimating cryogenically frozen heads. Attaching it to a physical body was something else again, but that could wait. Once contact was established, the 'patient' could be reassured and placed back into their deep-freeze limbo until … whenever.

"Meaning … the process …."

"The process is fine. We've done three. They're testaments to the reign of Dr. Zanoun and his colleagues from way back when. They were brought back over the optimum time, you know, just up to the temperature where we could get the brain to function, then they were given twenty-four hours to … er, acclimatise. Look, I'll not beat about the bush. There's something wrong. They're fine, they've got memories, they can reason. But … *something's* missing."

"Uh?"

"And, Dr. Wise, one of them is asking for *you*. By name!"

Jared stood in front of a cylinder of invisible liquid. At the level of his face floated an aged human head. It reminded him of a realistic wax head, the kind of thing they used to have in those wax museums in the old movies. The only difference was that this head was hairless. Suddenly, its eyes opened and blinked, looking directly into his. The thin lips twitched, then formed the semblance of a smile. A voice came through a transducer – pleasant-sounding, affable. "Hello Jared."

"Hello …," he glanced at a label … "Mr. Hawking."

"Please, call me Al."

"Well, welcome, to the year 2612, Al. There's been some changes since you were last … around."

"So, I understand."

"What do you remember?"

"I have memories of a hospital. That's all."

"After you died?"

"Nothing, not till yesterday."

"Well, you understand you'll have to go back into cryo, Al. Till we have the technology to put you back on a body."

"Time doesn't matter to me, it's a great adventure. But there's one thing."

"What?"

"That thing from yesterday."

"What happened?"

"Well, a being, an … angel, I believe, came to me. He spoke about *you*."

Jared started to worry. The process couldn't have worked right. He'd need to discuss this with Dr. Klein right away.

"Yes, you see. You've got my soul. It passed into the world of spirit when I died and eventually reincarnated … into you! The angel told me."

"What!"

"I've got memories. Memories of Alexa, my wife, my job, I worked in the fire brigade. Kids, we had three, Ginnie, Dawson and Arnold. But you know that too, deep inside."

Jared had a flash of memory – burning buildings, sheets of orange-red flame, a fire-engine careering through streets with sirens blaring, men in reflective uniforms running. He could smell the smell of fire and smoke and that thing he hated most – burning flesh. And Alexa, twenty-five, a sensual young brunette mashing her lips on his, her heavy hard-tipped breasts against his nakedness …. He forced himself to come back to reality, of a kind. "Well, how can I help?"

"I want it back!"

"Sorry, you're the one who chose not to die properly!" It was *his* soul now. He turned the audio channel off, then pressed a button to restart the initial stage of the cryogenic process. Not daring to look at Al's face again, he headed back to Dr. Klein, wondering what on Earth to say.

Appendix 1 – Word Count of Stories

No.	Title	No. of Words
1	A Flying Visit	1300
2	A Girl Like Alice	650
3	A Tall Story	1450
4	A Visit from Saint Nicholas – 2017 Version	495
5	An Eye for an Eye	1400
6	Arse from His Elbow	550
7	A Kind of Peace	750
8	Billy Bunter's Christmas Surprise	2000
9	Blind Hope	500
10	Boxed into a Corner	1200
11	*Brother, Oh, Brother!*	650
12	But Can You Hide?	600
13	Chateau Courdermaire	850
14	Circles and Stones	1400
15	Clarissa's Missives	3200
16	Cruising Down the River	1300
17	Comic Tragedy	900
18	Death by DVD	850
19	Doing Time	700
20	Dreams on Board	650
21	Don't Dig for Bombs!	1200
22	Earthbound	850
23	EC was Here	750
24	Evil Versus Evil	900
25	Femme Fatal	100
26	For She Had Eyes …	1200

Appendix 2 – Answers to Riddles

Instructions: cover the answers you *don't* want to see and hold the page up to a mirror.

- I can only live where there is light ... a shadow.

- In 1990 a person is 15 years old ... the years were before Christ.

- Four men were fishing in a boat on a lake ... all the men were married!

- What disappears the moment you say its name? ... silence.

- It is greater than God and more evil than the Devil ... nothing.

- The more there is of me, the less you see. What am I? ... darkness.

- What comes once in a minute, twice in a moment, but never in a thousand years? ... The letter m.

- You can see me in water, but I never get wet. What am I? ... a reflection.

- What English word retains the same pronunciation ... queue.

- If Teresa's daughter is my daughter's mother ... if subject is female, then daughter. If subject is male, then son-in-law.

"They are the architects of greatness, their vision lies within their souls, they peer beyond the veils and mists of doubt and pierce the walls of unborn Time. The belted wheel, the trail of steel, the churning screw, are shuttles in the loom on which they weave their magic tapestries. Makers of Empire, they have fought for bigger things than crowns and higher seats than thrones. Your homes are set upon the land a dreamer found. The pictures on its walls are visions from a dreamer's soul.

"They are the chosen few – the blazers of the way. Walls crumble and Empires fall, the tidal wave sweeps from the sea and tears a fortress from its rocks. The rotting nations drop from off Time's bough, and only things the dreamers make live on."

– HERBERT KAUFMAN